"I'VE WAITED YEARS

Beth stopped in front of Tanner, her hazel eyes flashing indignantly. "To have someone who would wake up in my arms each morning, a baby to rock to sleep. Isn't that what all women dream of? So why am I so bad for wanting the same things?"

"You're not as things?"

"You're not as bad as you know I'm not good husband material." Tanner could see beneath her sheer nightgown. "But you think you can soothe my hurts and make me care about you enough that I'll change my ways."

"I don't give a fig about your hurts."

Tanner didn't want to stop. "You think that beneath this rough exterior there's a man worth saving, worth turning into a husband. You're wrong."

God, how he wanted her even when she was pushing him, making him feel things he'd long forgotten. He still wanted to feel her arms around him, even while he was trying his best to push her away.

"I have a man waiting for me. Why would I want a coldhearted bastard like you?"

"Because the man waiting for you, doesn't make you feel like this," he said as he pulled her into his arms.

Dear Romance Reader,

In July, we launched the *Ballad line* with four new series, and each month we present both new and continuing stories set everywhere from medieval England to the American West—written by the most kind of passionate, romantic stories you love book, by the most *en* you can find the back of book, we'll tell have captured subsequent book in the se your heart.

This month dark new author Lynne begins *The an Maclean se*, the passionate and dramatic stories of three brother orn apart in the aftermath of Culloden. In **Summer's E** one of these proud Scottish men must choose betwen fulfilling a debt of honor . . . and losing the woman he has come to cherish. Next, talented Cynthia Sterling completes the *Titled Texans* trilogy with **Runaway Ranch**. What happens when a reformed rogue and brand-new vicar finds himself at a shotgun wedding—where *he* is the groom? New favorite Sylvia McDaniel continues the funny, sexy saga of *The Burnett Brides* when a man haunted by the Battle of Atlanta rescues a woman from stagecoach bandits. Soon enough, **The Outlaw Takes a Wife!** Last, rising star Gabriella Anderson offers the second book in the charming *Destiny Coin* series, in which taking a headstrong American girl's hand in marriage becomes **A Matter of Pride** for one rakish British bachelor. Enjoy!

Kate Duffy
Editorial Director

The Burnett Brides

THE OUTLAW TAKES A WIFE

Sylvia McDaniel

ZEBRA BOOKS
Kensington Publishing Corp.
http://www.zebrabooks.com

ZEBRA BOOKS are published by

Kensington Publishing Corp.
850 Third Avenue
New York, NY 10022

All Kensington titles, imprints and distributed lines are available at special quantity discounts for bulk purchases for sales promotion, premiums, fund raising, educational or institutional use.

Special book excerpts or customized printings can also be created to fit specific needs. For details, write or phone the office of the Kensington Special Sales Manager: Kensington Publishing Corp., 850 Third Avenue, New York, NY, 10022. Attn. Special Sales Department. Phone: 1-800-221-2647.

Zebra and the Z logo Reg. U.S. Pat. & TM Off.
Ballad is a trademark of the Kensington Publishing Corp.

First Printing: January, 2001
10 9 8 7 6 5 4 3 2 1

Printed in the United States of America

To Paula Thomas for over twenty years of friendship, through good times and bad. A friend with a strong shoulder and a good ear is a blessing.

To Sharon Blankenship, Nicki Carter, and Cheryl Sidler, one of the best teams I've ever had the pleasure of working with. Thanks for your sacrifice and hard work; we were good!

I miss you guys.

One

Tanner Burnett sat in the stagecoach dressed like a banker, the string tie around his neck feeling like the noose he'd been running from for the last ten years. The wooden coach rocked and rattled along the bumpy road, dust rising from the spoked wheels, through the open window, and settling on the black suit he detested.

God, he didn't want to be here, dressed like this, waiting. Yet there was no way to change the past, and he didn't feel like trying. But there was a box of gold on this stage; the contents of the strongbox could go a long way toward his freedom.

He sighed and glanced across the seat at the beautiful young woman with burnished red hair and hazel eyes; she was the only thing about this trip that had been pleasant so far. She'd definitely made the scenery much better than the rolling hills of the Texas hill country.

The other passenger, who sat beside him, was an older woman on her way to visit her daughter. The three of them were cooped up inside this hot dust catcher rolling toward Fort Worth.

The name of the city conjured up images of home and family, images he quickly pushed away. Those memories belonged to another man, another lifetime, and he could never go back. He could never face his family again and let them see the man he'd become.

"Mr. Tanner, what kind of business are you in?" the older woman asked, jarring him from his casual perusal of the lovely young lady across from him.

"Banking," he said, thinking it sounded important. He glimpsed out the window, wishing the woman would leave him alone and let his eyes feast on the beauty across from him.

"What about you, Miss Anderson? What brings you to Texas?" the nosy old woman asked. "Do you have family here?"

Tanner couldn't help but glance at the young woman. She had ample curves, and with her high forehead and well-defined cheekbones, her face was both beautiful and full of expression. He watched her contemplate the grandmother's question, her hazel eyes large and vivid.

"Of a sort, yes," she said, vague with her response. "I'm originally from Jonesboro, Georgia."

She glanced at him, her gaze distant and aloof. Her lips were full and ripe for kissing, and before his mind traveled in that direction, he reached into his pocket, pulled out his watch, and glanced at the time.

The waiting and wondering were nerve-racking.

"Lord have mercy, the Texas heat can sometimes strangle a body right into suffocating." The grandmother picked up her fan and stirred a breeze in the dusty confines. She took a deep breath. "Miss Anderson, do you have kinfolk you left behind in Georgia?"

Tanner couldn't help but turn his attention from the window back to the woman. She probably came from a large family with brothers or sisters, similar to the smaller group of kin he'd given up. He pushed the pesky memory away, unable to think of them now. Yet since he'd crossed the state line back into Texas, they had hovered on the fringes of his mind.

"No one of any importance. My mother and father are buried there." Miss Anderson twisted her small handbag in her lap and then gazed up at the grandmother, her hazel eyes shimmering softly in the dim light of the coach.

He glanced out the window again. He needed to get out of Texas before his relatives found out he was alive.

"But you'll have family in Fort Worth," the older woman reminded her.

Miss Anderson hesitated, "Yes. Yes, I will."

"What's your kinfolks' name? I know a lot of people in town. I just might know them."

Just then a loud pop drew Tanner's attention back to the window.

Finally.

The snap of the driver's bullwhip sounded above them, and the stagecoach took a wild lurch, the horses picking up speed. The burst of gunfire and the whine of a bullet whizzed by the window, and Tanner grabbed the ladies by the arm.

"Down on the floor, both of you." He shielded their bodies with his own as the gunfire got closer and closer.

"What's happening?" the young woman asked, trying to raise her head.

"I think it's called a holdup," he said, pushing her head back down.

A voice yelled close to the stagecoach, "Stop this damn coach before I shoot you."

The stage slowed and finally, after several minutes, came to a halt.

"Everyone out!" the man commanded, his voice gruff. "Now."

"Ladies, do what the man says," Tanner said, rising up, hating what he did for a living.

Opening the door, he stepped out of the stagecoach, his hands high in the air. He turned slightly to his right and gave a hand first to the older woman and then to the stunning Miss Anderson. Her eyes were wide with fright, but she gazed about the group, her chin held high, her eyes taking in every detail. She wasn't panicking like most women he'd encountered in a holdup.

The mens' faces were covered with bandannas, their cowboy hats pulled low over their foreheads. Their only visible features were their eyes. Tanner stood to the left of the women, waiting and watching.

"Where's the driver?" Sam asked, looking around. "I want that gold."

No one responded, but stood quietly at attention, their hands held up.

Seaborn Barnes slid off his horse and started toward the women. "Off with your jewelry, ladies. Hand over your money and your valuables. Keep those hands up in the air until we get to you. If everyone follows the rules, then you'll all live to see another day."

Suddenly, the driver of the stagecoach stepped from behind the stage, a rifle in his hands. He swung the gun up and aimed the barrel at Sam Bass, the leader of the gang.

"You ain't robbing my stage," the driver yelled, intent on killing Sam.

Tanner reacted without thinking. He shoved the point of the rifle away just as the gun went off. The bang of the gunshot exploded in the still countryside, sending birds skyward.

The impact of the bullet knocked Miss Anderson to the ground. Slowly, a crimson stain appeared on the

beautiful woman's pink blouse, marred by the gunshot.
A cry ripped from Tanner's throat, echoing in the hills,
as he gazed at the woman lying in a crumpled heap in
the dirt.

Dear God, he'd pushed the barrel of the rifle right at
her.

He'd killed Miss Anderson.

Stunned, Tanner stood there while the past collided
with the present, and once again he was on the battlefield
fighting for his life, dodging bullets, fighting beside Carter.

"I'm obliged to you, Jackson," Sam Bass said, jolting
Tanner back to the present. For a moment he was confused by the name Jackson, but then he slowly realized
that was how he was known—Jackson to the law and to
everyone who hadn't known him before the war.

"Somebody help that poor girl," the grandmother
cried.

But her pleas for help were ignored as the bandits
grabbed the last bit of money from the older woman,
emptied the gold from the bank's stronghold box, and
finished collecting their loot.

"Let's get out of here," cried Seaborn as he kicked
the empty box out of the way. In shock, Tanner watched
as the raiders jumped back on their horses. In a matter
of moments, they spurred their horses, galloped down
the lane away from the stagecoach, and left him behind.

This was where he was going to rejoin them, where
he should jump on his own horse and ride with them to
their hideout. But Miss Anderson lay bleeding on the
ground.

Torn, he watched them riding away, their horses'
hooves thundering in the still prairie, his chance for a
new life sprinting off into the countryside. The urge to

follow them was insistent, but the woman lay still as death on the ground.

Another person dead because of him. His future didn't matter, but if he could save Miss Anderson's life, maybe hers would.

The stagecoach driver turned on him, suspicion darkening his eyes. "They knew you!"

"No, they mistook me for someone else. The name's Tanner, not Jackson." Tanner shook his head, concerned for the woman. "I'm a banker, not an outlaw."

"Then why in the hell did you push my gun away? I had a clean shot on him."

Tanner didn't spare a glance at the driver as he knelt beside Miss Anderson. "You'd be dead, and there's been enough bloodshed."

"Instead, she's dead," the man said with a spat. "It's all your fault."

Gently, Tanner stretched her out on the ground; her auburn hair spilled from its chignon into his hand. He tried not to think about how soft and silky the strands felt in his fingers; rather, he concentrated on the wound to her shoulder.

Tanner yanked off his suit coat, wadded it up into a pillow, and then gently slid it under her head. Up close he could see her chest barely moving beneath her blood-soaked blouse. Her heartbeat throbbed erratically, but she was breathing. She wasn't dead, but with every beat of her heart, she lost more blood.

He reached down, lifted up her petticoat, and ripped the worn yellowed material. He peeled back the torn blouse, away from her injury. The wound was a small hole. He grimaced at the sight of the visible tissue and muscle of her shoulder. Lifting her slightly, she moaned, and he saw there was no exit wound. The bullet had lodged in her shoulder, probably in the bone.

If someone could get her to a doctor, there was a chance she could live, though the bullet would have to be removed.

He held the piece of petticoat against the wound, trying to suppress the bleeding.

"Where's the next layover station?" Tanner asked.

"About ten miles up the road. But they don't have no sawbones."

"She needs a doctor," he said, frustrated. Tanner pressed the rag against the wound. How many times had he done this during the war? How many times had he failed to save a fellow soldier?

He glanced down at the woman, noticing how fragile she appeared. Her porcelain skin had turned an unhealthy shade of white that contrasted with the sprinkle of freckles across her nose and cheeks. She was beautiful, and near death because of him. "There's a doctor in San Antonio."

"We just came from there. I can't return," the stagecoach driver insisted. "She got shot because of you. You take her back."

Tanner glanced down at the woman, even unconscious she was still beautiful. As he pressed the strips of cloth against her wound, he wondered about the people who were waiting in Fort Worth for her, about her life and how this could affect her. The blood was starting to slow to a trickle.

Ripping another section of her petticoat, he packed the bullet hole with the extra strips of material he'd torn. He knew it was imperative to keep her arm immobile or the gait of his horse could possibly cause it to bleed again. Finally, he tied her arm in a sling.

The grandmother walked over, carrying a small carpet-bag and a small reticule. "Here, this belongs to Beth. She'll need it."

"What's her full name? Where did she say her family lives?" Tanner questioned.

He hadn't been paying much attention. He'd been too intent on eyeing her good looks and watching for the gang that had now departed without him.

"Elizabeth Anderson. She's from Georgia, but she told me she had no kinfolk or anyone left to take care of her. You make sure she gets to a good doctor."

He nodded. "Don't worry."

Tanner went to the back of the stage, where his chestnut mare was tethered. He untied the horse, grabbed the reins, and pulled the animal closer to the woman's body. He stepped one foot up into the stirrup and then swung a leg over the saddle and slid gently onto the back of the animal. The stagecoach driver hurried over and lifted the young woman's still form up into his arms. He settled her against him, the feel of her warm woman's body against his own, soft and vulnerable. He pushed the thought out of his mind.

She'd been shot, and it was his fault.

He glanced at the driver and the old woman. They watched as he tipped the edge of his black hat with one hand and then turned his horse in a southerly direction, away from the stage.

Hell of a way to end a holdup, a robbery that hadn't gone well from the start. He was supposed to rejoin the gang here, not ride in the opposite direction. Oh, well, it would have to wait until another day.

With a careful gait, his horse moved down the road, bouncing the lovely young woman in his arms. Tanner glanced at Miss Anderson's drawn face. Maybe he could save her, unlike his best friend, Carter.

Tucker Burnett watched his older brother, Travis, and his bride giggling on the loveseat together. He shook his head. It was almost more than he could stomach to believe that this hopelessly infatuated man was his older brother. The same man who had held Rose Severin, the woman he finally married, captive for months, believing she had stolen his mother's wedding band, which now glistened and shone on Rose's left hand.

His own mother had played matchmaker by hiding the ring, hoping all along that Travis would fall in love with Rose. They were just lucky the incident had turned out as well as it had.

Though he did think that his aging mother's hair had turned a bit grayer during the ordeal, her brown eyes still held a twinkle in them whenever she talked about the episode.

Eugenia Burnett walked into the parlor, and Tucker couldn't help but glance at her empty left hand. Although he missed seeing his mother wear her wedding ring, he knew she had wanted Rose to have the band of gold. Somehow it was the least Eugenia could do after everything Travis had put Rose through.

"Tucker, would you mind accompanying me for a walk?" his mother questioned. She winked at him and nodded her head toward the happy couple on the loveseat.

He shook his head knowingly.

God, why had he decided to come out to dinner today?

He should have used the excuse he was too busy. He could have lied and said there was no one to watch the jail. Instead, he had agreed to attend this little get-together. And now the sight of his smitten brother was both funny and irritating. Funny because responsible Travis had fallen and fallen hard; irritating because Tucker would never have a chance to experience love.

"Sure, let's go, Mother," he said, walking across the room, his boots clunking softly against the oval rug covering the parlor floor.

His mother slipped her hand in the crook of his elbow. "Are they always this mushy?" he asked.

She laughed. "They're in love, dear, and the emotion is so new. Let them enjoy it before the newness wears off and the babies come."

Tucker swallowed. "Babies?"

"Well, I certainly hope they have children. After all, I've not gone to all this trouble for nothing. I want grandchildren. Can you imagine a little girl with Rose's dark curls and green eyes or a little boy with Travis's brown eyes and sandy hair?"

Eugenia sighed. "It's what I hope for you, too. To meet a nice young woman, fall in love, and give me lots of grandchildren."

"So, how's the new barn," he asked, trying his best to change the subject. Surely, since Travis was settling down, his mother would be happy that one of the Burnett boys was finally married, and maybe she would leave him alone.

He pushed open the front door, and they stepped out onto the wooden porch.

"I know you're trying to shift my attention to other matters, Tucker, but I really must speak with you about a pressing issue."

Tucker glanced down at his aging mother and noticed for the first time that she seemed nervous. "What's wrong, Mother?"

"Well . . . you know, dear, sometimes in the heat of the moment, you do things that later you regret. Things that you know you should have left alone, though you do them with the best intentions, especially where your children are concerned."

"What did you do, Mother? Travis has not gotten over the fact that you lied about your wedding ring. I hope you aren't keeping anything else from him."

"No, dear." She took a deep breath and released it slowly. "Come sit on the swing with me."

She led him over to the porch swing, and they both took a seat. His mother picked up his hand and patted it. "Tucker, you have to remember that I was really upset when your brother Tanner disappeared, and then, when it looked like Travis and Rose were never going to get married, well . . . I did something I shouldn't have."

Tucker felt his heart speed up. Whatever his meddlesome mother had done affected him. "What, Mother?"

"I—I placed an ad for a mail-order bride." She paused. "For you."

"What?" He jumped up out of the swing, unable to sit beside his mother another moment. She had really gone too far this time. It was bad enough what she'd done to Travis, but she was not going to mess with his affairs.

"Well, things just sort of got out of hand. I started writing to this young woman who responded to the ad, and then the next thing I knew, I started signing your name to the letters. And now, well, now, she's on her way here." She paused. "To meet you."

"Me! You're the one who's been corresponding with her. You meet her."

How could his mother do this to him? He could never

marry. A gunslinger turned marshal didn't need a wife, didn't need to make someone a young widow.

"Now, son, I know you're upset. But remember, you don't have to marry her unless you want to. But since I've been signing your name to her letters, you would be such an understanding son to be nice to her."

"This is an out-and-out lie, Mother. What have you been telling her? How can I act like I know what you've said?"

"Well, I thought of that, so I've saved her letters so you could at least see her replies back to you." Eugenia threw up her hands. "I never should have done this, but she is such a nice young woman, I just didn't have the heart to tell her the truth after I got to know her."

"Mother, she's going to figure out I never wrote those letters. I hardly think we'd say the same things." He took his hat and hit the side of his leg with it. "Besides, did you ever consider that just maybe there was someone I was interested in already?"

"Really? Who, dear? You've never even mentioned seeing anyone."

Tucker clenched his fists in anger. Once there had been someone he really cared about, but he wasn't about to tell his mother. Nothing could ever come from the situation, for he wasn't a marrying kind of man. And he was not about to give his mother the ammunition she needed, because she would soon have an arsenal.

"Never mind."

"No, dear, tell me if there is someone else."

Tucker couldn't stand this. Now his mother had turned her matchmaking sights on him. He pushed his hat down on his head.

"There's no one, Mother. Absolutely no one." He

walked to the edge of the porch. He had to get away. He was in a fine pickle now.

"So will you at least meet the woman?" she asked earnestly.

Tucker strode to his horse, his steps heavy and hard. "No. You meet her stage; you marry her."

"Think about it. You don't have to give me your answer today. You have until Wednesday before she arrives."

"That's just great! When were you planning on telling me, Mother? As we drove up in the wagon?"

"Don't take that tone with me, young man. This is the first time I've seen you in weeks. If you came out more often, I would have told you."

"Between you and the lovebirds, I'm safer with a jail filled with criminals," he muttered under his breath.

"What did you say, dear? I couldn't hear you."

"Between you and the lovebirds, it's hard to stay away."

His mother looked at him, puzzled, and watched as he swung up into the saddle. "Tell Rose and Travis I said good-bye."

She ran to the edge of the porch and leaned over the white railing. "So are you going to go with me to pick up Beth?"

Beth. The woman his mother had chosen for him to marry was named Beth. He turned his horse toward the gate. "I'm working that day, Mother."

"But . . ."

He shrugged and rode away. Let her stew over the situation for a while. She needed to be nervous about his going with her to pick up this woman. It was the least he could do to teach his mother to stay out of his business.

Hell, Beth probably had buck teeth, stringy hair, and bad breath. Why else would a woman travel hundreds of miles to marry a man she'd never met?

Elizabeth Anderson never awoke during the ride to San Antonio, and Tanner wondered if she would live. He gazed down at her ashen complexion, her freckles standing out against her pale skin. She moaned several times as if she were in pain, but she never opened her eyes and looked at him.

When he arrived in town, Tanner found the doctor's house. As gently as he could, he lifted Beth off his horse and carried her up the steps to the infirmary, grateful he had managed to get her there alive.

A sign directed him to the side of the house, where a shingle hung over the door with the word Doctor painted in bold letters. He rapped on the door.

A man in his late fifties with graying hair slid open a small wooden window on the door that he could simply peer through. "How can I help you?"

Tanner stood there holding the woman while the man never even opened the main door. "She's got a bullet in her shoulder. I think she may have lost quite a bit of blood. She hasn't awakened since the accident. I'd like to leave her here."

The doctor glanced at her. "That's impossible. I'm not accepting any more patients right now. I have a patient who may have cholera. It's best you take your wife on to the hotel in town. I'll come meet you there in an hour."

The man assumed that Beth was his wife and that she would stay with him. But Tanner hadn't planned on staying in town. He had a gang to find. Though what kind of reception he would receive after they rode off and left him, he didn't know. Yet he was the one who'd told them of the gold shipment.

He hadn't planned on delaying, but he couldn't walk away from the woman, either, even if that meant not meeting up with the Bass gang as originally planned. They would just have to wait.

"I'll meet you at the hotel," Tanner acknowledged.

He carried Beth back to his horse and lifted her up in the saddle, then rode back down the main street of town, where he'd seen a hotel.

A little later, Tanner walked into the hotel with Miss Anderson in his arms. "Which room is available?"

The clerk stared at him open-mouthed. "Ah, number fifteen on the second floor is ready."

Tanner took the stairs two at a time, carrying the woman. She was light, but he felt as if he'd carried her everywhere and he noticed that the wound was beginning to bleed again.

With a quick twist of the doorknob, he threw open the portal and strode into the room. Gently, he laid Beth on the double bed, centered against a wall in the room.

Her long auburn lashes lifted slowly, then fluttered briefly before she focused her hazel eyes on him. She glanced up at him in surprise and tried to rise from the bed. With a gasp of pain she sunk back down.

"Don't move," he commanded.

She looked at him groggily. "Where am I?"

"You're okay. You're in a hotel in San Antonio."

"San Antonio?" She tried to rise up off the bed again and then groaned. "Stage? What happened?"

"We were robbed, and you were shot," Tanner said, hovering over the bed.

"The stage," she said, her eyes fluttering as if she were

trying to focus. Her voice became distant. "I've got to get back on the stage."

He laid a hand on her chest, just below her good shoulder, and applied pressure. "You're not in any shape to go anywhere."

She opened her eyes and gazed up at him in confusion and then winced in pain. "My arm. What's wrong with my arm?"

"You've been shot, Miss Anderson," he said, feeling so guilty that she'd taken a bullet because of him.

He could see her trying to remember and when she glanced at him, her eyes widened with fear. "You . . . you were on the stagecoach?"

"Yes, I'm trying to help you. I carried you to town, and a doctor is coming to see about that shoulder," he clarified, hoping she would accept his explanation.

Her eyes were dazed and frightened. "I—I can't stay here."

"You have to. The doctor is on his way to get the bullet out of your shoulder," he said, gently trying to ease her fears.

She eyed him warily, a frightened expression on her ashen face. He could tell she was still not convinced he was not going to hurt her.

"I've got to get out of here. I have to get to Texas," she said deliriously. She tried to rise off the bed again, but he held her down.

"You're not going anywhere right now."

"But I can't be in a hotel room with a strange man," she whispered, her strength ebbing.

"You don't have any choice, lady. You're hurt. Now lay still before you open up that wound again. The doctor is supposed to be here soon. He'll fix you up, and then we can both be on our way."

"I . . . can't stay," she said, drifting off again, her eyes slowly closing.

Gratefully, she sank back into unconsciousness once again. He took a blanket from the bed, covered her, and then took a step over to the window and leaned against the wooden frame.

The people of San Antonio bustled on their way to some unknown destination as Tanner looked out onto the street below. He gazed upon the men and women going about their lives and felt more alone than he'd felt in the last ten years.

Coming home to Texas had disturbed his concentration, even his sleep. For the last three months he'd pushed the memory of his family away while trying to focus on the task before him, with little or no success. Now, just when it was almost in his grasp, it had been yanked away by fate.

Staring out the window, Tanner watched as a buggy pulled up in front of the hotel and the doctor, carrying a black bag, made his way inside. A few minutes later, there was a pounding on the door.

Tanner opened the wooden portal, and the doctor rushed in. "Sorry, I got here as quick as I could." He held out his hand. "I'm Doc Benson."

Tanner grasped his hand. "Tanner."

The man walked in and glanced at the still figure lying on the bed. "Any change in her condition?"

"She woke up for a little bit, then passed out again," he said, running his hand through his hair.

"Well, if we're lucky, she'll remain out while I dig for that bullet," the doctor said, sitting down gently on the side of the bed, placing his bag close at hand.

The doctor pulled away the torn pieces of petticoat that Tanner had applied to stop the bleeding. The outer pieces of material were caked with dried blood; the ones closest to the wound were still damp. Searching for the bullet, the doctor pressed his fingers against the wound, causing Beth to moan, a deep, pitiful sound that left Tanner aching with regret for the woman's pain. If it weren't for him, she would still be on that stage headed for Fort Worth. She wouldn't be experiencing this pain if Tanner hadn't walked into her life.

"You're right. That bullet is deep, but I don't think it broke any bones. Once we get the slug out, your wife should be all right," the doctor said, glancing up at Tanner.

Tanner started to correct the doctor, to tell him that Beth wasn't his wife, but then thought twice. Why complicate matters? Years ago, he'd have been thrilled to have a woman like Beth as his wife. Now his life had changed, and he'd never marry.

"Extracting a bullet is never easy, and it's going to hurt plenty. I'm going to need your help holding her down," the doctor informed him.

"All right," Tanner said. Memories of hospital tents and the cries of the men inside rushed back with startling clarity. Recalling the sick, sweet smell of laudanum made him inwardly shudder.

The doctor opened his medical bag and took out a surgical knife, gauze, scissors, a bottle of antiseptic, and forceps. He stood up and went to the water basin and poured water over his hands. Tanner watched as Doc Benson soaped his hands up past his wrist, scrubbing his skin meticulously.

When he finished, he turned to Tanner and said, "Let's get started. Pull her down on the bed to where you can hold her head and shoulders. I'm going to angle my body over her, holding her chest down, while I try to extract the lead."

"Can't you give her something for the pain?" Tanner asked, knowing how much this was going to hurt Miss Anderson.

"I'd rather not. She's weak, and I don't want her so drugged she never comes awake."

Tanner swallowed, suddenly afraid for the beautiful young woman. He glanced over at the girl with the auburn curls and hazel eyes and speculated about her life. Who was waiting for her? Who would miss her when the stage arrived?

The doctor motioned for him to lift her shoulders. Tanner walked to the side of the bed and gazed down at Elizabeth Anderson. He grabbed her by the shoulders, and as gently as he could, he shifted her down on the bed while the doctor pulled on her feet.

Beth groaned, moving her head from side to side. Tanner felt the urge to comfort her, to tell her everything was going to be all right. Yet he resisted. She was a stranger, a woman who happened to take a bullet because of him.

The doctor sat down beside her and started to cut away the material of her blouse from around the wound. "I need to get the bullet out; then I'll have to wrap the shoulder. So I'm going to have to cut this blouse off your wife."

"That's all right." Tanner acknowledged, feeling strange giving such permission for a woman he'd known only since the stage had left early that morning.

Dr. Benson swathed the entire area with turpentine, cleaning away the dark gunpowder left by the bullet. Then he glanced up at Tanner. "Hold on to her."

Tanner grabbed her shoulders and held her firmly to the bed while the doctor took his knife and cut the bullet hole wide enough to get the forceps into the wound.

Beth jerked at the first cut, her hazel eyes fluttered open, and she moaned. "Stop! It hurts."

"It's okay, honey. The doctor is going to remove the bullet from your shoulder," Tanner whispered in her ear, trying to soothe her.

She glanced at him, her big hazel eyes confused. "Hurts. No! Stop!"

"We've got to remove the bullet," he repeated, taking his left hand and brushing back the silken strands of hair away from her face while his right hand continued to keep her from coming up off the bed.

She screamed as the doctor inserted the forceps into her flesh, groping for the bullet.

"It's almost over, young lady. Hang in there and we'll be done soon," he said, his voice breathy as he struggled, trying to get the bullet out. "I found it."

Beth started to cry, tears rolling down her face and Tanner leaned down and put his face against hers. "I'm sorry," he whispered. "It's going to be all right. Just a few more minutes and it will be all over."

"I got it!" the doctor cried, pulling the forceps with the bullet out of Beth's shoulder.

Tanner glanced up and saw the bullet between the clasps of the instrument. "Look, Beth, it's out."

He glanced down and saw that once again Beth had lost consciousness.

Quickly, he looked at the doctor. "Is she all right?"

"Let her be. She needs the rest." He dropped the bullet, and it landed with a clang in a metal bowl.

Tanner released his grip on Beth's shoulder and stepped back to watch the doctor finish his task. He took what looked like a needle and thread from his bag. Once again he swathed the area with antiseptic before he began to close the wound, stitching the skin back over the gaping hole.

"I don't believe you told me how your wife got shot," the doctor asked nonchalantly while he worked over Beth.

"No, I didn't," Tanner said in a clipped tone.

Five stitches completed the job, and then he put a salve on the area and began wrapping Beth's shoulder in clean gauze.

The doctor tied off the gauze in a knot and then began to pick up his instruments, wiping each one carefully with a clean cloth.

"Make sure she drinks plenty of liquids. She'll probably run a fever for a day or two before she starts getting better. I'll come by tomorrow to check on her, but if you need me before then, just send someone to the house." He paused and looked at Tanner. "I think your wife is going to be okay."

"Thanks, Doc."

Tanner escorted the man to the door, and with a tip of his hat, the doctor was gone.

Shutting the door, Tanner returned to the side of the bed. He glanced at the woman lying there. She was breathtakingly beautiful, her pale skin as white as parchment paper, her freckles standing out clearly against her skin.

If he were a boundless man, without the scars of war, Beth Anderson would be the kind of woman he'd court, but he wasn't free, and his past shadowed his days and tortured his nights.

No, as soon as she was well enough, Beth Anderson would be on the next stage out of San Antonio, and Tanner would be back to riding with the Bass gang. The very gang that had robbed Beth's stage.

TWO

Tanner knew he was dreaming, but he couldn't stop the nightmare any more than he'd been able to stop the real-life event when it happened. *Once again he was in Georgia in a pasture turned battlefield, littered with dead bodies, men he knew, their limbs blown away. The front line had fallen. The Confederates were being beaten, and Tanner had never been so frightened.*

He fought hand-to-hand combat and jabbed his bayonet into the belly of a Yankee soldier. Pushing and shoving, jabbing and stabbing, he made his way to the front line, looking for Carter. He'd been beside his friend a moment ago, and now Carter was gone, lost in the midst of the worst battle they'd ever fought. The cannons roared . . .

The roaring changed into pounding, and Tanner shook himself awake, realizing someone was beating on the door. Instantly, he came awake, jumping up and reaching for his guns in one smooth, quick move. As he made his way to the entrance, he passed the bed and glanced down at Beth, who was still blissfully unconscious.

The morning sun filtered through the window, and he realized he'd slept later than he'd intended.

Out of habit, he pulled the gun out of his holster, cocked it, and stood to the left of the door hinges. "Who is it?"

"Open up, you bloody fool."

Recognizing the voice, Tanner released the hammer on his gun and shoved it back into his holster. Dreading opening the door, he freed the lock and pulled the portal open, letting in the man who held Tanner's life in his hands.

Tall and muscular with graying hair, the man strode in, his size and attitude filling the empty spaces of the room.

"What the hell are you doing in San Antonio? Some woman was shot during the holdup yesterday and . . ."

Abruptly, the man halted and stared at the woman in the bed. He glanced back at Tanner, questioning.

"Keep your voice down. She's been out ever since the doctor removed the bullet yesterday evening. How did you find me?"

"Been checking hotels all morning. Who is she?"

"Elizabeth Anderson. The woman who was shot yesterday."

"Huh?" the man asked, clearly not understanding.

"Miss Anderson took a bullet meant for Sam that the driver fired." He gazed down at the woman, her face flushed with fever. "The stagecoach wasn't going anywhere near a doctor and I couldn't very well leave her and have her murder on my hands."

"You fool." He waved his hand toward the woman. "The people on the stage would have gotten her to a doctor. You didn't have to take care of her."

"No, I didn't have to take care of her, but I did," Tanner said, his voice rising.

"Well, you better do something with her quick, because the Bass gang won't wait for you while you're holed up inside this hotel playing nursemaid."

"They won't go far. I'll find them when I'm ready."

"I wouldn't count on it." The man strolled around the room, then turned and faced Tanner. His eyes were fierce. "You know what's riding on this."

"I said I'd catch up with them." Tanner shrugged his shoulders nonchalantly. He wasn't in that big of a hurry to join back up with the outlaws. It just didn't seem to matter whether or not he found them.

The man stared at him, weighing his words, his hands on his hips. "I'll be checking in on you soon. Get rid of the woman." He started toward the door and then glanced back. "Did you try the local doctor to see if he'd take care of her?"

"He's quarantined with a case of cholera."

The man grimaced. "Find some local woman who needs the money and then telegraph Miss Anderson's family. She shouldn't have been traveling alone, anyway."

Tanner opened the door, hoping his visitor would get the message. "I'll take care of it."

"Be sure you do—soon."

He strode through the door. Tanner shut the portal firmly behind him. Arrogant bastard. He just wished he'd go away and leave him be. But he knew that wouldn't happen, and he really had very little choice.

A moan from the bed drew his attention to Beth. What was he going to do with her? The doctor couldn't take her, and Tanner couldn't just leave her to anyone's care.

Her injury was his fault, and he took his responsibilities seriously.

She thrashed about in the bed, her voice suddenly crying out. "No! General—I can't. I'm a good woman. Really, I am!"

Tanner hurried over to the bed, his gaze taking in her feverish state. He laid the back of his hand against her brow. She was burning with fever, her sweat-soaked skin hot to the touch. He took a rag, dipped it in a bowl of water, and laid the cool cloth against her forehead.

Beth jerked at the touch of the damp rag; her eyes opened, but they were dazed and feverish. "Mother, it was the only way. I had no other choice."

"Shh, Beth," he whispered. "I believe you. Everything is going to be all right."

She turned at the sound of his voice, her demeanor relaxing, and she stared up at him, not really seeing him but whoever was in her dreams.

"Mother . . . I had no choice." Her voice faded away, and she drifted back into unconsciousness.

How many times had he soothed a soldier's fears or listened to his confession as he lay dying, pretending to be the person the injured sought resolution from?

More times than he ever wanted to remember.

Whatever disturbed Miss Anderson, she could never face in the light of day. But her fever broke down her barriers and exposed her nightmares.

Tanner gazed down at her. What did a beautiful woman who obviously had poise, grace, and charm have to fear? Over and over she'd said she had no choice, it was the only way. But what choice was she referring to, and why did she appear frightened?

Tanner had made the wrong choices in life, but he had made them of his own free will. And he hoped to God his own nightmares weren't as easily exposed as Miss Anderson's.

Through a misty haze Elizabeth saw the dark, coffee-haired man hovering over her, his face anxious, worried. She wanted to reach up and soothe his troubled brow, but her arms felt constricted and heavy. She thought she was moving her limbs, but they went nowhere.

She tried to open her mouth and request a drink, but only a groan escaped.

"Water," she finally managed to croak.

The touch of cool wetness bathed her lips, and she drank from the glass, grateful for the refreshment.

Only after the wetness eased her parched throat was she able to get coherent words out. "Where am I?"

"A hotel room in San Antonio," he acknowledged, pushing a strand of hair away from her face.

She shook her head, becoming agitated. "Fort Worth. I must get to Fort Worth."

"Once you're well," the man soothing her burning brow stated.

"Can't wait. I need to go."

He bathed her face, trying to soothe her.

"What happened?" she asked, wondering why she hurt.

"Your shoulder. You were shot during a holdup."

Groggy, she glanced at her shoulder, bare except for the white gauze bandages covering the wound. She tried to move the joint, and pain assaulted her in undulating waves.

With a cry, she lay back against the pillows, closed her eyes, and breathed deeply, trying to ease the throbbing.

"Are you all right?" he asked. "Stupid question."

She nodded her head, feeling dazed from the pain and fever.

"You're the man from the stage. You were sitting across from me."

"Name's Tanner."

The memory of sitting across from him and the elderly

woman who had talked most of the journey slowly returned. She remembered thinking he was a handsome man in a unique sense. Not classically handsome but more rugged and rough. There was an edge to him that spoke of danger and defiance. The evidence of a man who had lived a hard life showed on his face. No, he was certainly no pretty boy, at least not like the boys back home.

"I'm going to get you some soup. I want you to take a few sips, at least. I'll be right back," he said, walking out the door.

Beth dozed off, but minutes later Tanner came back into the room, a tray in his arms. The aroma of beef broth teased her long-denied stomach, which insisted she open her eyes.

"I got you some broth. You need to eat a little, just to keep up your strength."

"Must get to Fort Worth," she whispered weakly.

"Later, Miss Anderson, when you're well."

But she didn't have later. She needed to be there on Wednesday. It was her only chance for the future.

With a great effort she reached up and pulled on his arm. "Have to be in Fort Worth."

He shook his head. "You've been shot. You're not well. You can't travel until that arm is better."

She shook her head, but he ignored her and lifted her gently to a sitting position in bed. The slightest jostle caused her to moan, and she closed her eyes until the pain subsided.

Pulling a chair up next to the bed, he sat beside her with a bowl in his hand. He dipped the spoon into the broth and gently put it to her lips. The aroma was delicious, and she sipped from the spoon.

"Stage," she croaked.

"Yes, you were on the stage, but you were shot during a holdup." He brushed her fevered brow. "You're safe now. Eat some more broth."

He put another spoonful to her lips. She sipped, the warm liquid somehow soothing. He held the bowl of hot broth in his hands, which were large and strong, rugged from hard work. She glanced up at him and noticed the way his long, dark lashes seemed to shield his blue eyes. She wondered if the brief flashes of pain she seemed to sense in him were real or just her feverish hallucinations.

It felt so odd to have someone feeding her when she'd taken care of her family members all their lives. Never the patient herself, she was the one who spoon-fed the others. But for a man to be taking care of her, a complete stranger, seemed odd and certainly out of character for the men she had known.

Yes, Mr. Tanner was certainly dangerous looking, but handsome and pleasant to look upon also. Quickly, she reminded herself that she was all but engaged to a man she'd never met.

He continued spooning the soup to her until she'd eaten almost half of the bowl's contents and pushed his hand away.

"No more." She grabbed him by the arm; her eyes felt droopy with fatigue. "Fort Worth. Must get to Fort Worth."

"If you'll relax, I promise you I'll find a way for you to get to Fort Worth. Now, rest and get well."

The strain of so much talking and her first meal since the accident overcame Beth. As she drifted off to sleep, she mumbled the same words.

"Fort Worth. I must reach Fort Worth."

* * *

The early-morning sunshine was warm against Beth's face as she slowly opened her eyes and glanced around the hotel room.

It was then that she saw Tanner sitting in a chair on the other side of the bed. The muscular man was sprawled out, asleep, in a chair close to her. His brown hair grazed his forehead in a curl that defied being combed away. His eyebrows were bushy and dark, and a full mustache covered his upper lip from view. He had the look of a man who even in his sleep looked more like an outlaw than a banker.

Gone were the stiff, formal banker's clothes. He was dressed differently, and somehow his clothes seemed more fitting than the three-piece suit and bowler hat he'd worn previously.

He still wore the same black vest and white shirt, but the tie and hat were gone, and his pants fit his muscular thighs and legs. A worn gun belt was slung low across his hips, the holster filled with not one but two Colt Navy revolvers.

Beth recognized those guns. They were from the Civil War. Confederate guns. She shivered, determined not to think about the war. Yet how had Tanner gotten those handguns? Certainly he had enlisted just like every other available man. The question was: Which side had he fought on?

She didn't care as long as he took her to Fort Worth. She had to get there and marry the man who had sent for her or starve.

Bits and pieces of the last week started to drift back. After leaving Jonesboro, Georgia, she'd caught the train in Atlanta and headed west. In Houston, she'd taken a stagecoach bound for San Antonio, where they'd changed drivers and continued on toward Fort Worth. Her mind slowed, and she swallowed. On the stage had been two passengers, an older woman and Tanner, who now sat sleeping in a chair across from her.

Bandits had chased the coach until they pulled over. She remembered getting out of the stage and then a loud explosion.

She stirred restlessly in the bed, and a sharp pain stabbed her in the shoulder. She tried to rise, but a moan escaped her as pain ripped through the tender flesh of her shoulder, and she remembered. She'd been shot.

Mr. Tanner's eyes opened, and she stared into the bluest gaze she'd seen since leaving Dixie. A tremor of awareness rippled through her, yet she felt almost fearful. She was alone with a strange man in a hotel room, hurt and eager to get to Fort Worth.

"Good morning. How do you feel?" he questioned.

"Sore, tired. What happened?" she asked.

"We were riding on the same stage when it was robbed," he said, brushing his hair back. "The stage went on to Fort Worth. I brought you back here to San Antonio, to the doctor."

"Oh, no! What day is it?" she asked, fear paralyzing her.

"Tuesday."

"Oh, my God! I'm not going to be there on time." She tried to swing her legs over the side of the bed but found they felt more like dead weights than her own legs.

"Whoa! Just lie back. You're not going anywhere."

Beth lay her head back against the pillow, the tears hovering right below her lashes. This was her last chance at happiness, at a respectable future with a husband and a family. She had invested all her money into getting to Fort Worth. Now she was broke, destitute, hurt, and inside a strange hotel room with a man who looked more like an outlaw than a nursemaid.

Bitter disappointment at once again being dealt a bad hand in the card game of life consumed her. It wasn't fair.

"It'll take a while for that shoulder to heal, but you'll be okay," Tanner said gruffly.

Beth could barely nod her head. She knew if she opened her mouth, the tears would start to flow, and a sob would escape.

She swallowed hard and rapidly blinked back the tears. She couldn't think about this right now. But there had to be a way she could fix this latest incident in a life gone awry. There had to be some way for her to get out of this town and find her way to Fort Worth.

"I bet you're hungry. You've only eaten that little bit of broth I brought you yesterday," Tanner said, jumping up and heading for the door.

"Actually . . . I need to use the . . . the slop jar," she said, mortified that she was forced to depend on a stranger to help her.

He glanced at her and then at the porcelain bucket sitting over in the corner. He looked uneasy, but she couldn't wait any longer.

"Uh, sure," he said, looking uncomfortable.

It was then she noticed that her good white blouse had been cut away. It looked as if scissors had snipped away the material, leaving her chemise exposed, her right shoulder carefully wrapped in a gauze material. Yet the bruising could be seen streaking down her arm.

She lifted the covers and anxiously peeked to see what else she was wearing. The rest of her clothes remained the same. Her shoes had been removed, her corset loosened, but everything else was intact.

Beth tried once again to swing her legs over the side of the bed but was just too weak.

She was bedridden, dependent on a man she'd met briefly and about to miss what she'd hoped would be the biggest day of her life.

This time there was no holding back. Everything looked bleak. She had no money, no way to get to Fort Worth; she was sore and weak and couldn't even perform bodily functions by herself.

The tears welled up and overflowed, running down her cheeks. She sniffed, and the tears fell faster as a little sob escaped.

"Hey, what's the matter?" Tanner asked. "You're going to be okay."

He leaned down beside her. "Are you hurting?"

She shook her head, the tears falling faster, almost out of control. "It's everything. I was supposed to be in Fort Worth tomorrow."

He took her in his arms and held her, being careful not to hurt her shoulder. As he pressed her to his chest, Beth cried for everything that had brought her to this point in her life. And there was so much that she felt she'd had no control over, including the bullet that had taken her off the latest road she'd chosen, the one that would have promised her a good future.

"Shh."

She laid her head on his shoulder and cried, her tears falling on his black silk vest as his hands rubbed small circles on her back in a comforting gesture.

"Shh. It's okay," he said against her neck.

Slowly, the tears subsided until there were only small hiccupping sounds, but she made no move to withdraw from his embrace.

It felt good to have a pair of strong arms holding her,

to smell the clean scent of a man, and to be held only for comfort.

The room finally became silent except for the steady rhythm of their breathing, which Beth was acutely aware of.

Eventually, he drew back and looked into her tear-streaked face. "Feel better?"

She nodded her head, unable to speak, awed that this big, strong man was still holding her, comforting her. His gruff mannerisms didn't give credence to the fact that he could be tender and concerned. It surprised and intrigued her about this man she hardly knew but was so dependent on.

Tanner glanced over at the slop jar and then at the bowl the doctor had left behind. "What if I brought over that small metal bowl that the doctor used to remove the bullet? Do you think you could use that for a bedpan?"

"I think so," she acknowledged.

He handed her the small metal dish, his eyes not meeting her gaze.

"I'll step out in the hall for a few minutes," he said awkwardly. "And give you some privacy."

She sniffed. "Thank you."

He hightailed it out the door, and Beth knew he felt as uncomfortable with this arrangement as she did.

Beth waited for the door to close, and then she struggled for a good five minutes to pull down her pantaloons. Only able to use her left hand, she tried to get a good grip on the pesky pantaloons to pull them down. Weakened from the bullet wound, she soon tired of struggling with the drawers. Frustrated by her inability to complete even this small task, she threw the metal bowl. It hit the wall with a clang and fell to the floor, where it rolled.

Mr. Tanner opened the door cautiously and peered inside. "You all right?"

"Uh, no. I have a problem," she said, embarrassed, the tears right below the surface, her modesty in serious jeopardy.

He stepped inside and shut the door. "What's wrong?"

Beth glanced up at him, then took a deep breath and released it slowly. "I . . . I can't get my—pantaloons down with just my left hand. I've tried and tried, but I'm not strong enough."

She watched his face for any sign he was amused or even uncomfortable, for she knew she certainly felt shy at asking a stranger to help her with this intimate task. His face was expressionless, and his eyes refused to meet hers.

"Let me help." He slipped his hand underneath the covers and found her skirt. Pulling it out of the way, he lifted the material just enough to find her drawers. Letting the blanket fall around his hand to shield her modesty, he found the waistband of her pantaloons and tugged on them gently.

Beth felt flames of embarrassment light up her face as she helped him tug down her drawers. As his fingers brushed against her naked flesh, tingles of awareness went through her lower body. She almost jumped at the contact of his rough hands against her thighs. Yet his touch was gentle, almost a caress.

She glanced up at him to see if he, too, had felt the ripple that had almost caused her to jump. But his face remained the same.

"Is that going to be all right?" he asked, his eyes still not meeting hers.

"I think so."

"Do I need to stay, or can you manage?" he asked gently.

"No. I think I'll be okay, now."

He had started for the door when Beth remembered.

"Uh, Mr. Tanner."

"Yes."

"Could you pick up that metal bowl and bring it to me?" she asked, feeling like a fool.

He walked back into the room, glancing around until he located the missing bowl. With a smile, he handed it back to her.

Now he found it amusing, though he didn't say a word.

"Thank you," she said, unable to meet his gaze before he left.

Three

Beth awoke with a start. She glanced around the room and realized she was alone. Gingerly, she moved to a sitting position on the bed, her back needing relief from the pressure of the bed's ticking. Even that little bit of exertion sent her shoulder to throbbing and left her breathless from the pain and effort. Though the wound still pained her, she no longer felt that she was running a fever.

The windows were open, and the curtains billowed from the warm summer breeze. The sound of horses and buggies moving down the street drifted up through the window. Men called to one another, and occasionally she could hear snatches of conversation. She felt isolated, cut off from the rest of the world, by her injuries.

If only she could dress and find her way to the telegraph office to send her intended a telegram. Just a brief message to let him know she'd had a slight delay but would be there soon. He'd wait, surely he'd wait, wouldn't he?

But the telegram was impossible. Whatever money she'd possessed at the beginning of the trip was now in the hands of a man who wore a mask and waved a gun. No matter how badly she needed that cash, she felt grateful just to be alive. But now she was destitute and had no way to reach Fort Worth, no way to contact the man she was to marry.

Beth leaned back against the pillows, amazed at the turn her life had once again taken. Since the war, her life had never been as she'd foreseen it when she was younger. Everything had changed, and now, on her way to Fort Worth to a fresh start, she'd taken a bullet and worried that her husband-to-be would think she had jilted him.

After all, they'd never met, only corresponded. How would he know she hadn't changed her mind, gotten cold feet, or decided against becoming a mail-order bride?

And maybe his fears were well grounded. After all, marrying someone she'd never met wasn't exactly what she'd had in mind when she considered taking a husband. But the war had left her little choice.

There was nothing to return to in Georgia. Everyone she loved was buried in the family cemetery. And the boll weevils had finished off what she'd managed to hold on to through the war. Now the tax collector held the keys to Pinewood, the family plantation.

The belle of the ball was no longer accepted by society. All she had left were poignant and bittersweet memories of the way life once had been.

She shook her head. Surely she had the worst luck imaginable. Her chance for a new beginning, a new start in life, had taken a shot in the shoulder and had suffered a serious setback.

Somehow she had to get to Fort Worth.

Though she didn't love her new husband-to-be or know much about him, his letters were nice. He promised to take care of her, and he wanted children. Everything she wanted in a mate, she hoped, or at least a provider.

Beth didn't need a lot in life. She'd seen enough death

and destruction to realize what was really important. She didn't even need a big, fancy house anymore or even riches to make her happy. All she wanted was a man who could accept her and her past, wouldn't let her go hungry, and was willing to have children.

Her dreams weren't big, had never been extravagant, but the war had robbed her of everything she'd held near and dear. Everything had disappeared or altered forever, changing her in the process.

Now she had to get well, find a way to continue on to Fort Worth, and catch up with her mail-order husband. For if she didn't marry, what would become of her? She had nothing left to return to, and somehow she knew her future was in Fort Worth. And this time her life was never going to be uncertain again. This time she would have more control.

"Carter," Tanner screamed into the roaring cannons. "Watch your back!"

Carter, a tall, lanky Texas boy, spun around and fired his Enfield rifle at point-blank range. The Yankee soldier crumpled at his feet.

"Thanks," he called, putting the rifle to his shoulder and taking aim once again.

The Yankees overran the first rifle pits, the blue-and-gray soldiers fighting hand to hand, but the steep terrain of the Kennesaw Mountain stalled the federal soldiers' forward progression. And Samuel French's Confederate division cut the soldiers down savagely until the blue uniforms ceased to run up the hill.

A loud cheer arose from the tired Confederate soldiers as they watched the federal militia retreat. The grassy meadow below was covered in a blanket of blue-and-gray

*bodies, their blood mingled on the field. Soldiers from
both sides lay bleeding, mortally wounded or dead, a
result of the trenches and cannons carved into the
wooded slopes of the Kennesaw Mountain.*

*It was barely noon, and the battle was over. Atlanta,
the heart of the Confederacy, lay safely thirty miles away.
Once again they had managed to hold off the Yankee
bastards.*

*Tanner glanced over at Carter, grateful they were still
alive, knowing the dead from this battle must be in the
thousands. Feeling odd about being grateful to be alive,
Tanner raised his hands in the air with the rest of the
troops whooping and hollering, celebrating the joy of life.*

A hand violently shook him, jarring him awake. He
opened his eyes, grabbing the hand, ready to come up
swinging. He was caught between the dream world and
the real world, and his eyes were not focused. A soldier's
face swam before him before it disappeared and the darkened room, lit only by moonlight, came into focus.

He glanced into Beth's frightened face, inches from
his own.

"I'm sorry, but you were thrashing around and moaning in your sleep," she whispered in the darkness. "I was
afraid for you."

Releasing her soft hand, she gently lay back against
the pillows that supported her. Tanner sat up and wiped
his damp face with his palm. Her voice had been soothing, her touch demanding, and he was grateful she'd
awakened him before he'd said too much.

It was early, just before dawn, he surmised, as he
leaned forward and propped his head on his hands, his
elbows resting on his knees. He'd slept in a chair pulled
up next to the bed where Beth lay. She'd grabbed him
with her good left arm, and he'd almost hit her in his

sleep. Would these cursed dreams ever leave him in peace?

"Why are you awake so early?" he questioned. "Are you in pain?"

"Not terribly, just a dull throb right now. I think I've had too much sleep the last few days, and I'm starting to get tired of just lying in this bed," she said, brushing a lock of her auburn hair with her good hand.

He nodded. It had been three days, and so far he'd been unable to find anyone to take care of Beth. He'd searched the newspapers, asked around town, but no one had seemed acceptable to take in the young woman.

"I'm also tired of sleeping in my clothes, and I need a bath," she said.

Tanner swallowed. The thought of trying to give Miss Anderson a bath was just a little more personal than he cared to get. Having to help her with the bedpan had been embarrassing enough for both of them. And the thought of her ivory skin, naked and wet, was more than he dared think about. She'd been safe to think of while delirious, but now she was recovering, and suddenly he was the one in danger of her tempting lips and seductive curves.

He was trying so hard not to notice that she was a beautiful young woman, that her skin was soft and supple, her lips full and tempting. But sleeping in the chair beside her bed for the last three nights had given his active imagination more than enough to envisage.

She seemed so vulnerable and in need of protecting; she brought out feelings he'd long since buried.

"I'll ask one of the hotel maids to help you this morning," he replied, the image of her warm and wet causing him to shift in the chair uncomfortably.

"That would be lovely." She sighed and moved in the bed. "So what were you dreaming of?"

Tanner glanced at her suspiciously. "Why?"

"I just wondered. You seemed anxious. Almost like you were frightened," she said, her hazel eyes gazing at him cautiously.

How could she know that?

With a sigh, he stood and walked to the window. "I don't remember what I was dreaming. I seldom do," he lied, unable to share with her the terror of his dreams.

He turned from the window in the predawn light and noticed she was staring at him. Her eyes suddenly appeared soft and luminous, and the urge to crawl into her bed and touch her almost overcame him. He didn't know why, but the sanctuary of her arms seemed inviting. The longing to seek comfort the only way he knew how was tempting, but he resisted.

Tension seemed to envelop the room as they stared at one another. It was that time of morning, just before the sun began its ascent into the early-morning sky, when night makes one last valiant stand against the dawn. A time when everything seems fresh and new and even lost souls have a chance once again.

Tanner wondered suddenly if the beautiful Miss Anderson would have given him a chance if he didn't have a past that shrouded him in guilt.

"I guess I'm keeping you from your job," she said awkwardly. "Will they mind that you've not reached your destination?"

"No."

"What do you do for the bank?" she questioned.

Tanner frowned. She was asking way too many questions that he was not willing to answer, so he lied. "I'm an auditor."

"Oh."

There was a moment of silence that seemed to stretch into forever. Finally, Beth cleared her throat.

"How much is the hotel costing us a night?" she asked.

He stared at her in the darkened shadow.

"Don't worry about it." He ran his hand through his hair. "If I hadn't pushed the barrel of that gun, you wouldn't have been shot. It was my fault."

"It was an accident. You should blame it on the bandit who held up the stage." She waited a minute, tilted her head, and asked, "Why did you prevent that bandit from getting shot?"

Tanner stared out the window. How could he tell her the truth, that he needed Sam Bass alive? That he'd saved Sam's life and hurt her in the process? He sighed. Would the number of people he'd managed to hurt in his lifetime ever grow smaller in number instead of larger?

"I thought there had been enough bloodshed," he acknowledged. "If we'd shot Sam, they wouldn't have hesitated in killing us all."

She reflected on his comments a moment and then said, "You're probably right. I guess we should be grateful that any of us came out alive."

"The Bass gang is a dangerous gang of robbers," Tanner said, inwardly cringing. They were renowned, and he was one of them.

The sun was beginning to peek over the eastern horizon, streaking the sky with orange and blue. The dawn was breaking, and he suddenly felt like a caged animal, restless and edgy. He had to get out of this hotel room, if only for a little while. He needed some distance from the beautiful Miss Anderson before he gazed at her luscious, full lips one time too many and decided to find out for himself if they were as succulent as they appeared.

"I'm going to go downstairs and get us some grub. Then I need to run some errands. I'll send the maid up with your breakfast and ask her to arrange a bath for you."

"Thank you." She gazed at him, her hazel eyes bright in the early-morning light.

He seized his gun belt, strapped it on, grabbed his hat, and was halfway out the door when he stopped and looked back. He couldn't rush out without saying what really was bothering him.

"Look, I'm sorry you got robbed on that stage. Don't worry about anything except getting well. I'll take care of you."

And he would help her, he had to, even though he could possibly lose his life in the process. He was in no hurry to catch up with the Bass gang. Besides, he had no choice. Although the tattered remains of his honor wouldn't let him leave her, he knew he could be sacrificing his freedom at the least, his life at the most. But then again, his life had been a hellhole for over ten years. Why would it matter if it ended now?

She looked up at him from the bed, her eyes wide and filled with concern. "Don't feel responsible for my getting shot. It was an accident."

He shrugged. "I'm not going to argue with you. I just want you to get well."

Tanner shut the door behind him. How would she feel if she knew it was the gang he'd recently joined that had robbed her?

Beth awoke at the sound of a noise she recognized and feared. Her eyes opened to the sound of a revolver spinning, the hammer being pulled back. She watched as Tanner held his Navy Colt revolver in his hands, a small can of oil on the table beside him, a rag in his hand. He held the gun intimately, stroking the barrel like a man well acquainted with the revolver. His hands moved swiftly over the open chamber, polishing and cleaning.

She watched as he tipped the can of oil against the cloth and then twisted the edge of it into the holes of the gun, swabbing it with the rag. His face was intent with a purpose, though he looked as if his thoughts were elsewhere, his mind miles away.

He was a man who had done this enough times, for it was clearly repetitive work, and he did it automatically. How many bankers knew how to clean a gun?

Bankers were smooth and polished, with no rough edges, Beth knew, because she'd dealt with more of them in the last few years than she wanted to think about.

Tanner didn't fit the mold of a banker.

He carried himself as though aware of his surroundings at all times. He was watchful and seemed more like a man who stood on the fringes and observed. The bankers she'd known had always been powerful men who wanted everyone to be aware of their status and to know they held the keys to their future. Bankers were ostentatious people who didn't blend well. Tanner didn't appear greedy, and blending was a word that somehow didn't fit him.

Since the accident, she hadn't seen his black tailored suit; instead, he wore a white shirt, black vest, and black pants with well-worn boots. The hat that she had thought looked ridiculous on him in the coach had disappeared, and in its place was a shabby black Stetson that had a tall crown and wide brim for shading the sun from his deeply tanned skin. He looked more like a hired gun than a banker.

And it was odd, but she felt comfortable in his presence.

Watching his powerful hands hold the gun as he stroked the chamber, she remembered the feel of his hands as he helped her. They were not smooth hands that handled cash; but rather, rough and work-hardened. They were textured, like those of a man who used his hands to earn a living.

Beth watched as he spun the cylinder on the gun, the clicking noise chilling in the silence. Who was this man, really? Was he who he claimed to be, a banker on his way to a business meeting? Or what exactly was his occupation?

A knock sounded at the door, and he glanced up, sliding several bullets into the chamber of the gun faster than she could think. He sprang to his feet, alert, then glanced at her and noticed she was awake. He frowned.

"Who is it?" he called.

"Dr. Benson," the voice replied. "I came by to check on my patient."

A sigh escaped him, and his rigid posture visibly relaxed.

"Just a minute, Doctor." Tanner rapidly put away his cleaning supplies and made sure his gun was in good working order. He slid both pistols back into the holsters, which lay against his hips. He looked up, his ice-blue eyes meeting and holding Beth's.

Why all the precaution for a visit from the doctor?

She'd never met a banker so completely at ease with his gun and yet as nervous as a rabbit in a hound hunt. He was a contradiction both frightening and intriguing.

Tanner walked to the door and pulled it open cautiously.

The gray-haired man Beth recognized as the doctor stepped inside the small room, and Tanner shut the door behind him.

"I would have been by sooner, but I had another patient come down with cholera." He shook his head. "Such a terrible disease. Kills so quickly and spreads so rapidly."

He glanced at Beth. "Well, you certainly appear to have a little more color in your cheeks since the last time I saw you. How are you feeling?"

"Better. But not great," she acknowledged.

The doctor stepped over to the chair beside the bed. "Well, let's have a look at that wound and see how it's coming along."

He reached inside his bag and pulled out a pair of scissors. He pulled the coverlet down past her shoulder and pushed the sleeve of the clean nightgown she'd donned after her bath out of his way. Very carefully he began to cut away the gauze covering the wound.

Beth had yet to see her shoulder since the accident, and she looked curiously, anxious to see the damage to her flesh. When the doctor cut away the last of the gauze, she was amazed at how small the wound actually was, though her flesh was bruised around the stitched area.

"I see no complications. You're healing quite nicely."

"When can I travel again?" she asked, anxious to know when she could leave.

The doctor frowned. "Not right away, but maybe in two weeks, definitely in three. Actually, I'd prefer that you waited the full three weeks. That will give you time to recuperate from this."

"Three weeks!" she exclaimed.

"You lost a lot of blood, my dear."

"But I have to be in Fort Worth," she exclaimed, feeling tears of exasperation filling her eyes.

"Traveling will only break open the stitches. I'd rather you waited." The doctor began to wrap new gauze around the wound.

"It won't be long, Beth," Tanner said.

"I'm going to change this bandage. After this one, I think we'll be able to leave it off completely." He quickly wrapped the material around her shoulder and tied it in a knot, leaving her arm in a sling. "You'll be well and ready to travel in no time, Mrs. Tanner."

For a moment, Beth was stunned. Had he just called her Mrs. Tanner? She glanced up at him quizzically.

"What did you say?"

The doctor began returning his equipment and supplies into his doctor's bag. "Don't worry. Your wound is healing very well, and I don't see any complications. The stitches will have to be removed in about four days, and after that you'll just have some tenderness and soreness left."

The man stood ready to walk out the door.

"No, what did you call me?" she asked.

Tanner came up behind her and leaned over, his gaze sending a clear warning. Then he kissed her on the cheek, his lips warm and supple. "It's all right, sweetheart. You're going to be just fine. We'll get you to Fort Worth, you'll see."

"But—"

Tanner stepped away and opened the door. "Thanks for coming by, Doctor. We'll see you in a couple of days."

The old doctor frowned. "Good-bye, then. Send for me if you need me."

The doctor stepped out of the room, and Tanner firmly shut the door behind him. Beth gazed at Tanner quizzically.

"Did he just call me Mrs. Tanner?" she questioned. She stared at the worried expression on Tanner's face. "Why?"

"Because the good doctor and everyone in the hotel thinks we're married."

Four

Eugenia sat nervously in the buckboard, glancing up and down the street. The stage was several hours late, and Eugenia feared what the delay meant.

What if the young woman didn't show? What if she'd changed her mind and decided to stay in Georgia?

Her imagination ran wild as she twisted her hands nervously around the umbrella handle, twirling it fretfully. The umbrella provided little shade from the hot Texas sun, but it occupied her hands and kept her from fidgeting quite so much.

"Eugenia, come inside out of this blistering heat. We'll have plenty of time to greet Miss Anderson once the stage arrives," Rose, her daughter-in-law, admonished.

"I promised her that I'd be waiting. That I would be the first person she saw when she arrived."

Rose glanced up at her, clearly annoyed. "Eugenia, did you promise her that you would be the first person or that Tucker would be the first person she saw?"

Sometimes the girl was way too smart. Yet she had fallen in love with Travis, and Lord knows, Eugenia had been ready to give up on that boy finding any woman to love him.

"Well . . . it was me, of course, but I signed Tucker's name."

"That's what I thought. So let's wait inside," Rose reproved.

Eugenia started to climb down from the wagon, and Rose held out her hand to help her disembark. "Thank you, dear. You're right, it would be cooler inside, in the shade."

"Much," Rose agreed.

"So where did my sons take off to?" Eugenia questioned.

"They're sitting inside sipping lemonade."

Eugenia looked at her in surprise. "Lemonade?"

Rose laughed. "I told them I would start reading tea leaves for everyone who entered the café if they even considered ordering whiskey or beer." She smiled. "Travis knew I would, too, so he told Tucker they'd get something stronger later."

Eugenia patted Rose on the arm and chuckled. "A woman who knows how to handle my son—I love it." She sighed. "Now if everything will work out for Tucker the way it has for Travis, I'll be so happy."

They stepped up onto the wooden sidewalk, underneath an awning, out of the sun. "Eugenia, why are you pushing your sons into marriage? Why can't you just leave Tucker alone and let him find a woman when he's ready?"

"Someday you'll understand, dear, when you've waited for years and none of your children seem interested in settling down. You lose a son, and a small part of you dies, and then your husband passes on and leaves you alone. These things make you realize time is running out. And you want more. More time to spend with your grandchildren and family. So you rush your children, and finally you do things you never thought you'd do just to see them settled and happy, with a family of their own."

Rose glanced at her. "But you can't keep interfering, Eugenia. You're going to hurt someone in the process."

"I sincerely hope not. I'm trying to be careful, but I love my children. I want to see their children." She sighed. "I'm just thankful Tucker came today."

The rattling of a coach as it turned the corner interrupted their conversation, and they both tensed.

"Oh, my God, here she comes," Eugenia exclaimed.

Rose turned to the men in the café and waved excitedly. The moment was upon them; the newest member of the clan was about to arrive. Travis hurried out the café door, urging his younger brother not to tarry. But Tucker hung back, trepidation on his usually smiling face.

Eugenia hurried over to him. "Come on, dear. All you have to do is meet her. That's all. If you don't like her, I would never expect you to marry her."

"Mother, I'm not going to marry her."

"We'll see, dear."

Rose took her husband's arm, and together the four of them walked toward the stage that had just pulled to a stop, in front of the El Paso Hotel.

The door swung open, and Eugenia held her breath as a woman older than herself stepped out.

"I knew it," Tucker said. "She's old."

She poked her son in the ribs. "That can't be her."

"Whew," Tucker said, winking at Eugenia. "I was frightened for a moment."

The grandmother glanced around the small crowd of people expectantly and then boldly asked, "Anyone here to meet Miss Elizabeth Anderson?"

Eugenia stepped forward. "We are. My sons and daughter and I." She glanced into the stagecoach and realized it was empty. "Where is she?"

The older woman's face became sympathetic. "I'm

sorry to have to tell you this, but we were robbed. Elizabeth was shot in the holdup."

"Oh, my God, is she all right?" Eugenia asked.

"A nice young banker feller who was riding with us took her back to San Antonio on his horse and promised to get her to a doctor. They have a marvelous doctor in San Antonio."

"Was she hurt badly?" Eugenia asked.

"Beth had a pretty nasty shoulder wound. But from what I could tell, I don't think it was life-threatening."

Suddenly, the older woman waved to a waiting family. "There's my daughter. I must go, but I think Miss Beth will be just fine."

"I'd better go to Elizabeth. I'll take the next stage to San Antonio and find her," Eugenia said, wringing her hands.

"That's really not necessary. This doctor helped my son-in-law one time, and he's very good. He'll take care of her." The grandmother patted Eugenia on the arm. "She was anxious to get acquainted with you, and right now might not be the best time for her. Let her recuperate before she meets you."

"But . . ." Eugenia frowned. "All right, but only because you think it's best."

"I really do. Now, I better run along and join my family." As the grandmother hurried off, Eugenia stood there, stunned. Robbed and shot at gunpoint!

She turned to Travis and Tucker. "The two of you should go to San Antonio and bring her home. She needs us now more than ever."

"Mother, you heard the woman, let's give her some time. Besides, the herd is almost ready to go to market," Travis insisted. "I need to stay here and help our foreman finish getting the herd ready."

"I have a job to do here," Tucker exclaimed.

"But your job is upholding the law. Protecting the citizens. You need to go after those men who robbed her stage," Eugenia persisted.

"Mother, it's not my territory, and besides, the sheriff in San Antonio will be investigating." He sighed. "I'm sure Miss Anderson will be contacting us as soon as she's well. If we don't hear from her soon, then I'll take some time off to go down and see if I can locate her."

Eugenia frowned. "I don't like it, but what can I do? Someone take me home. This day has simply lost whatever joy it held."

"Why did you tell everyone we were married?" Beth asked Tanner as she sat up in bed, the covers tucked around her. "I'm on my way to meet my fiancé."

Her fiancé? So that was why she was going to Fort Worth. Tanner swallowed, feeling uncomfortable in the intimate setting of the hotel room with the beautiful woman before him. They had been in this hotel room alone, together, for almost a week, and the close proximity was starting to wear on him.

"People assumed we were married when I carried you into the hotel." He shrugged his shoulders. "It just happened."

Her hazel eyes were troubled, and he could see she was worried about something. "Did you consider how it would look if the man I'm to marry tried to find me?"

She took a deep breath, and the covers clung precariously to the material of her nightgown, just above her breasts. He couldn't help but imagine how her breasts would look beneath her nightdress, how they would feel—soft and full to his touch.

"No, I didn't know you were getting married. After everything happened, I thought maybe it was better this way. No one would think less of you for sleeping in a strange man's hotel room."

Plus, it was a good cover for him. No one would think to look for him with a woman in the room.

"But will the man I'm going to marry take that into consideration?"

Tanner was beginning to feel exasperated. "Look, I didn't do this to hurt you. I just let them think what they wanted. I was trying to protect you."

"This marriage is very important to me. I can't return to Georgia," she said, anxious.

"Your family would take you back, wouldn't they?" he questioned, curious about her traveling all this distance alone.

She glanced down at her hands and then back up into his eyes. Her hazel eyes brimmed with tears. "There's no one left in Georgia. Whatever family I had is all dead and gone. Except for my aunts and uncles, and they don't want me."

The sadness he saw reflected in her eyes made him feel awkward. Why didn't her family want her? How could a woman as beautiful as Beth be so alone in the world? He had an overwhelming urge to take her in his arms and soothe her until she smiled again.

"No one would take you in?" he questioned, finding it hard to believe she had no one.

"No! You don't understand." She took a deep breath and leaned back against the pillows. "There's no one left to care about me. No one that would be willing to take in an invalid."

He shrugged. "People will usually do just about anything for a price."

She stared at him in wonder. "So why are you doing this? What's your price?"

"What?" he asked, stunned she'd turned his question on him.

"Why are you taking care of me? You didn't have to."

"No, I didn't have to. But I couldn't very well leave you behind. And my price, lady, you can't afford," he said, disgusted.

"I can't afford any price. But surely there was some place you could have left me?"

"There was no place. And I wouldn't have left you even if there was," he admitted, knowing that after the robbery he had to see to her well-being. He could never have just ridden off and left her to die.

At that bold admission, he suddenly felt very uncomfortable. "You were too sick to leave with strangers." He stood and walked to the window, presenting her with his back, the conversation clearly at an end. She'd gotten a little too close, and he felt the need to remove himself.

He glanced down at the street and realized that dusk would soon be upon them.

"Are you hungry?"

"Yes, I am," she said, nodding.

"Well, at least your appetite is returning," he said.

"Yes," she acknowledged. "I know you must be ready for me to get well and out of your life permanently."

He glanced at her puzzled. "Why do you say that?"

"Well, I'm certain I've slowed you down."

He shrugged.

When a man had no good place to go, he certainly wasn't in a rush to go nowhere. His only pressing business was the Bass gang, and even though catching up with them was urgent, it could wait. He was in no hurry. And though he was loath to admit it, he had enjoyed her company this last week, since she'd regained consciousness. She had been an easy enough patient, and she had an agreeable personality. It had been so long since he'd enjoyed the company of a woman that he had to remind himself she would be leaving soon and not to grow accustomed to her presence.

They stared at one another, feeling awkward in the cramped room. He gazed at her tasty mouth and wanted to run his finger along her full bottom lip, feel the texture of her skin, her warm breath on the tip of his finger. His thoughts were disturbing, and he knew it was time to get out of the room for a while and let his overactive imagination contemplate what lay beneath that nightgown, cool down several notches.

Finally, he cleared his throat. "I'll go down and get us a bite to eat."

"That would be nice."

He strode to the door and then glanced back. "You know you don't have to worry about being in the same room with me, don't you?"

She glanced at him, her forehead puckered in a frown. "I haven't worried about being alone with you, if that's what you mean."

He couldn't say that he would never touch her, for he longed to do just that, but she was safe with him.

"Good. I just wanted you to know you're safe with me."

"Thanks," she said, and watched him close the door.

He stood outside the door and took a deep breath. Yes, she didn't have to worry about his forcing himself on her. But being in the same room with Beth and not touching her was starting to become a challenge. For she was the type of woman that reminded him of his previous life. She reminded him of home.

* * *

Beth took a sip of her soup, wishing she didn't tire out quite so fast. Though she napped several times a day, she still became exhausted faster than expected.

Tanner sat at the small table eating roast beef and gravy, but he had brought her soup. And while she loved the taste of chicken vegetable, his roast beef smelled absolutely succulent. When was the last time she had tasted good roast beef? Before the war?

She couldn't remember.

"How are you feeling?" he asked.

"All right," she said.

They finished eating, and he cleared away their dishes. She leaned back against the headboard of the bed, several pillows at her back. She felt tired from the simple task of eating, but she knew that with each day she was getting stronger and soon she would feel like moving about. Then she could somehow catch the next stage to Fort Worth.

He picked up a newspaper and began to read, but Beth felt edgy and bored. The walls of the room were beginning to close around her, and she needed a diversion.

"Anything interesting in the paper?" she asked.

He pulled the newspaper down and glanced at her over the top. "Not much. There is a small article about the shooting."

"What does it say?" Beth asked anxiously.

He lifted the newspaper and read:

While traveling on the Fort Worth stage, Mrs. Tanner was shot during a holdup. The Bass gang is believed to be responsible for robbing the stage and leaving Mrs. Tanner to die. Her husband, who happened to have his horse tied to the back of the stagecoach, carried her into San Antonio, where Doc Benson removed the bullet. Mrs. Tanner will recover according to the doc. Once again this gang has struck an innocent victim.

He looked up from the newspaper. "That's all they wrote."

Beth tilted her head and looked at him sideways. "The Bass gang—that's who robbed the stage?"

He nodded his head.

"If they know who did it, why haven't they caught them? They could go and arrest them right now, and I could get my money back."

"That money has already been divided and probably spent. As for bringing them in, they'd have to know where the Bass gang is to do that. The hill country of Texas has plenty of places for an outfit to hide. And this group of outlaws has been working this road clean up to Fort Worth."

"This wasn't the first robbery on that road by that bunch?" she asked indignantly.

"Of course not."

"Then why hasn't the law done something to stop them? Why hasn't the Bass gang been caught?"

Tanner shrugged. "Don't know."

Beth glanced at Tanner and noticed the tight expression on his face. "I'm sorry for getting so upset. It's just that they acted like it was not important in the paper. But that gang robbed me, and I was shot."

He folded the newspaper and set it aside. "Happens often enough in the West. You'll soon learn and be glad all they did was rob you." He paused. "Any chance your fiancé will see the paper?"

"I don't know," she said. "Hopefully, if he does, he'll think it was a misprint regarding the name."

"So when are you getting married?"

She glanced at her hands, her stomach churned into a knot. "We haven't set the date yet. For that matter, we've not even met in person." She gazed into his sky blue eyes. "I'm a mail-order bride."

There was a long moment of silence as he stared at her. Then his face wrinkled into a frown, and he looked confused. "Why would a beautiful woman like you become a mail-order bride. I thought that was for homely women."

She blushed at his compliment. "There was no one left back home. I needed to get away and make a fresh start."

There was a moment of silence. "So why have *you* never married?"

Tanner picked up the paper, rolled it into a tube, and then slowly released it. "I'm a rover, constantly on the move, never staying long in one place."

"You can do that as a banker?" she asked in disbelief.

He pulled his paper back up. "I don't just work with one bank."

Beth licked her lips nervously. "I would think that would be a lonely life."

She hated to think of him alone.

"Never thought much about it."

Tanner confused her. Though hard and rugged, there was a quiet sense of vulnerability about him that intrigued her, that drew her to him. His blue eyes were cold, but occasionally there was a flash of warmth and even laughter. There was nothing soft about him, and his good looks were unique in a tough, masculine sort of way. And there was a growing sense of consciousness of him as a man, one she was attracted to and shouldn't be.

"Don't you want to get married someday, settle down and have children?" she asked, curious about this man who appeared gruff, yet had taken care of her since the shooting.

Tanner laid down the newspaper and then glanced at Beth. "No."

"Why? I thought bankers needed wives for social reasons?"

"You ask a lot of questions."

"Sorry. I guess I'm just curious."

He got up and walked across the room. "It's just not possible for me to get married."

She tried to scoot up in the bed, using her left hand, and Tanner hurried over to help her. When he reached for her, the blanket covering her breasts fell to her waist. He lifted her up easily into a sitting position, his hands warm through the cotton material of her translucent nightgown. As soon as he released her, she quickly pulled the covers back up over the top of her bosom, hoping that nothing had been revealed.

Her cheeks flamed in embarrassment.

Glancing quickly at Tanner, she noticed that his eyes had widened, their color changing to a smoky blue, which left her feeling warm as he gazed at her. Even if he'd seen nothing, the thought of his gazing at her breasts left her with a feeling that was completely unfamiliar but nice.

She flicked her tongue across her bottom lip to moisten them, feeling a flush of heat she'd never experienced before, and wondered at the emotions Tanner evoked in her. A breathless stirring seemed to encompass her as she returned his stare.

Nothing could come of her growing awareness of Tanner. She had no choice but to wed the man she was to meet in Fort Worth. Tanner was just a man who had taken care of her since she'd been shot, and she must be feeling grateful for his kindness. That's all it could ever be.

She was lying to herself, but she didn't dare explore her feelings for Tanner any further. He swallowed, glanced away, and she felt a keen sense of disappointment. No, she refused to feel anything for this man. She had a respectable man waiting to marry her, and she was not about to let him go. She needed a husband, a supporter, or she would be destitute.

Tanner cleared his throat. "I'm going out for a while. You'll be safe here alone."

"Where are you going?" she asked, and then realized her mistake as he sent her a look that showed his disapproval. "I'm sorry, that's none of my business. I . . . I guess being cooped up here in this room has given me a case of nosiness. You go out. I'll still be here when you get back."

As if he'd just been released from prison, he stood, grabbed his hat and gun belt off the table, and began buckling it around his hips. He made his way toward the door, his actions hurried. She knew without asking that he wanted to get out of this room, and she was envious of his freedom.

"I don't know what time I'll be back," he said as he walked out the door, not looking back.

Beth stared at the closed door that Tanner had just gone through and felt more alone than on the day she buried her parents. She had to get out of here before she did something she'd regret, like exploring the feelings this man stirred within her.

* * *

The next morning, Beth awoke to the sound of the door closing. The sun was shining through the open windows, and she knew that Tanner had just left. She couldn't help but wonder where he'd gone the night before and whom he'd been with. She had no right to question his whereabouts or even wonder what he'd done, but still she was intrigued. And as much as he'd been on her mind the last few days, she had no business thinking about this man.

Living in close proximity with Tanner had certainly awakened parts of her she thought had died with the war. But Georgia lay behind her, and she couldn't lose sight of her goal—to reach Fort Worth and marry. And the attraction she felt for Tanner was beginning to plague her every waking moment and could not be acted upon. In fact, the sooner she left, the better.

He was such a complex man, part nurse and defender, part rogue and gunslinger. Whenever she thought she was beginning to understand him, he seemed to change right before her eyes. He was intriguing in a way she'd never before thought a man could be. And she had to get away.

Beth reached over and touched her shoulder. It was still sore, but she felt stronger, the swelling was going down, and it hadn't bled in several days. Why couldn't she leave today? Right now?

Surely she was strong enough to get dressed, sell the pieces of jewelry that had been stowed in her luggage, and walk to the stage office. Once she was on that stage, she could rest all the way to Fort Worth. If there was a stage leaving today, she could be on it. And suddenly the need to be gone from this town, this room, and Tanner was urgent.

The sooner she was away from Tanner, the less she would feel compelled to act upon the apparent magnetism that had developed between them. Yes, he was an eye-catching man, and yes, she appreciated what he had done for her, but Tanner was not a man prone to settling down. And there was another man waiting for her in Fort Worth who wanted to settle down, who wanted a wife. Her future lay with him. She was thankful for Tanner's help, but nothing could come of this temptation.

Rising from the bed, she swung her feet over the side and slowly stood. Her legs felt wobbly and she swayed, surprised at her own weakness. She hadn't felt this frail in bed. Holding on to the furniture in the room, she walked to where her satchel sat and found her corset. There was no way that she could put it on by herself, so she packed it in her bag. She tugged and pulled until she removed the nightgown. After resting for a few moments, she then tackled putting on her petticoat.

The garment slipped over her head fairly easy, and she tied the string on each side. Letting go of the dresser, she took her dress in her hands, determined to get it on by herself. She glanced at her dress and knew it was going to be a struggle. She looked at her arm and the dress and wondered how she would get her sore shoulder in the garment without passing out from pain.

Finally, she lifted her dress with her good left arm and almost cried at the pain that shot through her right shoulder. She managed to get the dress over her head. Her left arm was in the sleeve, but the right one still hung limp at her side. She knew it was going to hurt before she even attempted to squeeze her arm through the sleeve. With a deep breath, she bent her arm and tried to slip the dress over it. Pain shot through her shoulder, causing her to gasp and double over, almost incapacitating her.

She stopped, leaned over the table, and took several

deep breaths, trying to ease the ache so that she could continue. The sound of the door opening startled her, and she glanced up into the hot blue eyes of the man she was running from.

"What the hell do you think you're doing out of bed?" he said, his voice rising as he strode into the room. "Are you trying to finish killing yourself?"

"I . . . I felt better and thought . . . thought I would try to go down to the telegraph office." She didn't have the courage to tell him that she was really trying to sneak out of town and leave him behind, that she was afraid of the feelings his nearness was beginning to evoke and how hopeless she knew they were.

"You're hardly healed, lady." He lifted her dress off her shoulders and pulled her good arm back out through the sleeve.

"What are you doing?" she questioned.

"I'm putting you back in bed," he snapped. "Whatever color you'd managed to put back in your cheeks is gone."

"No, really, I think I'll be okay. I'll keep the dress on," she said. "I'm tired of being in that bed, in that nightgown."

He threw the dress on the bed. "Your shoulder is not ready."

"But I am," she said stubbornly.

She stood before him dressed in her chemise and petticoats, feeling exposed, almost naked. A flush started at the base of her neck and warmed its way past her cheekbones.

He shook his head. "No."

"I've got to get to Fort Worth. I can't spend another minute lying in that bed," she said, her voice weak, tears dangerously close.

She spun around and bumped her arm into the table. She gasped and stumbled, almost fainting from the pain.

Tanner reached out and grabbed her waist, pulling her up against his solid chest. She stood in his arms, half-dressed, a feeling of protection and shelter overwhelming her. The pain slowly subsided, until she relaxed and was able to take a deep breath.

His hand reached up and smoothed back her tangled hair, and she laid her head against his shoulder. A feeling of warmth and safety stole over her. "I guess I'm not as strong as I thought I was."

"No," he said, his voice a deep, husky tone that reached inside her and stroked her like a lover.

She raised her head from against his chest and glanced at his stony expression. Her breathing became quick and shallow as she looked up into his blue eyes and became lost in their smokiness. She watched with fevered antici-pation as his mouth hovered over hers. He moistened his full lips, and she almost moaned with need, fearful he wasn't going to kiss her, needing the feel of his lips against hers. Then, swiftly, his lips descended, and she eagerly met him halfway.

His mouth covered hers, and she felt whatever strength remained drain from her body. He clasped her waist and pulled her gently against him. He tasted of potency and masculinity, and he kissed her like a man who had been denied passion for a long time. His lips devoured hers, his tongue running along the edge of her mouth, testing and tasting. And she met his every stroke with one of her own.

She gasped, and his lips covered hers once again. He seemed famished for her, and she reveled in the feel of him. She felt protected, safe and secure, as though she had found a haven from the ugly world and he was her strength, her fortress. She felt cosseted and coveted and more secure than she had for many years.

And she'd never been kissed so thoroughly that she felt on fire with desire. The general's kisses had certainly never left her quivering with need. They'd never incited her to want more. They'd never left her feeling faint.

His hands caressed her shoulders, trailing down her back, touching her, clasping her to him. She realized she was standing in the arms of the man who had saved her, who was taking care of her, and she was clothed only in her chemise and petticoat. Her intended waited for her two hundred and seventy miles to the north, in Fort Worth, and she was acting like a wanton in a hotel room with a man whose full name she didn't know.

Beth pushed away from Tanner and gasped, her lungs rapidly filling with air. She staggered away, her hands gripping the nearby table for support. When she felt confident she could stand, she raised one hand to her chest and the other to her bruised lips. Finally, she lifted her gaze to his.

Desire—hot, raw, naked need—shone from his eyes, and she was stunned at the impact. He desired her, and she couldn't deny she wanted him just as badly. But it was impossible. She was on her way to meet the man she intended to marry. Tanner was a man she knew so little about, and what she did know seemed dangerous— much more than the image he portrayed.

"I—can't. I can't do this," she gasped.

His expression changed from one of desire to remoteness.

"It won't happen again." He ran his hand through his hair. "Get back in bed. I'll go get you some breakfast."

Tanner strode quickly from the room, the door slamming behind him. It was almost as if he ran, and Beth couldn't help but think she would run, too, if only she could.

Five

Tanner leaned against the closed door and wondered what in the hell was wrong with him. He'd kissed her. Like a starving man, he'd put his lips to hers and drank of her sweet nectar until she'd pushed him away.

The sight of her standing there in her chemise and petticoat had left him rigid with desire. But the feel of her soft curves molded against his limbs had surprised him. He hadn't been prepared for the onslaught of craving that had rocked him. He hadn't been prepared for the protective feelings that had suddenly awakened within him when he'd seen her standing there weakly trying to dress. Damn, but he could ill afford the complications a woman would bring to his life, especially now.

The kiss had been a mistake, one he could not repeat. In fact, the sooner Beth was on her way to Fort Worth, the better. He could not afford to become involved with any woman for more than a night no matter how beautiful, how kind, or how intriguing. Good women, the kind who wanted marriage, were just simply not for him. He didn't deserve them, and they certainly didn't merit being shackled with a man like him. When he was younger, he had wanted a wife and a family, but now his life had no room for those simple trappings. The thought saddened him, but he knew he could never marry, he didn't want to tarnish a woman with his soiled reputation.

Beth Anderson already had a man she was going to marry. Tanner just needed to finish taking care of her and then put her on the next stage to Fort Worth without kissing her again. But that was easier said than done. Every time she gazed at him with those hazel-green eyes, he felt a response unlike anything he'd ever experienced before, and those full, pouty lips of hers were almost irresistible.

The feel of her curvaceous body in his arms, the touch of her satiny skin, was more tempting than a bank filled with gold, and he couldn't help but think he'd be safer in jail than in this hotel room with Beth.

God, how could he keep from touching her when all he wanted to do was lay her down and find the release he so desperately needed? Her recovery had better come soon or he could be seriously jeopardizing her future and his.

In a fog, Beth awoke to the sound of raised voices. For a moment she thought she was home—her father and the general were arguing—but then she remembered that the war was over. Her papa was dead, and the general had returned to his wife.

"What the hell are you still doing here? Do you not give a damn about our agreement?"

She didn't recognize the furious voice and almost opened her eyes to see who had come into the room. Instead, she lay still as stone and pretended to sleep.

"Keep your voice down, she's asleep."

Tanner's voice sounded strained, but there was a dangerous edge to it that she'd never heard before. It was just another facet of the man she realized she didn't know.

"You said you'd find someone to take care of her. Why is she still here?"

Stunned, she realized they were discussing her.

"I said I'd take care of Miss Anderson," Tanner said. The tone of his voice almost made Beth shiver at the cold briskness. "Don't worry, you'll get your piece of me, just not quite yet."

"Don't play games with me, Tanner. I'll jerk you out of here so fast you won't have time to think of Miss Anderson. Men like you are a dime a dozen, and I won't put up with your bullshit."

The mystery man knew her name, and a shiver of apprehension almost had her shaking. Who was this man, and what did he want with Tanner? She resisted the urge to open her eyes, for now she was afraid.

"I said I was working on it."

"Well, you better work faster, because I'm about to lose my patience with you."

Could this be Tanner's employer?

"She's getting better. It shouldn't be long now. You know where I am. What more do you want."

"I want you to get your butt out to the Basses'. I don't give a damn if Miss Anderson's getting better. The Cisco bank was robbed yesterday."

There was a lengthy pause, and then the door opened. "Out in the hall," Tanner demanded.

But before the door closed, Beth clearly heard the gruff voice say, "You should have been with them."

The door shut quietly, and all Beth could hear was murmured voices. What did he mean, Tanner should have been with them? With the bank? Certainly he didn't mean the robbers, so it had to be with the bank. The man must be from Tanner's job, and she was holding him back, keeping him from his employment. But what exactly did he do for a living? He'd said he was an auditor, but she was having a hard time believing him. Certainly a banker or auditor didn't seem to fit him.

She had to get well so that they could both resume their lives, though suddenly she wasn't in such a rush to reach Fort Worth. Until this moment there had been a sense of security here with Tanner that she had never felt before. Fort Worth seemed a scary unknown, but this intrusion was just another indication of how little she knew Tanner. Combined with yesterday morning's kiss, maybe it was time to move on.

And that kiss had just about caused her to pass out yesterday morning. It had stayed in her mind all day. She reached up and touched her lips as if she could still feel the impression of his mouth. Never before had she enjoyed a kiss as much as that one. In fact, none of her previous experience at kissing had ever affected her like Tanner's kiss. When he'd put his lips to hers, she'd felt as if she were coming undone in his arms.

What was she doing? Although she had a man waiting for her, her thoughts were more and more on the man she owed her life to. Tucker awaited her, but Tanner intrigued her.

The door opened, and Beth quickly closed her eyes. He walked in and went directly to the bed. He leaned over her, and she smelled his masculine scent, a unique blend of man and leather. The sound of his boots rapping against the floor faded, and she knew he had walked to the window. Soon he began to pace relentlessly, his boots tapping patterns on the floor. She opened her eyes a peek and glanced at the worried look on his face, wondering again at her protector. Who was this man that had managed to awaken her youthful interest in men once again? Something she'd all but given up hope of feeling again.

A shiver passed through her. What did she know about Tanner? He was a man who said he was in the banking industry, yet his appearance and mannerisms were not like any banker she'd ever met. And he didn't seem the type of man who could sit quietly in an office and deal with people all day long. No, the man she was beginning to know was more of an outdoorsman who would seem more at home herding cattle than sitting behind a desk.

There was a ruggedness about him that somehow didn't belong in a bank.

She opened her eyes and watched as he paced the floor. He'd yet to see that she was awake, that she watched and wondered what it was that troubled him and brought that worried countenance upon his handsome face. His blue eyes were darkened with worry, and she knew that something distressed him.

"What's wrong?" she asked, unable to watch him pace any longer.

His head jerked up, and he stared at her. "You're awake."

"Did we have a visitor?" she questioned.

"Just a man from the hotel," he replied.

She knew he was lying. Whoever the man was, he hadn't been from the hotel. Beth was holding Tanner back from something, and she didn't know what. But he needed to be rid of her, and that disappointed her. Though why she should be saddened, she didn't know. After all, only yesterday she herself had been trying to leave.

"Funny, I thought I heard raised voices. I thought I overheard the word bank and considered maybe the man was from your employer."

Tanner's stare was relentless and cold enough to make

her shiver, but she met his gaze head-on with a look of her own. He was lying; she knew it, and she wanted him to know she realized his deception.

Finally, he turned and gazed out the window. She hadn't accomplished anything, and it was plain he wasn't going to divulge any information that would satisfy her curiosity.

She sighed, her frustration mounting.

"I'm feeling better. Don't you think we could go for a walk? It's the only way I'm going to get my strength back."

He turned his head and glanced at her. "Are you sure?"

"Yes."

"Good. The sooner you get your strength back, the sooner I can put you on the first stage to Fort Worth."

She should feel glad, but somehow she didn't. There was nothing for her here, yet this man drew her, surprised her and frustrated her.

"What about you?"

He shrugged. "For now my destination has changed. You'll be going to Fort Worth without me."

Tanner turned to face the window once again. She gazed at his stance, his hands were on his hips, his legs spread apart. He looked like a pirate in control at the helm of his ship. Suddenly, she didn't want to go to Fort Worth without him. Tanner intrigued her, and she wanted to know more about him. But her intended was waiting, and she needed no other delays.

Beth leaned against Tanner's arm and took small steps down the wooden sidewalk. The touch of her hand on his arm left him with a warm feeling that wasn't generated by the sun. Somehow he knew this heat would be there with or without it.

The sunlight touched her face, and she raised her cheeks to the light. She was one of the most breathtakingly beautiful women he'd ever met. And the sight of the light bathing her with radiance had him thinking thoughts he had no right to entertain. He was taking care of Beth because he'd accidentally shot her, not for any other reason. Though he'd like to explore other possibilities.

He'd like to spend time examining every delectable inch of the lovely Miss Anderson. But she was promised to someone else, and he was a man who needed no connections to a decent woman. His women were more of the saloon variety, and he knew that as soon as the pleasant Miss Anderson was on her way to Fort Worth, he'd be seeking some release with the nearest saloon girl.

Besides, she was starting to become way too curious about his background, his life, and even his visitors. This afternoon had been a close call. Evidently, she had overheard part of the conversation. She'd heard enough that she'd formed her own opinion, and he was not about to confirm or deny anything. The less she knew, the better.

If Sam Bass thought she knew anything, it could be dangerous.

Beth took tentative steps, and he knew their walk could not be a long one that would overtire her. However, the pleasure of being out of that small hotel room was clear on her expressive, beautiful face. She was getting stronger; soon she would be gone, and he would return to being alone.

She turned to him, and her face brightened like a flower in springtime. He wanted to moan but restrained himself.

"Can we go down to the jewelry store? I want to see what I can get for my rings," she asked, her hazel eyes snapping.

"Why?" he asked. They had no business being seen in a store. "The stage owes you a trip to Fort Worth."

"But how else will I pay you back for the doctor and the hotel room."

"That's not necessary." He couldn't let her sell her jewelry. Not after he'd been involved with the holdup that had caused her to lose her cash and become injured. Not after he was the one who was responsible for getting her shot. No, her troubles were a result of being on the same stagecoach as he. He wasn't about to let her sell her jewelry.

"Of course it is."

"I'm not going to help you sell your jewelry," he said, the feel of her hand heavy on his arm, like the weight of his conscience on his soul.

"Look, the robbers took all my cash, and I need some money to continue on to Fort Worth. If I don't sell the jewelry here, I'll have to sell it later, when I'm in Fort Worth."

Inwardly, he cringed. Surely they hadn't taken everything. She must have some money stashed away someplace.

"Everything? You mean you have no cash left?"

"Nothing."

He clenched his fist. He didn't need to hear this, he already felt bad enough that she'd been shot, but to lose everything because of him? He hated what he was doing, stealing for a living.

"Miss Anderson, never put all of your money in your purse. Put some in your suitcase or even your boot. But never put everything in one place." He helped her up a step. "Robberies are pretty common on the road, and you never want to be left without cash."

"Your advice is great, but it comes too late. I need to sell my jewelry," she insisted.

"I'll give you a loan until you get to your destination."

"You don't understand. My reticule contained my entire life savings. I have the clothes on my back, what's in my valise, and the little bit of jewelry I'm carrying. That's all."

He gazed at her and swore.

"If I don't get married, I don't know what I'll do."

They had taken her life savings. The robbery he had helped execute could possibly cause a good woman to become destitute. Another blight on his soul.

They continued walking down the sidewalk. People passed them, and carriages rumbled down the street.

"Consider it a wedding gift, then."

"I cannot accept charity from you."

"Look, lady, I'm attempting to help you. You're starting to try my patience. Accept my help."

"You've already helped me more than most people. I want to sell my jewelry."

He stopped on the sidewalk and stared into eyes, the color of springtime, but didn't say a word.

"You have helped me considerably. And I know I'm slowing you down from your job," she said.

"Don't worry about my job. It will still be there when you're gone." Scowling, Tanner knew he'd be lucky if he ever got away from his profession. "Forget selling your jewelry."

She frowned and turned away from him. It was then he noticed they had stopped in front of the local sheriff's office. There on the wall were sketches of men wanted for crimes. She gazed at the pictures, her face a silent mask.

"Do you think the pictures of the men who robbed us would be posted here?" she asked, staring intently at the display of Wanted posters.

God, he hoped she wouldn't recognize any of them. It could only be dangerous to describe the men who had robbed the stage.

"I swear, I think I would recognize them if I saw one . . ." she said, her voice trailing off.

Tanner glanced at the wall and felt a swift surge of fear as he gazed at the poster with a drawing of a younger version of himself, one in which the ravages of war gave his eyes a haunted look and the strain of losing Carter still followed him. The man in the Wanted poster hadn't cared whether he lived or died; he'd had nothing left to lose—not much different from today.

It had been a while since he'd seen a likeness of himself on a Wanted poster. The sight always stunned him and didn't seem real.

Suddenly, he noticed that her interest seemed to have shifted to the picture of him, and he took her arm and pulled, trying to get her away from there quickly, the fear of recognition causing him to sweat.

"Come on, let's keep going."

"Jackson . . ."

"We're going," he said, his hand gripping her elbow and leading her away.

She turned and looked at him, her eyes questioning. "All—right."

They started to walk away, and she glanced behind her at the posters one last time.

Damn, he was the biggest fool to let her stop and stare at the Wanted posters and find one with his face hanging on the wall. Jackson was the name on the poster, and Tanner hoped that would be enough to deter her from realizing it was he. He glanced at the mutinous look on her face. Maybe not.

"Come on; we need to get moving," he said. They walked along the wooden sidewalk not saying anything, the handkerchief in her free hand crushed beneath her palm.

He didn't need her asking questions, he didn't want her to find out that he was not really a banker but made his living stealing from banks and stages—something he wasn't proud of.

"Let's go a little farther," he said.

She glanced at him, her features tight. He tensed. Did she realize that the face on the poster had been his? She seemed anxious, but wouldn't she be frightened if she recognized him?

With one unintentional stop at the sheriff's office, the atmosphere had changed from relaxed to strained. How could he have been so stupid not to have known where they were walking? He'd been too busy noticing how delectable Beth looked, how the color had returned to her cheeks, giving her skin a healthy glow, the way her lips were full and pink and so perfectly kissable. And the urge to put his lips to hers was almost more than he could bear. She was so vulnerable, so innocent, and so tempting that he knew he couldn't take much more of their confinement. He had to get his attention back where it belonged.

Tanner glanced up and noticed a man walking toward him. Something about the man was familiar. Something about him set off warning bells, and he tensed as he realized who the man was. He watched the outlaw approach, wondering if he would stop and say something to him on the street.

Sam Bass tipped his hat at Tanner and glanced curiously at Beth. That single glance at Beth almost caused Tanner's heart to stop beating.

Curses filled his mind, and he muttered one under his breath. He was endangering Beth by being seen with her. If Sam Bass recognized her from the holdup and realized that Tanner was with her, there was no telling what he might do. While Tanner wasn't too worried about himself, Beth was entirely a different story. Sam Bass was a cruel man who would do whatever he felt was necessary to get rid of anyone he thought was a threat to his safety.

Tanner watched him walk away. As soon as he felt Bass was out of sight, he slowed Beth down.

"Let's cross the street," he said, deliberately taking her by the arm and all but dragging her to the other side. He had to get her out of here. "I think it's time we went back to the hotel. There's no sense in wearing you out on your first trip out."

"But we haven't been gone that long." She gazed at him, a bemused expression on her face. "I'm not even tired."

He took her by the arm and turned her toward the hotel, his mannerisms clearly showing that the walk was over. "Let's go."

He knew his manner was abrupt. He knew she was gazing at him with a stunned expression on her face, but he'd already endangered her life once; he couldn't risk her safety a second time.

Tanner was not going to be responsible for yet another death.

* * *

Beth watched Tanner close the door behind him as he walked out of the room.

As soon as they had gotten back to the hotel, he made an excuse and left Beth alone to sit and wonder about their odd walk through town. Part of her wanted to rebel, run out the door after he left. She wanted to find the stage office and redeem the rest of her ticket to any city but here. But she knew there was no stage this late in the day, and she had no money.

And Beth had lied when she said she wasn't tired. Even though they had only walked for a short distance, it had been long enough to completely wear her out and make her realize she needed to rebuild her strength slowly.

Beth sank in a chair by the open window and looked down into the streets of San Antonio. She watched Tanner hurry down the street. Her blood seemed to thicken within her body, her heart pounding as she watched him go. His hips moved in a rhythm that was more swagger than walk, his guns clinging to his thighs.

No banker she'd ever known had worn guns like a gunslinger. And after today's outing, she doubted more and more that he was a banker. His mood had changed dramatically from the time they started until he brought her back.

In fact, the entire outing had been strange. He had started out friendly, laughing and talking. But once they stopped in front of the sheriff's office, he'd grown tense and snappy. And after she noticed the Wanted posters, he'd become quiet and stiff, practically bruising her to force her farther down the street. Then he had completely withdrawn, leaving Beth to feel as if she were alone.

So what had made him suddenly so moody, so remote?

One minute he'd been fine, and the next he'd blown colder than a spring blizzard.

What about the sheriff's office had caused him to react? They had halted there for just a few moments while she gazed upon the Wanted posters, hoping to find the bandits that had held up the stagecoach. There was only one thing that could have possibly upset him, and that would have been the Wanted posters.

The sketch had borne a striking similarity to Tanner. However, he hadn't given her the chance to read what the man was wanted for. Moreover, the man's name had been Jackson, not Tanner. He had practically yanked her down the street when he'd noticed her gazing at the sketches. But why would looking at the faces posted on that board have upset him?

Something about Tanner was wrong. She couldn't quite put her finger on it just yet, but somehow she knew that he was not telling her the complete truth, and she wanted to know the realities about Tanner. How he could be so gentle one moment and tough the next.

Was Tanner the man on the Wanted posters, or was he someone else she didn't know?

Six

When Tanner came in later that evening, Beth sat her body in front of the window, stiffer than a male virgin in a whorehouse.

Questions whirled through her mind like a dust storm. The events over the last two weeks had shaken her more than she cared to admit, and today's walk had left her head spinning.

"You been sitting there all afternoon?" he asked, staring at her from the open doorway.

"Yes," she informed him.

She had gazed out the open window, not really seeing the street below, instead reflecting on Tanner, comparing him to the drawing on the Wanted poster. Had it really been him?

The urge to ask about that Wanted poster was strong, but she resisted. If he were a criminal, why had he stayed and cared for her? She wanted to know about his background and if it really was his likeness on the Wanted poster, but she was afraid. She couldn't rest, however, until she knew more about Tanner.

If that was even his real name. Could he be this outlaw called Jackson?

Tanner shut the door behind him with a decisive click, his expression uncertain as he stared at her. He pulled off his hat and sat the black Stetson on the table. Slowly, he removed his gun belt and methodically laid his Colt navy revolvers next to the bed, where he could reach the pistols quickly. He looked every bit like a dark and dangerous gunfighter, and her pulse pounded, not from fear but from a feeling that began somewhere lower.

He glanced at her, his dark blue eyes questioning. "What's wrong?"

"Nothing," she said, unable to ignore the way, with just one glance, her breathing quickened at the sight of the solidly built man.

"You feel all right?"

"I'm fine," she said, her voice quivering, her eyes unable to meet his gaze.

"Dinner will arrive in about an hour," he acknowledged. "I'm going to wash up."

Before she could protest, he pulled his shirt out of his pants, unbuttoned it, and let it slide off his back to expose his rippling muscles. He pitched the garment on the bed and walked to the pitcher and water bowl sitting next to the window. She was so close she could almost touch him, and he was naked from the waist up.

It was the first time she had seen him without his shirt, and the urge to close her eyes was strong, but something inside her resisted.

She wanted to stop him, but the sight of those muscles undulating as he bent over and splashed his face with cool water halted her protest.

As he stood before the water bowl, his chest gleamed in the dwindling sunlight, his hardened muscles clearly outlined for her perusal. And the trepidation she'd felt all afternoon suddenly dimmed as she stared at the man she realized could never be a banker.

Counting money could not give a man the kind of

physique Tanner possessed. She'd never seen a banker without his shirt before, but she doubted that any of them had muscles that rippled down their stomachs, arms that bulged beneath their shirts, or a back that appeared strong and healthy.

No, Tanner had a body that was well-toned, hard, and tanned, with a scar that ran around his muscled back, from beneath his rib cage, before disappearing beneath his waistband to . . .

Her face flushed, and she thought she was beginning to break into a sweat as the heat suddenly felt oppressive.

She turned away from the sight of him splashing water over his glistening muscles and reminded herself that she knew little about this man. Nothing except that she was afraid it might have been his face on that Wanted poster hanging outside the sheriff's office that afternoon.

She glanced at the bed and noticed how normal it looked for a man's shirt to be lying across the quilt. This was how married people lived every day, sharing intimacies in close proximity. But she and Tanner weren't married, and he wasn't the type of man to want marriage. Yet her body responded to his in the way a woman responds to a man. She had to remind herself that she was practically engaged to someone else.

"You're awfully quiet this evening," he said, drying his face with the towel.

And he seemed unusually talkative and more edgy than normal.

"Uh, the walk tired me out more than I thought," she said, focusing her gaze on the streets below the window and not on the man whose half-naked state she was trying to ignore.

What was the harm in asking him what he really did

for a living? He was probably nothing more than a hired gun. A man who did another man's dirty work.

He took the towel and briskly dried the droplets of moisture from his chest and back. She looked away, her eyes searching the room for something to focus on. Anything besides the man whose very presence seemed to engulf the small room, suffocating her with his nearness.

A warm feeling came over her, and she knew he was watching her, wondering about her silence.

"What's wrong?" he questioned.

His query surprised her. He was not the type of man to ask about feelings, to inquire about the other person's emotions.

But the Wanted poster had resembled him so much, and he didn't seem like the type of man who worked in a bank. Beth couldn't stand not knowing a moment longer. "Are you really a banker, Tanner?"

She swallowed, the feel of his blue eyes staring at her intently, shredding what little confidence she had managed to retain. His face was unreadable, almost as if he were bored with her question.

"I've worked in a bank before," he said with a drawl that sent tingles down her spine.

"But you're not a banker now, are you?" she asked. "Who are you really?"

He drew the towel around his neck, sat down in a chair at the table, and let his hands rest comfortably between his legs, his elbows supported by his knees.

All she could see was his glistening, rock-hard flesh glowing at her, filling her mind, tempting her to run her fingers down the smooth expanse of his flesh.

"Lady, here in the West people don't ask these types of questions. They just accept a person as they see them."

He stared at her, his blue eyes intense. "If you're going to stay, you better learn that principle."

"I don't know who you are, and I can't help but wonder who I'm sharing a room with. And what you were doing on the stage that day."

He shrugged, his face a bored expression. "I was traveling, just like you."

A shiver passed down Beth's spine as she looked at him. From all outward signs, he appeared relaxed, but she sensed a tenseness about him that, although subdued, was there just the same.

Though Tanner didn't like the fact that she was asking questions, at a casual glance he appeared just fine with her interrogation.

"Elizabeth, do you think I'm going to harm you?" he asked, watching her carefully.

He'd drawled her name, not the shortened version but her full first name. Her mother had only used Elizabeth when she was in trouble, her father, when he was trying to convince her his way was best. So what did it mean when Tanner used her full name?

She stared at his lips and briefly remembered the way they had felt against her own, how he had tasted and his unique smell, which somehow soothed her when he was near. No, she didn't think he was going to hurt her.

"I'm not worried you're going to harm me," she said, her voice almost a whisper in the dwindling sunlight. "I just want some answers."

"To what?" he asked. "You know my name. I told you my profession. I've taken care of you since the accident. Why are you questioning my motives now? If I'd wanted to hurt you, I wouldn't have brought you back to town."

He used her name just as her father had, to convince

her to see reason. And everything he said seemed so logical, while she appeared a melodramatic fool.

She couldn't even tell him the reason for her sudden suspicions: a Wanted poster that held a certain resemblance to his handsome face papered on the outside wall of the sheriff's office.

No wonder he was looking at her as though she'd lost her mind, maybe she had. Now that he mentioned her fears, they seemed so minor, so inconsequential.

She shrugged. No, the pit of her stomach was telling her that he was not only handsome; there was so much more that he wasn't telling her. And that's what made her nervous.

"You're right. I guess being ill has made me edgy." She glanced at his naked chest. "I just need to relax."

How did she loosen up when a half-dressed man whose very presence reeked of masculinity and danger stood before her? She needed to ignore the feelings being near Tanner evoked. She needed to forget about the handsome man she had every reason to suspect was a hired gun, or worse.

All her energy needed to be focused on getting to Fort Worth, and to Tucker Burnett, before she did something really foolish that could jeopardize her future.

The afternoon sun cast a hazy glow through the smoke-filled air. The cannons roared, each shot sending more white smoke spiraling throughout the battlefield.

Tanner put the gun to his shoulder and pulled the trigger again; the reflex of the gun jerked him back each time he fired. The smell of gunpowder filled his nostrils. The cannons boomed, and the sound of bayonets clashing sounded closer, but still they stood and fought, determined to stop the Yankees at Peachtree Creek.

They were losing. The tide of the battle was turning and they were in danger of being soundly beaten.

Around him the moans of the wounded could be heard during the brief silences of the cannon, and the dead lay scattered like fallen leaves. With a worried glance, he searched for Carter. His friend still stood, and Tanner wondered how he ever thought that war was glorious and heroic.

They'd run away from home to join the army and whip the Yankees, only to find that their foolish dreams of glory were anything but grand. And he missed his family more than he'd ever thought possible, even his formidable father.

A whistle sounded, and a signal passed down the line, the bugler having been wounded days before. They were retreating, moving out once again and Tanner could only guess what that meant. They were thirty miles from Atlanta, with a precious railroad line that supplied the Confederate army with supplies somewhere between them and the heart of the South. He knew in his gut the Confederacy was losing, but his mind refused to acknowledge that the glorious cause he'd left his family for was a dying mission. He wanted to go home, he wanted his mother's apple pie, he wanted to tell his father he was sorry, but he couldn't.

He'd be damn lucky to get home alive. A man had his pride.

A bullet slammed into the dirt beside him, and he quickly returned fire. Blue soldier boys were racing toward them, and somehow he knew he was going to die right there, on this field in Georgia.

Running backward, he fired his rifle again; he contin-

*ued firing over and over, pausing only long enough to
reload. But the Yankees were coming faster than he could
fire.*

*A quick glance showed that Carter had seen his pre-
dicament and was struggling, fighting hand to hand, to
make his way toward him. They would die together on
this field. Go down together like brothers.*

*He gave up reloading and used his bayonet to fight
off the attackers. An uncanny feeling came over him, and
he swung to the left. A boy dressed in blue stared him
in the eye. The young man's eyes were as brown as a
freshly plowed patch of earth.*

*Tanner raised his bayonet; then a cry of anguish filled
his throat.*

He felt a hand on his arm. He grabbed the arm, twisting the soldier to the ground. A soft moan filled his
sleep-muddled mind and he slowly realized that he
wasn't on a battlefield and he wasn't about to die. It was
only a dream. The same dream that plagued his nights
and haunted his days.

But the moan had sounded real. And there was a softness surrounding him that smelled as fresh as a spring
rain, not rank, sweaty, and fearful.

Slowly, he opened his eyes, not wanting to face the
real world. Beth lay beneath him, her soft curves molded
to his body. He was lying in her bed instead of in the
chair beside her. He held her good arm in a viselike grip
while she murmured soft words to him.

"Wake up, Tanner," she said. "It's all right," she
soothed.

A shiver passed through him as the dream slowly
faded, and he realized he was back in Texas, not on a
bloody battlefield in Georgia. What had moments ago

seemed so real was only his mind taking him back to the place he dreaded most. He released her good arm.

"I'm . . . I didn't hurt you, did I?" he asked, his voice ragged and rough.

"Not really," she said in a breathless whisper that twisted his insides. "You just jostled my shoulder a bit."

For a moment, neither one of them said anything, but she patted his back gently, as a mother soothes a small child. He willed himself to relax in her embrace, to let the dream and all its ugly memories fade away.

Her arms were around him, her breasts crushed against his chest, but she was stiff and tense beneath him. He knew he was too heavy to be lying on top of her, but she felt so good that he didn't want to move. He wasn't ready to abandon the cocoon of pleasure in which he unexpectedly found himself.

He glanced down at her face, checking to make sure he wasn't hurting her. She gazed up at him, her lips full and inviting. In the moonlight, the darkness couldn't hide the way her eyes were wide with wonder, her pupils dilated. Her tongue flicked across her bottom lip nervously, and he swallowed back a moan.

God, he wanted to kiss her again. Their brief kiss had lingered on the edges of his mind, teasing him with flashes of her taste and the feel of her in his arms. Now she seemed to fit in the hollows of his body's embrace, and he marveled at the way they melded together. How had they ended up tangled in the bedsheets together?

Her breathing quickened, and when her tongue darted out to wet her lips one more time, that was all he could stand. He lowered his mouth to within scarcely a breath away and paused, knowing he shouldn't kiss her. He gazed into her eyes, amazed at the desire he saw reflected there.

"Oh, hell," he whispered, and gave up any intention of resisting the taste of her full mouth one more time.

His mouth plundered hers, greedily consuming what he'd long denied himself. Her sweet lips tasted of pleasure and madness, and he sampled her mouth, sweeping his tongue across her full bottom lip.

He wanted to consume her, become lost in the insanity of this moment, never returning to the real world, which was filled with uncertainty and pain.

His hands reached up and gripped her face, slanting her mouth for a deeper exploration. One hand tangled in the mass of curls at the back of her head, bringing her closer.

Her arms wrapped around him, urging him still closer, and he gladly complied. She was a distraction he didn't need, a temptation he had to indulge, and now she lay beneath him.

Shifting on the bed to avoid hurting her shoulder, he gently turned her sideways, facing him. Though his lips never left hers, his fingers began to slowly unbutton the top buttons of her nightgown. He promised himself that he only wanted to touch her breasts, see how they felt, before he'd once again retreat and leave Beth alone.

But when his hand slipped inside her gown and he caressed the hardened pebble of her nipple, he moaned a low, throaty growl. She was soft as satin for sale in a shop window, and he trailed his hand over her breasts, enjoying the feel of velvety smoothness.

Beth was a lady, a sweet, beautiful woman who with one glance managed to send his heart thundering like a stampede of buffalo. Yet she was a fighter, a tough woman who had survived a gunshot, a holdup, and the fall of the South.

Opening the last button on her nightgown, he shoved aside the material and put his lips to her breast. She gasped a deep breath and arched her back toward him. Suddenly, her hands were in his hair, holding his mouth to her hardened kernel.

This was madness. A sweet lunacy that enveloped him, making him forget he was a man who couldn't afford a complication like a good woman in his life. He was a man haunted by the war, by the decisions of his youth, and no decent woman should want him.

But that didn't mean he couldn't pretend for just one moment in time that he was good enough for the woman beneath him and that she desired him. For just a moment he wanted to act as if he were unscarred by life.

He slid his hand past her ribs, down her smooth stomach, to the waistband of her pantaloons. He slipped his hands in her drawers, past her belly button, down past her stomach to the wispy curls of hair covering her center. He touched the folds of her womanhood, and she moaned a deep, throaty purr.

Unable to resist her sweet mouth, his lips covered hers once more. He drank from her greedily, consuming her with a pleasure he had long denied himself. Her hands were urging him on, pulling him tighter and harder against her as she moaned repeatedly.

Then, suddenly, those same hands were pushing him away. She went stiff beneath him and shoved him with all her might, breaking the contact of their lips. He stopped touching her, the moisture of Beth on his fingertips, and pulled his hand from her drawers.

Tanner took a deep breath urging his body to relax from the pleasure that consumed him.

"I . . . can't," she whispered in the darkness.

He rolled to the edge of the bed, his body breaking the contact they had shared. He sat up and rubbed his hands through his hair, trying to calm his racing heart and pounding pulse.

"It wouldn't be right," she whispered, her voice filled with anguish.

She was right, but that didn't mean her decision was a welcome one. No, in fact, he felt damn foolish. He never should have kissed her.

He stood, unable to listen to her protests any longer. He strode to the table, grabbed his gun belt and his hat, turned, and walked out the door. He couldn't say anything, couldn't tell her he was sorry. He knew deep in his heart that he wasn't going to apologize for what they had done. His only disappointment was that they hadn't completed the act. He had wanted Beth since that very first day.

Though the hour was early, Tanner shoved his hat on his head and was out the door before she could say goodbye.

When he shut the door behind him, he took a deep breath and shuddered. He had to get Beth out of his room, out of his life, quickly or find himself in her bed.

Tanner spent the day at the local saloon, drinking away the memories of his dreams and the remembrance of the lovely Miss Beth Anderson. He should have been looking for a place in which she could stay until she was well enough to continue on her journey, but he didn't have the energy or the enthusiasm to find her a safe haven.

Now it was dark, and though he'd had meals sent to her room, he had not seen or talked to her since before dawn. Slowly, he made his way back to the hotel. He had to go back, check on her, make sure she was all right, but he feared seeing her face. He dreaded wanting her, seeing her reaction to his kiss, knowing he couldn't have her. And he refused to go on apologizing for what had happened that morning between them.

He made his way up the stairs until he stood outside the door, knowing he should enter, anxious about this first meeting since he had almost—

Tanner turned the knob, pushing himself past that troubling thought. He walked in and found her where he least wanted to face her, in bed. Beth sat propped up, reading a book of poetry, her auburn hair curled softly around her face.

"Hello," she said, her hazel eyes wide and doelike.

"Evening," he replied curtly. "You feeling all right?"

"Stronger every day," she replied curtly.

"Good, then I'll be able to leave you soon."

It was then that he heard the first moan, and he glanced at her sharply. The sound hadn't come from Beth. Had it come from the room next door?

He walked over to the table and noticed several pictures sitting out that previously had not been displayed. "What's this?"

"Today was my mother's birthday." She glanced at him. "I took those pictures out . . . I was looking at them . . . remembering."

It was a tintype of Beth dressed in a ball gown with a scooped neckline that revealed the swells of her bosom to perfection. An older woman dressed in finery and a gentleman in a fancy suit stood beside her.

"Those are my parents," she said, an undercurrent of sadness in her voice. "That picture was taken the night of my debut ball."

Clearly she came from a sphere of society that he could never reach. They had very little in common except that he wanted to crawl into that bed with her and finish what they'd started that morning.

"Looks like you lived high before the war." He walked away from the table, to the window facing the street.

Beth glanced at him, her eyes filled with pain. "We did all right."

The sound of a female moan echoed through the room, and he glanced at Beth. She grimaced.

"Is that noise coming from next door?" he asked.

He watched as she glanced at the wall; her eyes widened, and her face seemed to turn a beguiling shade of pink.

"It's . . . it's the couple next door," she said, stammering. "They're . . ."

About that time, the mattress began a telltale squeak, and suddenly the very thing that had kept him holed up in a saloon most of the day was occurring next door. He stared at the woman whose image he had tried to drink away.

"Good God," he said, the sound of moans penetrating the thin walls of the hotel room. "How long have they been doing this?"

"Huh, the noise usually stops in about twenty minutes." Beth acknowledged, her eyes not meeting his.

"I bet," he said, his voice clipped. The couple's moans of pleasure were getting louder, and the sound of squeaky bedsprings grated on his tightly strung nerves. He wanted

Beth so bad, and now the image of a faceless couple filled his mind as his imagination filled in the pictures to go with the sounds.

"I've heard it on and off all day," she said, playing with the covers that were tucked beneath her breasts.

A moan, along with the rhythmic bump of a headboard thumping against the wall, all but drowned out the sudden pounding of his heart.

"All day, huh." No wonder Beth seemed a little tense tonight. He'd have gone crazy having to listen to another couple doing what he kept dreaming of doing with Beth.

"Where have you been?"

"I felt the need for a day of drinking," he said, staring at her, almost daring her to say something to him.

His head echoed with the crude sounds coming from next door, the hammering pulse of his heart, and the cadenced swish of his own blood as it rushed through his veins. Her skin looked so smooth, and he knew it would be velvety soft.

She glanced at him, her eyes raking him with a harsh glance. "You're not drunk, are you?"

The corner of his lip turned up in a smile. "I tried, but I was unsuccessful."

Beth looked at him warily as the moans from next door grew louder. The sound of someone else in the throes of passion made him want to lose whatever control he had and finish what he had started that morning. He wanted to push Beth back onto the bed and lose himself within her.

"So, if you didn't drink all day, what did you do in the saloon?" she questioned.

"I didn't say I didn't drink," he said, raising his voice even louder, trying to cover up the sounds of the lovers as their tempo seemed to increase, banging the bed against the wall. "I just said I wasn't drunk."

She glanced up at him, her eyes sparkling, and she licked her full lips, her breathing shallow and fast.

He threw his hat, and it sailed across the room, landing on the table and knocking the picture of her parents down.

Tanner walked across the room to straighten the pictures, but before he could pick them up, she had jumped up out of bed and fairly flown to the table. In a huff, she grabbed her precious pictures and pulled them in close to her chest.

"If you're not drunk, would you please be careful around my things? I don't disturb your guns."

He glanced at her in surprise. Maybe Beth was more than edgy; perhaps the sounds of the couple next door had gotten to her also. Tanner crossed the room to the table beside the bed and began to unbuckle his gun belt. "Good! Keep it that way. I don't like people bothering my weapons."

Her nightgown flowed behind her as she marched across the room and touched the cold metal of his gun. The hazel orbs of her eyes flashed with challenge; her auburn hair glistened with defiance.

Tanner grabbed her by the arms, the rhythmic banging of the bed next door gonging like a warning. The currents flowed thick like smoke between them, and he knew that if he sank his lips down onto the fullness of her mouth, as he so desperately wanted to, he would never cease. He would never stop until they reached a fully sated state, and that wouldn't be until the debutante was lying beneath him, wrung out from desire.

"A man's guns are his personal property. They're like his woman. You don't touch her, you don't look at her, unless you want trouble. He pulled her closer. "Do you want trouble, lady?"

"I think trouble found me the day I got on that stagecoach to Fort Worth," she whispered, her hazel-green eyes exhibiting rebelliousness as her gaze never left his.

He pulled her still closer until her breasts were smashed against his chest, his arms around her. "For once you're right."

The moans crescendoed, the pounding of the headboard suddenly ceased, and then there was silence. Sweet, blessed silence that left his breathing harsh and loud to his own ears in the suddenly deafening quiet.

Sweet, merciful God, he wanted her.

She was gazing at him, a proud lift to her chin, her eyes bright with fierceness, and suddenly he knew that sweet, innocent Beth could become a tiger when pushed too far. And he was close, real close, to sending her over the edge.

"Release me this instant," she said, her voice taut with anger.

"Why? What are you afraid of, Beth?"

"Nothing. You're hurting my arm."

He eased his grip. For a moment he considered holding on to her, but he knew if he didn't release her soon, he wouldn't free her all night.

Tanner let go of her, rocking her back on her heels.

He had to get out of there. The silence was even more deafening than the noise of a few moments ago. He took two steps, reached for his hat, and shoved it onto his head.

"Where are you going? You just got back after being gone all day."

"None of your business, lady."

In two large strides he grabbed his guns and was out of the cramped room and into the hall. Just as he pulled the door shut, he heard her yell.

"Damn you, Tanner."

He smiled. Good. Her anger was better, safer, than her warm awareness and unconscious invitation. He had no business getting involved with a woman, any woman. And she damn sure didn't need to get involved with a man like him.

Seven

Tanner spent the night in the White Elephant Saloon until closing time sent him to the livery stable and he bedded down in the hay. He couldn't face her, not yet. He'd walked in last night with a chip on his shoulder, just daring her to knock it off. It hadn't been Beth who had jarred that chip off his shoulder but the voracious noises coming from next door and his already heightened awareness of Beth as a woman. The copulating couple had almost undone him.

Instead of taking charge and convincing the innocent debutante they weren't meant for each other, his hard erection had sent him fleeing from the room. Anything to escape the raucous noises that had been both titillating and disturbing. Anything to escape the visions of him and Beth entwined together, their bodies slick with passion, that the sounds seemed to conjure up in his mind.

In his attempt to ignore the noise from the room next door, his behavior had been detestable. He had acted like a complete ass, and now he owed her an apology.

Yet he couldn't help but think that she was getting to him. Every inch of delectable skin that showed, each smile or touch, any little nuance he recognized as Beth, were mounting up. And, like a geyser, he was bound to erupt soon if he didn't do something to relieve the pressure.

Though he'd tried to postpone the inevitable, it was past time that he found someplace to leave her so that he could continue on with his business. Not that he wanted to. In fact, he dreaded going back and facing Sam. He wouldn't go at all, but he had no choice. And he'd put it off longer than he should, because the thought of parting from Beth was not a pleasant consideration.

At dawn, Tanner saddled his chestnut horse and rode to the doctor's house at the edge of town. He had to see if the man would take Beth in until she was completely well. Somehow Tanner knew she would be safer with the sawbones than with him.

When he arrived, the sun was barely over the horizon, yet the doctor met him at the door at his first knock.

"Good morning, young man," he said, opening the full door to Tanner in the bright morning sunshine. "What brings you to see me? Your wife feeling okay?"

Wife. That one word brought up so many images that Tanner thought better left alone. Beth would make the man she married an excellent helpmate. Tanner could see her several years from now, a couple of children tugging on her skirts. He felt jealous of the man who would be by her side, fulfilling the duties of her husband, envious of the life she would be living, while he would be forever wandering, forever alone.

"My wife," he said, stumbling over the words, "is fine. But I must go out of town, and I wondered if she could stay with you at the hospital until she was healed."

"Oh, no, I don't think that's a good idea, not with the threat of cholera still possible. After everything she's been through, I don't think it would be good for her to be here, where she might catch something so deadly."

He shook his head and rubbed his chin thoughtfully. "Just to be cautious, I'd rather she wait another week before she travels. But there are several boardinghouses in town you might look into."

"Thanks!" Tanner said as he turned and walked down the steps to his waiting horse.

"Say, young fellow, how long the two of you been married?" the doctor asked.

Tanner turned around and waved at the doctor. "Long enough," he replied, and put a foot up into the stirrup, anxious to get away before the doctor began asking more questions.

Riding back into town, Tanner couldn't help but wonder how it was going to feel to say good-bye to Beth. He should get back to his life, yet suddenly she had become an integral part of it, and he didn't like the thought of being alone again. Still, there was no way she could stay with him permanently. In fact, it was past time he got rid of her, before he did something stupid—something a hell of a lot more than just kiss her. And every day it was harder to resist her.

Though Beth was a complication he could not afford, he was not willing to abandon her, and he couldn't put her on the stage until she had healed. There was no way he was going to have another person's death on his hands, especially Beth's.

When he reached town, he found the rooming house the doctor had suggested. An older woman wearing a spotted apron and smelling of onions answered the door and let him inside. As soon as he walked into the room, the filth of the place almost made him gag. Smells he did not want to identify made him want to retch. Chamber pots that needed emptying, rotting food, and something that smelled like wet animal fur filled his nostrils, and he took a step back.

The woman sighed and brushed back a stray hair that stuck to her cheek.

"The price is twelve dollars a month; plus cleaning and meals are extra," she informed him. "I've got two extra rooms right now."

She was charging for cleaning? He nodded his head and quickly backed out the door.

"I'll let you know," he said, stepping into the clean outside air, resisting the urge to gasp.

As she shut the door behind him, he breathed deeply, ridding himself of the putrid air that had occupied the house.

Mounting his horse, he rode to the next rooming house, two blocks away.

The female proprietor who answered his knock seemed pleasant enough, but he sensed something wasn't right. He knew immediately that the place was clean, but the atmosphere seemed too relaxed, almost too friendly.

"I charge the ladies who stay here by the night or by the week; it doesn't matter much to me," the young woman said, smiling at him coyly.

"How much?" Tanner asked, thinking maybe this would work out and he would pay Beth's first two weeks' rent.

"Fourteen dollars a month," she said.

The door to the room next to where Beth would be sleeping suddenly opened, and a woman stepped out in a robe that clung to her curves, that was open low to expose her cleavage and split up the front to show off her calves. She stepped out into the hall, followed by a man.

"Same time next week?" the woman asked the man, her hand brushing a piece of lint from his shirt.

He smiled. "Yep. See you, Mary Lou."

"You bet, honey," she said, and patted him on the butt. The calico queen glanced at Tanner, winked, and went back into her room.

"The women are free to host gentlemen in their rooms," the young proprietor told him.

"I don't think this is what I'm looking for," Tanner said, and started walking toward the door.

"Well, if we can be of any other service, let us know," the woman said, smiling at him as he walked out the door.

After he left, he visited three more rooming houses and found fault with each of them.

Slowly riding back to the hotel, he wondered what he was going to do. So far every place he'd looked at had either been unclean, a whorehouse, in an unsafe neighborhood, or just didn't feel right. He'd found no place he was willing to trust, where he felt safe in leaving Beth behind, none where she would get the care that he had given her.

He didn't want to be rid of Beth. No place would satisfy him because he didn't want to leave her behind. The only solution was to keep her until he could put her on a stage to Fort Worth, which shouldn't be much longer. A week at the most, the doctor had said. Meanwhile, he would need to stay away from their hotel room as much as possible, and keep his overactive thoughts and his eager hands to himself.

The sun was starting to slink toward the western horizon, and Tanner realized he hadn't been back to the room in almost twenty-four hours. The urge to go back and see her, to make sure she was all right, was powerful enough that he couldn't resist. He hurried back to the hotel room, anxious to see her. The decision he made that day to wait another week could possibly cost him everything he'd been working toward, but he really didn't care. Somehow it didn't seem all that important, and he couldn't leave her behind. His future looked bleak, so why be in a hurry to rush to his destiny.

They had the next week, after which he would put her on a stage for Fort Worth. Then she would be out of his life forever. How much could one more week of waiting hurt?

Beth spent the morning pacing. When she awoke to an empty room and realized Tanner had not come in the night before, she'd begun to pace the floor, worried that something had happened, that he'd never come back.

Questions revolved over and over in her mind until she thought she would go crazy with worry. And why was she so upset that he had walked out on her last night after the way he had treated her? Certainly he'd acted less than a gentleman.

The memory of the sounds of the couple next door coming through the thin walls still made her blush. Yes, she knew everything that went on between a man and a woman. The general had seen to that. He'd delighted in training a young girl in the ways a woman pleasured a man. But to overhear the intimate sounds while trying not to think sexual thoughts about the man right before her eyes had been awkward to say the least.

The moans of pleasure had been disturbing, and when she'd gazed at Tanner, all she could think about was the way he looked without his shirt, her urge to touch him, to feel his strength beneath her fingers.

Beth pushed the unwelcome thoughts from her mind and continued her pacing. She had to build her strength in order to leave the hotel before the emotions Tanner evoked consumed her. She needed to get on a stage and continue to Fort Worth, to join the man who was waiting for her.

She picked up the picture of herself and her parents taken before her debut ball, before the war had changed their lives forever. The girl in the picture no longer existed. Elizabeth had died with the war, and now the woman who promised herself to an unknown man existed in her place.

The woman in the picture had lost everything. But Beth hoped to regain some of those aspects of her life, like her self-respect, dignity, and sense of self-worth.

Beth glanced over at the dress that lay strewn on the table where Tanner had flung it several days ago, after she had attempted to pull it over her head.

She would put that dress on, go down the street, sell her jewelry, and send that telegram. She would be on another stagecoach as soon as possible. Mr. Tanner was not going to bully her with his cold silences, hot stares, and sultry kisses.

Beth would be on the next stage out of town. She had a man waiting for her, a man who wanted to marry her, and she had no reason to stay in San Antonio. Her future was in Fort Worth with a good man, not someone with a questionable background like Mr. Tanner.

She picked up the dress and raised the skirt high, the material bunched together to slip over her head. The folds gently fell to the floor as she managed to get her pained arm into the dress without as much fuss as several days earlier. The wound throbbed, reminding her of her injury, warning her of the consequences of her actions. Still, the arm was better, though it was in no way completely healed.

A quick glance in the mirror revealed that her hair, twisted up off her neck, looked presentable. She grabbed her reticule and stepped out into the hall.

It felt so odd to be out of the room without Tanner at her side. And she was amazed at how quickly they had become accustomed to one another. The thought of leaving him behind while she moved on to Fort Worth seemed strange, yet she knew they could not be together. He was too dangerous, too unsettled. However, unlike any man before, she was drawn to the gunslinger.

But he had to move on, and she had a stage to catch.

Walking carefully down the stairs, she was surprised to see the number of people bustling about the lobby of the hotel.

Beth walked to the front desk, where a young man was working. "Excuse me, can you tell me where to find the nearest store that buys and sells jewelry?"

The young man dragged out a hand-drawn map and proceeded to give her directions. "Go up the street two blocks and turn right. You should see it on your left."

"Thank you."

She stepped out the front door of the hotel and stopped, startled by the brightness of the afternoon sky.

She hurried down the sidewalk, intent on getting to her destination. It didn't take long to walk the two blocks, and when she arrived at her destination, she took a seat outside on a bench and rested for several minutes.

It took less than fifteen minutes to sell most of her jewelry. She'd already disposed of the very best pieces trying to hold on to the land, but these were smaller ones: an emerald brooch, a diamond pendant, and a set of pearl earrings her father had presented her mother. She saved only two pieces, her mother's wedding ring and a necklace her parents had given her.

The rest was now in the hands of the shop owner, and she refused to think sadly of the exchange.

Passing in front of the jewelry store, she realized she was beginning to tire and needed to get back to the hotel room as quickly as possible.

A block from the hotel, she stopped at the telegram office and quickly penned a message to Mr. Tucker Burnett. WILL BE ARRIVING IN THE NEXT TWO WEEKS. LOOK FORWARD TO MEETING YOU. MISS ELIZABETH ANDERSON.

Exhausted, Beth hurried back to the hotel, feeling tired but pleased at the results of her outing. She ignored the niggling disappointment that Tanner would soon be out of her life.

Beth turned the knob of the door to their room and was surprised to see Tanner pacing the floor.

"Where the hell have you been?" he asked harshly.

"I . . . I went for a walk." She didn't know why she didn't tell him the truth—maybe it was the anger in his voice—but she didn't. The jewels had been hers, though Tanner had already expressed his disapproval of her selling them. And she was too tired to argue right now or do anything more than gaze at the unyielding man.

He stared at her and then pulled out a chair. "Sit down before you fall. You look exhausted."

"I am rather tired. I pushed myself today."

"I see that," he said. "Don't overtax your strength."

"I have to get well. I need to become stronger," she said, walking across the room to the nearest chair.

She watched him pace the floor, his brow furrowed deep in thought. He seemed genuinely concerned that she hadn't been here when he returned. Yet the surly man from last night wasn't a distant memory, and she was wary of just who had returned to their hotel room, the real Tanner or his evil twin.

He paced for several more moments while she rested and stared out the window.

"I . . . I owe you an apology," he said, breaking into her reverie. His voice, calmer, still held a strident note.

"What?" she asked, stunned.

"I said, I owe you an apology," he repeated. "For the way I acted last night."

"Oh," she said, surprised.

"I was rude," he acknowledged.

She sat and stared at him, astonished that he was admitting his wrong.

"You didn't do anything to deserve to be treated badly, and I apologize for my behavior," he said, not looking at her.

Beth felt as if someone had just kicked her in the shin. Before this moment, she had begun to doubt that he had ever felt any sympathy regarding her injuries, yet she knew better. It was just so much easier to think of him as a scoundrel she would be glad to be rid of than the man who had taken care of her, fed her, and seen her at her very worst. A man she had been forced to depend on.

Although she didn't want to be beholden to him for anything, whenever they were in the room together, everything seemed intensified. Smells were stronger, tastes were richer, feelings were deepened, and Beth was afraid. Tanner evoked emotions she had never explored and couldn't afford to discover at this time in her life.

"Your a . . . apology is accepted," she said, stumbling over the word and still reeling from this unexpected turn of events. She'd never heard a man, other than a family member, express regret, especially one who looked capable of taking on the world by himself.

He took a quick look at her dress. "Since you've already been out of the hotel, I was thinking, if you aren't too tired, maybe we could go downstairs tonight and eat."

She glanced down at her hands. "Just let me rest for about fifteen minutes and then I think I'll be well enough."

"Why don't you rest while I change clothes?"

Oh, God. How could she lie on that bed and watch him shed his clothes? The sponge bath he'd taken the other night had almost done her in, and now he was going to change in front of her?

She wasn't prepared to face Mr. Tanner without his clothes on today—maybe never.

"I . . . think maybe I'll meet you down in the dining hall." Before he could object, she all but ran out the door.

Tanner glanced around the crowded dining room and realized immediately that he'd made a mistake. He should never have brought Beth down to dinner. The waitress had asked her how she was feeling, he'd overheard the words "shot during a hold up" several times, and he knew they were being observed by the other guests of the hotel. And she was with him.

From the moment they appeared in the doorway, people had turned and stared. Not only did Beth's auburn hair attract attention; the emerald-green dress that clung to her curves brought out the brilliance of her eyes and reminded him of a Georgia Pine forest in summer. She was by far the most beautiful woman in the room, and Tanner was awestruck at her beauty.

Yet she appeared completely unaware of the sensation she had caused when entering the dining room of the hotel. Seated across from him, she daintily wiped a crumb from her bottom lip and smiled. "I'm so glad we didn't eat in the room tonight. I was tired of staring at those same four walls."

"Well, it shouldn't be much longer before your life will be back to normal," he said, his voice deepening. "I spoke with the doctor this morning, and he said in another week you should be able to ride."

Beth picked up her wineglass and twirled it between her fingers. "Where did you see the doctor?"

Tanner couldn't tell her he'd been looking for a place to leave her, so he lied. "He was on his way to visit someone when I ran into him."

"One more week." She glanced up at him, her emerald eyes dilating in the candlelight. "Soon I'll be meeting the man I'm going to marry."

Tanner knew their time was limited, that another man was waiting for her, but that didn't mean his thoughts didn't wander down paths he knew he could never travel. Paths that he wanted to explore with Beth.

She took a sip of the wine, her tongue running along the curve of her lips.

"Why did you decide to become a mail-order bride?" he asked, suddenly curious about her. "I would have thought that you would have more marriage proposals than you could handle."

She shrugged her shoulders. "I lived in a rural section of Georgia, not far from Atlanta. I was barely of age when the war began, and then so many of the boys from back home died. There wasn't anyone left to marry."

"So you decided to take your chances in Texas with a man you've never met?" He scowled.

Her smile seemed to droop as her eyes changed, the green turning a shade darker, and she took a deep breath.

"I answered an ad. We corresponded for a while, and then he asked me to come to Fort Worth, Texas."

Tanner felt a pang of homesickness rattle his bones at the sound of Fort Worth. Home, where he could never return.

He didn't ask the man's name. He didn't want to know Beth's new name once she was married. That way he could never be tempted to look her up. Or even worse, he might know her husband. No, it was better if he didn't know who she was marrying, and she didn't seem inclined to tell him.

She tilted her head to the side, and the candlelight reflected off the smooth plane of her cheekbone, bathing her in a luminous glow that made her even more beautiful. If only his life had been different, he could have been the man Beth was going to marry.

"What about you? You've not told me what bank you work for. Or even much about yourself."

He cleared his throat, determined not to let the glow of the candles on her satiny skin, dainty nose, and full lips distract him. But somehow all he could do was stare at the beautiful woman before him, knowing he was losing the battle. He wanted to run his fingers along her chin and touch her skin to see if it felt velvety soft beneath his fingertips.

"Not much to tell. I work for whoever needs me."

"I know you served in the war."

She was referring to his dreams at night. He glanced away. "Yeah, so did everyone else."

"You must have family somewhere."

He shrugged and watched the elegant way she put her fork to her lips. Beth was a refined lady who, like so many others, had been misplaced by the war. Unlike himself, she'd dealt with her loss and moved on.

"Yeah, I have two brothers. How about yourself? Any brothers or sisters?"

She laid her fork on her plate and dabbed her mouth with her napkin. "No, I was an only child. My parents were older when they had me."

He remembered her saying they were dead, and suddenly the image of her, feverish and pleading with him that she was a good girl, came back, and he wondered at the memory. The lady was so proper, so refined, that he couldn't imagine her doing anything unseemly.

Yet there was a certain mysteriousness and worldliness about her that led him to believe she was not an innocent but a woman who knew about the intimacies of life. He couldn't help but wonder about the man who had showed her how to be a woman.

He couldn't help but stare at her; the fiery highlights in her hair flittered in the candlelight like tiny shooting stars. She was warm, responsive, and if he had been a less honorable man, she'd be doing more than just sleeping in his room.

It was surprising he had some measure of honor left after all these years that still held him in check.

He took a deep breath to calm the erratic beating of his heart. "So you were an only child."

"Yes," she said breathlessly.

"Is it true that only children are spoiled?" he asked, not really caring about her answer, just wanting to hear her talk, to see the vivid expressions on her lovely face.

She laughed, and he couldn't help but think how nice it was to hear the sound.

"Somewhat. But what people don't tell you are the high expectations placed on an only child. After all, your parents only have one chance to do it right. Not to mention the fact that there's no one there to share the laughter, the responsibilities, and the burdens. I would have loved to have had siblings."

Beth had gone from laughing and playful to serious, and he resisted the urge to reach across the table and hold her hand. He wanted to, but somehow he knew it wasn't appropriate. Damn the proprieties! He wanted to touch her, feel her silky skin beneath his own.

She smiled, though the sadness in her eyes still lingered. "I've talked all evening, and you've said very little. So where is home?"

He raised his hand and signaled for the check. It was time to go. Her questions were becoming more focused.

The waiter brought over the check, and he reached into his pocket and pulled out the necessary coins.

"Wherever I lay my head, that's where I call my home." He stood and pulled back her chair.

"I think you're avoiding the subject," she said, rising from her seat, her interest clearly piqued.

"Maybe. It's been so long since I went home that I'm sure they've forgotten about me."

"I don't believe you."

"I didn't leave under the best of circumstances," he said, taking her by the arm and leading her toward the staircase.

"Even more reason for you to go home and straighten things out," she said.

"Not likely."

He could never return home and face his father, mother, and brothers. His past was anything but honorable, and having to face his father was impossible.

The comfortable atmosphere that had enveloped them

since Beth's return evaporated, leaving Tanner feeling uneasy as they trod up the steps of the hotel.

A thought crossed his mind. What would he do if the couple next door were as busy tonight as they had been last night? Surely the man next door wouldn't get lucky two nights in a row.

He opened the door, and Beth stepped into the hotel room that had been their sanctuary, their home, since her accident. A feeling of dread came over Tanner.

The air seemed thick and heavy with the remembrances of the night before. Every little creak and groan caused Tanner to jump for fear the couple next door were about to repeat their performance.

"I bet you're feeling tired, since you went for a walk today," he asked, hoping that she would just go to bed and he could slip out for a while.

"Not really." She sat down in the chair, watching him expectantly.

"Have you read today's newspaper?" he asked, starting to pace the floor.

"Twice."

She glanced at him, and her eyes darkened to a deep green, her pupils wide and dilated. She swallowed nervously. God, just looking at her left him with little doubts as to what she was thinking.

"Want me to set up the checker board tonight?" he asked, a restless energy preventing him from sitting down.

"No." She went to her reticule, which lay open on the dresser. "Why don't you go smoke one of those cigars you're so fond of while I get ready for bed. I think I'd like to take a quick bath and slip into my nightgown."

He swallowed. The thought of her slipping into that soft nightgown, the one that was a luminous white, that clung to every curve, every voluptuous inch, the one that shadowed the nipples of her breast, was too tempting, and he agreed. It was time for a cigar.

"Take your time. I'll be back in a little while," he said, hurrying out the door, and shutting it firmly behind him. He leaned against the frame and took a deep breath. God, he didn't know how much more close proximity to this woman he could take. She was soft, appealing, and sexy as hell, but worse than that, he enjoyed being with her, and that scared him worst of all.

Tanner found himself sitting at the counter of the White Elephant Saloon, a block from the hotel. He'd needed more than a cigar. He'd needed a sip of whiskey to dull how much he wanted Beth.

She was a lady. He was an outlaw. And she would soon be married, though the idea of seducing her was a temptation dreams were made of. But it was a deed he could never attempt. He'd caused more heartache in his short life than one person should be allowed, and he was not about to accrue yet another offense.

Still, the thought of her languishing naked in a tub filled with warm water was enough to require a second drink.

And that was the one that got him into trouble.

Tanner sat at the bar thinking about Beth, dreaming of the way her breasts peeked through the cotton material of her gown, the way she appeared, so gentle and kind, but with such a strong spirit. He couldn't help but remember the way she had withstood the pain while he had held her down and Doc Benson removed the bullet.

Yes, she was a lady, but she was a strong, decent person, and he wasn't going to corrupt her with his ways.

"So I finally caught up with you without your lady friend." The voice came out of the blue, sending his heart into rapid pulsating.

Tanner jerked around at the sound of a voice he immediately recognized.

He tried not to let his surprise show. "Hi, Sam, sit down and I'll buy you a beer."

"Thanks, don't mind if I do."

The bartender drew a draught of beer and sat the mug in front of Sam, the man who had robbed Beth's stage.

"We'd just about given up on you ever riding with us again. Where you been?" the outlaw asked.

"Had some things here in town that I needed to take care of," Tanner drawled, trying to slow his racing heart and get his nerves under control.

"Yeah, I saw what you've been taking care of. She's a right pretty little piece, too."

Tanner only smiled.

"So why don't the two of you come out to where we're staying. You know where it is. After all, you've been there before."

"Yeah, I know where you're at. I've been busy."

Sam drank from his glass, greedily gulping almost half the beer.

"You know, Jackson, I've gotten the feeling you don't want to be with us anymore."

"No, I've just been busy, that's all. Women can take up all your time."

Sam stared at him, picked up his drink, and downed it. "I'm going over to the Palace and try out Miss Jane's girls. Why don't you come with me? We'll make a night of it."

"Sounds like fun, but well, she's waiting for me, and I think I'm going to finish my beer and call it a night."

Sam set his empty glass on the counter and then stared at Tanner.

"Bring her out soon, Jackson. We'd all like a piece of her."

Anger flared like an explosion in a mine shaft, but Tanner managed to hide it.

He shrugged. "I'm not much good at sharing, but I'll be out there soon enough, Sam."

"You do that."

The outlaw stood and walked out the door, leaving Tanner alone, trying to hide the fact that he was shaking, he was so angry.

Sam wanted him to bring Beth out to the hideout where his men would insist on sharing her.

That was it. He would not harm Beth deliberately even if it meant destroying the rest of his life. Though the doctor had wanted her to wait another week, Beth's life suddenly seemed to be in more danger here in town than from a horseback ride.

Tanner couldn't just put her on a stagecoach and send her on to Fort Worth, where Sam and his boys might hold it up again. He couldn't just let her fend for herself. But taking her to Fort Worth would mean days together on the trail. No matter what he did, Tanner was going to come out the loser, but he really had no choice.

He was taking a huge risk, and he knew it. But it seemed small compared to the danger that Beth would be in if she stayed here, where Sam could find her. Tanner couldn't let anything happen to Beth.

It was too late to leave tonight, but they would be departing at first light.

Eight

Tanner opened the door and was greeted by the sight of Beth wrapped in a towel, her long, bare legs exposed to his gaze.

She blushed. "I . . . I took longer than I expected."

"I'll come back," he said, stepping back into the hall, determined to go anywhere to get away from the sight of Beth in that clinging wet towel and all that exposed skin.

"No, uh, I'm almost done," she said hurriedly, her hazel eyes warm and languid. "Just turn around and close the door."

Reluctantly, he stepped into the room and shut the door. He turned to face the portal, feeling as if he were confronting a firing squad. How could she be almost done when she'd been wearing nothing but a towel?

This was torture. He could hear her rustling behind him. The noises were intimate swishes of cloth brushing against naked flesh, and his mind supplied the picture while Beth provided the sounds that made him want to groan. Why had he come back to the room so soon?

For a brief moment he wished that he were that piece of cloth being rubbed against her satiny skin, over her lovely breasts, between her thighs and down her long legs.

The image of her naked was so vivid that this time he did groan, which he promptly covered with a cough.

"Are you getting sick?" she asked, her voice breathy from her actions.

"I'm fine," he snapped.

God, he was lying. He was about to die from just standing there in the same room while she finished toweling off.

"You can turn around now. I'm dressed," she said.

When he faced her, she was sitting before the dresser, running a comb through her long auburn locks, which hung almost to her waist. Her cheeks were rosy and flushed from her bath. Damp tendrils of hair clung to her nape and face; the luminous nightgown flowed over her curves like a river clinging to its banks.

He drank in the sight of her and knew there was no way he could abandon her. He could never leave her to the mercy of a madman like Sam Bass. No matter what the consequences to himself, he had to take her to Fort Worth and deliver her safely into the hands of her new husband-to-be. But he wasn't ready to tell her of their change in plans just yet.

"How's your shoulder?" he asked, knowing that the next few days would test her strength.

"It's better. It's still sore, but I can move it a bit now."

She was getting well, and while he was glad, he knew that their time together was drawing to a close. Though it was for the best, he wasn't ready for their brief idyll to end. Unbeknownst to her, tomorrow morning he would take her to the man who was waiting for her.

Irrational anger surged through him. He didn't want to take her to any man, especially one who was going to marry her. But he had no choice, and he needed to accept the fact that at this time tomorrow he and Beth would be on their way to Fort Worth.

He walked over to the table and began to remove his gun belt, taking his Colt navy revolvers out and laying them close at hand.

He took a seat in the chair, then reached down and tugged on his boots. He was tired, and it was best they make it an early night, for dawn would find them on the road.

"If you'd like, I could ring for a bath to be brought up for you?" she offered, glancing at him from the dressing table, where she sat.

Bathing here in the same room with her was more than he was willing to risk. As it was, the whole evening had taken on an intimate hue. First with her bath and now with his sitting here watching as she combed the curls that wound down her back, fighting the desire to run his fingers through her tresses.

"No, thanks."

She shrugged and continued pulling the comb through her long auburn locks. The greenish tint of her eyes caught his attention, and his gaze held hers in the mirror. A look passed between them that seemed to ignite a flare along the base of his spine, sending hot flashes of need curling through him.

Damn, but he wanted her.

She cleared her throat nervously.

"Did you have a nice smoke?"

He gazed at her, his frustration mounting at the way his body responded to her. "Yeah."

For the first time since before he left for the war, he had found a woman who interested him. She was not only beautiful but intelligent, and he was attracted to her in ways he'd never even thought about. And now he was going to take her to her new husband, and there wasn't a damn thing he could do but hand her over and say good-bye. Life could be so unfair.

"So, are you looking forward to meeting your new husband?" he asked, his curiosity prompting the question.

He couldn't help but wonder about the man who would have all Tanner's fantasies come true. The man probably thought that because she was a mail-order bride, she was homely, but was he in for a surprise.

"I'm a little nervous." She shrugged and absently ran the comb through her hair. "This is a new beginning for me. I'm twenty-seven years old, and this is a chance for me to start my life over. It's an opportunity for me to finally have the family I've always wanted."

Her words surprised Tanner. He never would have guessed she was the same age as he. She looked young but somehow worldlier than her years. Part of him was a little jealous. He'd like to have a second chance at his own life. There were things he would have done differently.

Something in her past had brought her to the decision to move miles away from Georgia and leave everything she'd ever known.

"What made you think you needed a second chance to begin again?" he asked. "Not enough husband material in Jonesboro, Georgia?"

"As a matter of fact, there wasn't. Besides, why shouldn't I start somewhere fresh?" She stopped brushing her hair and stared at him. "The war took away the only life I've ever known. It changed me in ways you'll never understand."

"The war changed us all," he replied gruffly, thinking of how his own life had been affected.

Sitting in the chair before the mirror, she turned and faced him. "Did it change you, Tanner?"

He gave a short, sarcastic laugh. "Yeah, I used to be a choirboy." His brows drew together in a frown. "Don't ask. There are things about me you don't want to know."

She frowned, his response obviously irritating her.

"Look, you're not the only one who has had to face things in life that you'd rather forget. I may not have been in the army, but I fought a battle just the same," she said, gripping the handle of the hairbrush.

Her response irritated him. What kind of battle could she have fought? Oh, yes, the blockade had kept her from getting the latest fashions from Paris.

"The war ended almost ten years ago," he said. "Get over it."

Her hazel eyes had darkened and flashed sparks of irritation at him in the lantern light. "The fighting may have stopped and Reconstruction has long since begun, but the healing is far from over."

He was getting to her, and for just a moment it felt good.

"How could a rich little plantation owner's daughter be ruined by the war?" He dropped his boot on the floor. "I guess it did wreck your social calendar for several years."

Her eyes narrowed. "You have no idea what happened to me during the war. I wasn't exactly sitting at home darning some poor soldier's socks."

"That would easily have gotten you a marriage proposal. Socks were a valuable commodity during the war. There's nothing worse than having tired, wet, cold feet."

He was weary and he didn't want to argue with her, but he was enjoying their verbal wrangling. The frustration of the last few weeks seemed to be building to a level he wasn't sure he could control. And suddenly he'd found a way to express his disturbing response to Beth.

Her face tightened as if she were clenching her teeth.

"If you think that my life has been easy, you're wrong. Making the decision to leave my home, everything I knew and come west, was by far the second-hardest decision I'd ever made."

"What was the first? What dress to wear at your debut?"

Sparring with Beth felt good. She was the first woman in years that had managed to make him feel something besides pure lust. It made him feel really alive, and that scared the hell out of him. The farther he pushed her away, the safer he'd be.

"No, the hardest decision concerned my family home. Whether to let the Yankees or the scalawags take it."

The memory of his family's ranch came to mind. What if he'd been forced to give it up?

Suddenly, he knew that the decision had been intensely painful for Beth, and for a moment he didn't like what he was doing. But he didn't dare try to comfort her. His gaze was steady as he stared at her and raised his brows expectantly. He stood and tugged on his shirt until the garment came free of his pants.

"No more talk of war. I've tried my damnedest to erase those years from my memory," he said, walking across the room.

"Maybe you should just accept what happened. Maybe then it wouldn't bother you as much," she said, pulling the brush through her hair.

He turned and faced her in his stocking feet. "I've seen things, done things, you could never understand. And you think I should just accept them?"

She took a deep breath and released it slowly. "I'm

sure you've done things you're not proud of, but that doesn't mean people can't change. Everyone has the power to become different."

She glanced into the mirror and pulled the brush through her hair, her movements jerky and ragged.

"Maybe I don't want to change," he said, knowing it was a lie but unable to admit the need to exorcise his demons to her.

Beth stared at him, her large hazel eyes round with sympathy, and seeing his greatest fear reflected in her gaze, he wanted to do anything to alter her opinion of him. The thought of her having pity on him was just too much to bear. He didn't need anyone's sympathy or compassion, especially hers.

"Everyone has things in their past they'd rather forget. I have a fair idea of what you might have done," she said.

He laughed, his voice twisted and filled with pain. "You have no idea. And I'm not going to enlighten you. You're some lily-white debutante whose life was destroyed by the lack of an available husband. You're looking for a man to take care of you; that's why you became a mail-order bride."

"That's not fair!" she said. "My choices were limited, to say the least."

"So why did you wait so long?" he questioned. "The war has been over for ten years. Surely you could have found someone before now?"

She swallowed nervously. "I had my parents to take care of, and there was Pinewood, our plantation, to see about. Then Mother became sick, and I had to care for her."

"Excuses, lady. You could have married."

"Why didn't you?" she said, her voice loud and strident.

"Because I'm not the marrying kind." He continued on, wanting to hurt her for making him feel, for making him want things he knew he could never have. "I'm not the kind of man a woman wants to tie herself permanently to."

"Even men who aren't the marrying kind fall in love and marry eventually." She stood and walked to his side, her white nightgown flowing around her hips. Her eyes flashed indignantly at him. She stopped right before him. "I've waited years for a husband. To have someone to wake up in my arms each morning, a baby to rock to sleep. Isn't this what all women dream of? So why am I so bad for wanting the same things?"

"You're not as long as you know I'm not good husband material." He took a deep breath and tried not to reflect on the circles of pink that he could see through the material. "But you think you can soothe my hurts and make me care about you enough that I'll change my ways."

He watched as a rosy flush covered her face. Her hands were clenched at her side.

"I don't give a fig about your hurts."

Tanner didn't want to stop. He wanted to inflict on her the pain she had made him feel. "You think that beneath this rough exterior there's a man worth saving, worth turning into a husband. You're wrong."

God, how he wanted her even when she was pushing him, making him feel things he'd long forgotten. He still wanted to feel her arms around him even as he was trying his best to push her away.

"I have a man waiting for me. Why would I want a coldhearted bastard like you?"

"Because the man you have waiting for you doesn't make you feel like this." He pulled her in his arms, and she struggled against him.

"I don't want to feel this," she whispered, her voice emphatic.

"Oh, yes, you do."

"Bastard!"

He laughed. "Call me that again—later."

Tanner lowered his lips to hers in a kiss that was both torture and pleasure. Torture because he could never have her and pleasure because nothing could stop him from taking her.

His kiss was rough as he held her face between his hands, holding her immobile as he took her lips between his own. With a sense of urgency, he traced her mouth with his tongue as if to burn the feel of her lips into his memory.

He'd resisted her for what seemed like forever, and he refused to wait any longer.

His hands became tangled in the mass of curls that hung almost to her waist, and he clenched them, holding her even tighter. Savagely, he slanted his mouth over hers. She was stiff and resistant, and he stroked her tender lips until they were pliant and yielding beneath his. Reluctantly, she wound her arms around his neck.

She tasted of peppermint and soap, of hidden pleasures and forbidden desires. She leaned into him, meshing her body against his until she suddenly broke away from his kiss.

"Coldhearted bastard!"

"You bet I am," he said, sealing her lips with his once again.

He lifted her up in his arms and carried her the few

short steps to the bed, where he gently laid her down, mindful of her shoulder.

Her eyes were dilated, her cheeks flushed, and her look was filled with a passion he could no longer resist. He ran his finger down her cheekbone. "I'm going to show you just how bad I can be. I'm going to make love to you tonight, and then in the morning nothing will have changed between us except we'll know each other intimately."

"Selfish, coldhearted bastard," she said, breathless.

His mouth greedily consumed hers before she convinced herself or him that this was wrong. He didn't want to think how wrong the joining of their bodies could be. He didn't want to be rational. He didn't want to feel anything but her body surrounding him.

Urgent and hungry for Beth, Tanner plundered her lips, devouring her with a fierceness that drove him blindly. He could no longer deny he needed her in his arms, needed her to comfort him the way only a woman could.

Surrounded by the scent of her, the consequences of his life seemed a hundred miles away. The smell of lilacs and roses, the taste of fresh mint, tempted and teased him. As his body sank onto the mattress beside her, he was filled with a sweetness he'd never before experienced.

A sense of belonging and of nostalgia overcame him that reminded him of home.

Home. That faraway place that he'd run from as a teenager, that place to which, as a man, he dreamed of returning but knew he never could.

His tongue swept the inside of her mouth, and all thoughts of right or wrong were quickly dispelled. He'd wanted this woman since before the accident on the stagecoach. He'd spent the last weeks caring for her, sleeping in a chair by the bed watching her and longing for her too long not to take advantage of this moment.

He would grant himself this night, this one brief moment of insanity before he took her to her soon-to-be husband. And though it was wrong, he could no longer resist. Tonight would be just one more sin against his badly tarnished soul.

But this woman had aroused more feeling in him than anyone since Carter. He deserved this brief respite to last him the rest of his life.

Beth ran her hands across his shoulders, down his back, to the edges of his shirttail. She reached under his shirt, and he felt the hot branding of her fingers trailing up his naked back. The touch of her hands massaging and coaxing his flesh left him gasping with need.

While his lips caressed hers, his hand moved to her breast. He touched her hardened nipple, stroking the tip until she moaned with pleasure and arched her back. Ever mindful of her shoulder, he unbuttoned the front of her nightgown and opened it. Her creamy white breasts lay exposed before his eyes, her pink nipples lay puckered in a rosy shadow.

Unable to resist the velvety delight, he brushed his lips across the furrowed kernel. She moaned a deep, throaty sound that only encouraged him. His tongue circled her areola, leaving a warm, damp trail across her breasts.

His hand skimmed down her stomach and over the material of her nightgown, pulling the burdensome garment out of the way until he reached her drawers. He continued the forbidden path down to the slit in the material between her legs. He slid his fingers into her moist, womanly center and gently massaged the velvety folds.

She clung to him, and he relished in the feeling as he

coaxed her intimately with his fingers. He didn't understand why this woman made him feel so much. But the world seemed intensified whenever he was with her, and for a man who never wanted to feel again, she left him reeling with emotion.

Her hands fisted around the sheets as he stroked her until she was shivering with the need for her release. She tossed her head from side to side, her hair splayed across the pillows as she called his name.

"Tanner . . ."

"No more talking, Beth." He silenced her with a kiss that sent his own passion spiraling out of control. He was so hard for her that he ached with a need that had been building since the day he saw her on that stagecoach.

His hand stroked her center while his lips covered her mouth. She was so beautiful, and he knew, no matter what, that he could never keep her. No matter how much he wanted to, he had to give her up and take her to her husband-to-be. He pushed the thought from his mind, determined to enjoy tonight, this moment in time.

Suddenly, her body tensed around him, and her lips broke free of his kiss. She arched her back against his hand and lifted her hips in response to his probing strokes. She cried his name, and shudders rippled through her like the tide against the shore.

For several moments she lay spent in his arms, her eyes closed as he let her catch her breath.

Patiently, he waited, longing to see her lush curves without the hindrance of that gown he longed to rip from her body. Finally, his own need spurred him into pulling the gown up over her head, and he threw the garment to the floor. Then he peeled her drawers off where they joined the rest of her clothes.

She lay before him, totally naked, exposed to his searching eyes, more beautiful than his mind had portrayed. He trailed his hand down her neck, all the way to her hips, the satiny feel of her flesh intoxicating. Timidly, she gazed up at him from beneath her long lashes, her eyes fairly smoldering.

That tempestuous gaze sent Tanner scrambling for the edge of the bed. Quickly, he sat up and shed his shirt, his pants and drawers. Everything went into a heap of clothes on the floor before he returned to the bed, naked and eager to experience Beth. His blood pounded with the primitive need to possess her, to feel her flesh sheathed around him.

She ran her hand down his side, where a long scar went from his rib cage around to his back—an old war wound that had long since healed, though the emotional pain still lingered.

Her fingers trailed down his chest over his ribs, down past his waist, and he grabbed her hand before she touched his manhood. He was on the edge, and he feared one touch from her would send him spiraling over without her.

He reached out and slid his hand down a smooth expanse of skin past her waist. Once again his fingers tantalized her until she was quivering beneath him. At the sight of her breasts, he leaned over and put his lips to her taut nipples. Her breathing became labored, and her flesh was once more wet and quivering. His blood pounded and roared with an urgency to bury himself within her soft folds.

She reached up and grasped the back of his head and pulled his lips close to hers. "I want you, Tanner," she said. "Now."

"I want you, too," he whispered, rolling onto his back,

taking her with him until she was on top. The feel of her covered him.

Her head tilted to the side as she adjusted herself to this new position, her eyes slightly closed in anticipation. He lay there for a few moments, enjoying the feel of her soft curves nestled against his own body.

Why did she have such an effect on him when so many before her had simply been used? This woman who had been dependent on him for her every need, who had trusted in him, who believed in him. Why had she been the one who had managed to get closer to him than any other human being in the last ten years?

Tanner lifted her hips and slid her over the top of his shaft.

She opened her eyes fully, her pupils full and dilated in the light of the lantern. She stared at him, her passion filling his empty soul.

With a rock of her hips, he plunged into her sweetness, pleasure gripping him. Sweet, sweet friction stroked him, surrounded him, as he gripped her hips with his hands. Beth lay straddling him, their hips moving in rhythm with a fierceness, an intensity, that surprised him.

In the glow of the lantern he watched as her eyes closed. She rhythmically rose over him, gripping his erection, consuming every pounding thrust of him. He reached up and pulled her face down to meet his. His lips covered hers in a drugging kiss that hungrily consumed him.

Deep, resonant pleasure emitted from each long, slow stroke and swirled him closer to the edge. He opened his eyes and stared into her desire-filled gaze. She whimpered a sound so touching, he cradled her closer.

"Am I hurting you?" he questioned. "Do you want

me to stop?" he offered, unsure that he could but making the offer just the same.

"Don't you dare stop," she whispered against his shoulder, her voice rough with need.

He rolled them to their sides, where he could see her more clearly, watch the expressions on her face, and witness her pleasure.

In the shadow of the lamp, he lowered his head and flicked his tongue across her breast. She moaned a sound so deep that the vibrations seemed to reverberate through his body, touching him intimately.

He rolled her onto her back, mindful of her shoulder. Rising above her, he lengthened his strokes, driving into her over and over. Each long stroke swirled him closer and closer. He wanted to prolong the pleasure, to slow the rising tide of desire hurtling him toward the brink.

Passion filled him until he thought he would burst from the feelings only Beth seemed to evoke. The sensations were so stirring and felt so right, he was in awe of their joining.

With each stroke she raised her hips to meet him, and soon they were plunging headfirst over the cliff. At Beth's first shudder, Tanner grasped her to him. His own release came quickly as he called out her name, imprinting her cry of pleasure on his soul.

He rolled them both to their sides and collapsed next to her, pulling her against him, needing to feel her softness surrounding him, careful not to hurt her.

Spent, Tanner simply lay there while his breathing slowly returned to normal, as worry began to encroach upon his feelings of completeness. Soon his weariness overcame even his anxiety, and he simply fell asleep.

* * *

Tanner's gentle snores came softly to Beth as she lay in his arms. She felt his body curled around hers, and the realization of what she'd just done hit her. Once again she'd placed herself in a position for the worst kind of social rejection. She'd been intimate with a man who wasn't her husband, and this time she'd been more than a willing participant. This time she'd relished the feel of his body joined with hers.

While she was promised to another man, she'd put aside her morals and done with Tanner the very thing that had sent her fleeing from Georgia. Though this time she hadn't been sleeping with the enemy; rather, a real flesh-and-blood man who seemed to touch her every sense and made her feel more than anything she'd felt since before the war.

Yet he was quite possibly an outlaw, a man who lurked on the fringes of society.

She closed her eyes, the comprehension of what she had done becoming more and more acute. What had she been thinking?

Obviously nothing; only feeling. Somehow tonight in his arms had felt so right, as if this were where she belonged. And Tucker Burnett of Fort Worth seemed a shadow filled with words and promises, not a living, breathing man.

Her joining with Tanner had been different from anything she had ever experienced. With the general, sex had always been quick and unresponsive. Never had she experienced the fulfillment she had tonight with Tanner. Though she hadn't wanted to compare the two men, they were her only experience.

Tanner was a quiet man who slayed demons and fought dragons and sheltered damsels in distress. Or at least he had healed and protected her, making her feel sheltered and special. No one had ever taken care of her as he had. Not only was she grateful; she also feared she could fall in love with Tanner so very easily.

Though she would welcome giving him her heart, she wasn't sure if he was capable of loving anyone in return. And she couldn't heal his hurts, only he could rid himself of his demons. But surely after tonight he'd reconsider their being together.

She shifted in his arms and stared into the darkness. Had she thrown away her only chance at a new start in life by giving herself to a man she could never marry?

Darkness filled the room, but Beth awoke to the feeling that something was terribly wrong. A hand was shaking her, a voice calling her name.

"Beth, wake up."

"Why," she moaned. "The sun hasn't even come up yet."

"I know," Tanner replied. "Wake up."

"Why? It's so early," she said sleepily.

"You've got to get up now," he said.

"Is the building on fire?" she questioned.

"No."

"Then there's no reason to wake me."

"Wake up, we're leaving," he said, shaking her a second time.

"Huh?" she said, suddenly focusing more clearly on his words.

"We're leaving," he repeated.

She sat up, bewildered, the tone of his voice jerking her out of dreamland. She rubbed her eyes. "What do you mean?"

"I've got to leave, and I'm taking you with me. I've been out and bought a horse for you."

"Where are we going?" she asked, not sure that this was what she wanted.

"I'm going to take you to Fort Worth and deliver you to the man you're going to marry," he said. His voice held no warmth, no passion, like earlier tonight.

For a moment she was stunned, feeling as if someone had doused her with cold water during a sound sleep. Then rage at his high-handedness flowed through her veins.

"I thought the doctor said wait another week?"

"We've got to leave now. We'll take it slow so as not to push you and take a chance on hurting your shoulder," he said, unaware of her growing anger.

She shook her head, trying to clear her jumbled thoughts. "You're taking me to the man I'm supposed to marry?"

He glanced away and then back, his face expressionless. "Yes, as soon as you get dressed."

It was then she noticed that he was completely dressed, down to his gun belt.

"Last night meant so little to you that you would take me to the man I'm going to marry?" she asked, her pain reflected in her rapidly rising voice.

"I told you nothing would change, and I meant it," he said, his voice cold and stern.

Yes, she'd heard him, but she didn't think even Tanner was capable of such heartlessness. Obviously, she'd been wrong.

"You really are a coldhearted bastard," she said, blinking rapidly to keep the tears at bay that suddenly sprang to her eyes.

He shrugged. "So I've been told."

"Just leave me here and I'll catch the next stage," she said, her voice quivering.

"Can't do that. Pack your things, we're leaving in fifteen minutes."

He stood and began walking to the door.

"I don't have to go," she yelled at his retreating back.

"Yes, you do," he said calmly but with certainty.

He said it with such conviction that she knew he meant every word. Beth watched him as he strode from the room and resisted the urge to throw something at him. He was taking her to Fort Worth, to Tucker, after they'd made love. She sat down on the bed and cried, great gulping sobs filling her.

Last night had just been a one-night disaster instead of the start of something new.

Nine

It took them ten gut-wrenching days to arrive in Fort Worth. There were moments when Beth wanted to tell Tanner to leave her and let her find her own way to the city without his handsome face and quiet presence.

She could almost count the number of words they had spoken since that awful morning they had departed from the hotel. Nothing more had been said regarding his insistence to take her to the man she intended to marry. In fact, they only spoke about meals, rest, and occasionally the hot Texas weather. There had been no acknowledgment of the night they had spent together, of the passion they had shared.

Nothing personal had been discussed, and each night Tanner slept well on the other side of the fire, away from Beth. Obviously she'd made a huge mistake in judgment concerning Tanner.

They spent ten grueling days riding horses during the day and sleeping on the ground at night. The man she had willingly given herself to now said very little to her. It was awkward, heartbreaking, and all she wanted to do was cry each time she glanced at him.

In addition to Tanner's silence, her shoulder had ached and throbbed, but so far no infection seemed to have set in. Tonight she was spending the night in a hotel with or without Tanner. He had fulfilled his duty of getting her to Fort Worth, and now she was going to cut him loose. Let him go, for her own sanity. For each time she glanced at him, each time his brown eyes met hers, she ached with the knowledge of the night she had spent in his arms.

Yet somehow, no matter what he had done, the thought of never seeing him again made her feel bereft. She had almost ruined her entire life because of this harsh, quiet-spoken man. She'd let her heart overrule her head, and it had certainly taken her down a wrong path. Still, the sight of him riding ahead of her, his hat tilted on his stubborn head, his back straight, his hips swaying with the rhythm of the horse's gait, moved her, and her breath caught in her throat.

Regardless of what he'd done, she still wanted him, and that's what irked her the most.

Why did this man stir her passion? What about him drew her to him regardless of the consequences? She had a nice man waiting for her here in town, and all she could think about was the one who didn't want her, the man who, for all she knew, was wanted by the law.

But the sweetest night of her life had been spent in his arms, and she knew from personal experience that it wasn't always that way between a man and a woman. She knew it could be worse, much worse.

Beth had no choice. She had to forget about Tanner and return to her original plan of meeting her husband-to-be. For no matter what she felt regarding Tanner, Tucker was the man who wanted to marry and support her.

Tanner turned sideways in his saddle and looked back at Beth, his gaze brief and impersonal. "We'll be spending the night at the El Paso Hotel. I'll get us two rooms, and then tomorrow afternoon, when the stage is due to arrive, you'll be there to meet him."

Two rooms, not one they could share but two, to complete the separation.

She nodded her head in agreement. "I would like a chance to rest and clean up before I meet him."

"Good, the hotel is down the street a ways."

He turned back around in his saddle, and Beth stared daggers at his back.

No, he hadn't made her any promises; in fact, quite the reverse, but she hated Tanner for what he was doing. She hated him because he'd made her feel more than any other person.

She cared about him, and that scared her even more. They had experienced one incredible night of pleasure in each other's arms, and now he was giving her up. For that reason, she could barely stand the sight of him.

Yet she couldn't endure the thought of never seeing him again. And then there was the man she had traveled to meet and marry. The man she had already betrayed.

Eugenia sat across from her youngest son in the restaurant of the El Paso Hotel, her family in tow, waiting to greet the afternoon stage.

"Mother, we've met this damn stage every day this week, and she hasn't shown up yet. When are you going to give up?" Tucker asked.

"Her telegram said two weeks. It's only been eleven days since we received the telegram.

"She'll be here soon," Eugenia replied, wanting to whack her youngest son on the hand as she would a troublesome child.

"I don't have time to sit here and wait every day for

a woman that I have no intention of marrying," Tucker informed her, his rebellion stronger than ever before.

"Would you just give this a chance? She may be the woman you've been waiting for all your life."

"I doubt that."

Before Eugenia could reply to her youngest son, Mr. Phillip Kincaid, the owner of the El Paso Hotel, stopped by their table.

"How was everything?" he asked.

Eugenia glanced up at the man and smiled. "It was lovely as usual. Your restaurant is one of our favorite places."

"It would have been even better if my mother and younger brother were getting along," Travis informed him.

The gentleman smiled. "The joy of families. So what brings the group of you to town?"

"We're awaiting the arrival of a soon-to-be new member of the family," Eugenia said, laughing. "Or at least I hope so."

"Oh? Who is this person?" he questioned.

"Elizabeth Anderson, Tucker's fiancée," Eugenia said as she smiled at the man. She'd known him for years, though since their children were grown and their spouses had died, they'd said very little to one another.

Tucker frowned. "Not my fiancée, Mother."

Rose, Travis's wife, lifted her brows and patted Tucker on the arm. "Your brother seems to have adjusted to being married quite nicely. He doesn't have any regrets, and neither will you if she's the right one."

"No one is going to force me to marry anybody," Tucker, a normally cheerful man, objected.

Eugenia sent him a look she hoped conveyed her irritation at his stubbornness and then returned her gaze to Mr. Kincaid. "Travis is finally married, and now I'm working on Tucker, but he's not cooperating, as you can tell."

The elderly gentleman laughed. "I keep trying to get my granddaughter to move back home from Arizona so that I can do the same thing, but so far she refuses me." He turned to Tucker. "You remember Sarah."

Eugenia watched as Tucker gazed up at the older man, a rapt expression on his face. "Yes, I remember Sarah. I ran into her at Tombstone several years ago, right before I came home."

"That's right," the older man said. "I remember her mentioning it. The two of you were friends."

"Yes." Tucker glanced at Mr. Kincaid. "Is she doing all right? Is she still a doctor?"

"She's doing fine. Wouldn't give up being a doctor; she loves medicine. I only wish she would come home and practice here, where I could visit with my grandson."

"Grandson? She got married?"

"Yes," the older man replied.

"Excuse me, Mother, Mr. Kincaid. I think I'll return to the jail, since the stage is not due for another hour. I'll meet you back here before it arrives."

"If you must!" Eugenia said, watching her youngest son stand. "Don't be late! She could arrive today."

"Yes, Mother." Tucker rolled his eyes and walked through the restaurant and out the door.

Tanner met Beth downstairs the next morning. They had checked in yesterday afternoon late, and he hadn't seen her since then. Since that fateful morning, he'd carefully chosen when and what he said to Beth, avoiding her as much as possible.

He had to. It hurt too much to think of her being in another man's arms. Yet he had nothing to offer Beth. Whatever feelings he had for her were better left unrealized.

He watched as she walked to his side, her auburn curls carefully coiffed and pulled up off of her neck. The dress, the same emerald green one she'd worn at dinner that night, displayed her curves to their finest. Though not the latest fashion, the material was made of fine brocade that he knew was quite expensive.

Beth appeared every inch the lady, and he envied the man who would be meeting her today. But Tanner could never be the man in her life. She deserved better.

"We're all checked out. Are you ready?"

"Yes," she said, her words clipped and short.

The stage was due to arrive at noon, and it was already eleven. Time was running out for the two of them, and Tanner knew it. But there was nothing he could do. Beth was meant for someone else, not him.

"Do you want me to wait here with you until he arrives?"

"No, that's not necessary. I'll be fine," she said, glancing down, twisting her gloved fingers.

A sense of relief swept through him. He didn't think that he could willingly hand her over to another man. And he certainly didn't want to know what that man looked like or even his name. Because then he would be tempted to find her, make sure she was all right, and that could never be.

"Look, I . . . I know that the last few days have been—" He didn't know what to say. His heart was in his throat, and he had to let her go.

"Tanner?"

The memory of a small boy calling his name, running after him, paralyzed him.

"Is that you?"

The voice sent chills down Tanner's spine. It was a voice from his past. It was a voice he had certainly hoped to avoid. He whirled around at the sound of his name.

There, before him, stood his baby brother. He stared in disbelief at the boy he had left behind who had become a man, a man who wore a badge.

Tucker gasped. "Well, I'll be damned, it is you. You're alive."

Tanner was suddenly grasped by his younger brother in a bear hug that almost squeezed the breath from his body. Reluctantly, he returned the man's hug, his body tense, his mind whirling with the realization that he was trapped. A surprising sense of joy filled him at the sight of his brother, but he quickly pushed it away.

Tucker held him at arms' length and stared at him in shocked surprise.

"My God, man, where have you been? We all thought you were dead. Wait! Everyone is here. They'll be so glad to see you."

Tucker leaned back and yelled at the top of his lungs. "Mother, Travis, get out here quick. You'll never believe who's here."

Tanner didn't have a chance to escape. He glanced up, and there in the doorway of the hotel restaurant stood his family, his mother, his older brother, and a lady he'd never seen before. Everyone was here except his father.

With a past like his, he'd planned on never seeing them again. Yet there was no way he could escape!

His heart almost stopped at the sight of his mother. It'd been so many years. Her hair was grayer, her body a little heavier, but her expression at the sight of him filled his throat with unshed tears.

"Tanner!" she cried.

The sound was a half-sob, half-scream, and then she rushed into his arms. She wrapped her arms around him and cried against his shoulder. He was stunned at her reaction, and a sense of pain he'd long ago buried wrapped its painful tentacles around his heart.

"Mother," he choked.

Her hands were touching his face, his cheeks, and she reached up and feathered kisses on his face, sobbing and crying.

He hadn't meant to hurt her so badly. He didn't know what he expected, but he'd never thought she would react this way to his coming home. He swallowed back the tears that suddenly clogged his throat and wrapped his arms around her, holding her tight.

"Oh, my God. I told them you were alive. I just knew I would feel it if you were dead. And now you've come home," she sobbed. "I've waited for this day for so long."

Tanner couldn't say anything; his throat closed with unshed tears at the sight of his family, so happy to see him. He'd never thought they would want to see him ever again.

He'd sneaked away like a thief in the night and thought they would only be angry if he ever returned home. He'd done them so wrong, and they were welcoming him home, like the prodigal son. He didn't merit this kind of reaction. He didn't deserve to be with them.

Wait until they found out he was an outlaw. Then they wouldn't welcome him home.

"We've waited so long for your return," his mother said, wiping a tear from her face.

His mother kept her arm around him and slowly dried her tears.

Travis, his older brother, stepped forward and wrapped his arm around his neck and gave him a brief hug. "It's good to see you again, Tanner. We've all missed you."

Tanner nodded his head, cleared his throat, and rapidly blinked back tears.

Travis stepped back and took hold of a woman's hand, then pulled her forward. "I'd like you to meet my wife, Rose. We've been married for several months now."

"Nice to meet you, Rose," Tanner said, grasping the woman's hand. She was a short woman with a mass of brown curls and twinkling green eyes. There was a certain mystique about her that was intriguing.

She held on to his hand a little longer than necessary. "Hmm. I'd like to read your palm a little later."

Travis laughed and rolled his eyes. "If you're smart, Tanner, you won't let her."

She shrugged and continued to watch him.

Eugenia spoke up. "Leave her be, Travis. She knows what she's doing."

Rose smiled at her husband and gave him a wink. Tanner watched as his older brother almost melted before his eyes. This was definitely a new side to Travis.

"Where's Papa?" Tanner asked, his curiosity suddenly overcoming him about where his father could be.

For a moment they all glanced at one another, and the air suddenly seemed tense. Then his mother squeezed him even tighter.

"Your father passed away several years ago, Tanner. He loved you and waited for your return right up until the day he died."

A deep sense of sorrow overwhelmed Tanner. His insides clenched with the knowledge that his father was dead, and he quickly shut out the pain that threatened to consume him. His father was gone; there would never be the chance to redeem himself. His father went to the grave not knowing that he'd been right about the war, that his son had run during the last battle.

"So, I guess you were on your way out to the house," Tucker said, hitting him on the shoulder.

Tanner glanced back behind him, looking for Beth. She stood off to the side, her eyes wide, taking in the scene of his family greeting him.

"Huh, yeah," he lied.

"Who's this?" Tucker asked, noticing Beth for the first time. He stared at Beth, a frown creasing his forehead.

"This is a friend of mine, Beth," Tanner informed them. He took her by the hand and pulled her forward.

Beth released Tanner's hand and gazed at everyone, her hazel eyes wide.

Tucker glanced at her oddly. "You look familiar."

Eugenia frowned, staring at Beth, and then she suddenly gasped. "Oh, my!" She pointed at Beth. "I recognize you from the tintype picture you sent us."

Tucker suddenly frowned. "You're the woman we're meeting at the stage today, aren't you?"

"I'm Elizabeth Anderson," Beth said quietly, the color draining from her face.

Tanner turned in slow motion and glanced from Beth to his brother Tucker.

"You're Tucker's mail-order bride," his mother said.

Tanner watched in disbelief as his mother left his side and greeted Beth with a hug. Tucker was Beth's intended?

Oh, God, don't let it be so! he thought.

* * *

Beth sat wedged between Tanner and Tucker in the wagon, their horses tied to the back. She sat rigid on the seat, in between the two men, staring straight in front of her at the countryside.

How could this be possible? Tanner's brother was the man she was supposed to marry, and worst of all, she had betrayed him by bedding down with his brother.

She wanted to cry, to scream, she felt so guilty about what she had done. She had certainly ruined things this time. She'd come here to start her life over and in the process had not only messed her own life up, but now it appeared she was damaging everyone's she came into contact with.

She'd betrayed Tucker by having sex with Tanner. It had been bad enough that she had done so while engaged to Tucker, but now, to find out the two men were brothers, was the worst.

With a sideways glance at the man she was supposed to marry, she took into account his handsome looks. Tucker was taller than his older brother, with brown hair tinted with hints of red, large brown eyes, and a nice smile. But he wasn't Tanner. All three of the brothers were similar in size and appearance, but their mannerisms were distinctively different.

Though she was destined to marry Tucker, Tanner was the one who appealed to her. Still, she had no choice but to get over that attraction. She could never notice again how his pants fit his hips snuggly or the way his eyes darkened right before his lips kissed her.

She had to forget about Tanner and concentrate on falling in love with Tucker. For Tucker had paid her passage to Fort Worth. He was the one promising to take care of her until death did them part. He had expressed a desire to marry her, not Tanner.

Beth glanced at Tanner and knew that no matter what, she would always be grateful to him for taking care of her. But to find out it was his brother she was to marry had stunned her. In fact, it had left her feeling dizzy, and for a moment she thought she was going to faint.

Somehow she had recovered enough to acknowledge that she was indeed Tucker's mail-order bride.

Then a newspaper reporter had gotten wind of what was happening at the El Paso Hotel, and the family reunion had been descended upon with questions. They had quickly bundled up Beth's valise, her missing trunk had been found, loaded, and then she and Tanner had been hustled into a waiting wagon, where they had escaped the nosy reporter.

Tanner had been as nervous as a cat in a dog pen since the reporter had showed up, refusing to speak with the man or let him use that newfangled contraption that took a picture. Beth was still reeling from the knowledge that she had sex with her fiancé's brother.

However unintentional it had been, the memory of spending the night in Tanner's arms would forever haunt her. No matter what the man had done, he would never know that the night they were together had healed her. For she had not known that it could be that special, that magical, between a man and a woman.

Sex had just been something to be endured with the general, not the tender, emotional union that had left her spent and more contented than she'd ever felt before.

Was this what it felt like to be in love?

Beth shook her head. No, she couldn't fall in love with Tanner; she was going to marry Tucker. She had no choice.

"So how is your wound?" Tucker asked her.

She glanced at him, feeling awkward with Tanner sitting right beside her. "It's much better. The constant riding the last few days has made it sore, but it's healing."

"How come you didn't ride in on the stage?"

Tanner cleared his throat, and Beth glanced at him. "We decided not to wait on the stage but to come on by ourselves."

Tucker shrugged. "It might have been better you weren't in that bouncing coach, anyways. As you found out, sometimes they get robbed."

"Tanner was with me when the stage was robbed. He saved my life," Beth acknowledged.

Tucker stared at his older brother. "Were you the one that took Beth to the doctor? The elderly woman who was on the stage told us that a young banker fellow had rescued Beth and was taking her to the doctor. Was that you?"

"Yes, that was me."

"I guess you were on your way back when this happened?" Tucker asked.

"Yeah," Tanner replied not very convincingly.

Somehow Beth knew he was lying. He'd never said a word about his family when she'd mentioned going on to Fort Worth. In fact, he'd never said anything about where he was going or what he was doing on that stage except that he worked for a bank.

She glanced at Tanner. Why did she get the feeling that he hadn't meant to find these people? That it had been years since he'd seen them and this morning had been an accident? She'd bet if they hadn't seen him first, he would have left town without their ever knowing he had been here.

She had to get ahold of herself. She swallowed and

tried to make conversation. Anything to fix this awkwardness that hung over the wagon.

"Your letters said that you were the marshal. How long have you worn a tin star?"

Tanner tilted his head and stared at his younger brother. Beth could feel his body tense beside her. She glanced at him and saw the worried expression on his face. His hands were clenched on his knees. He'd been acting strange ever since his family joined them, not at all jubilant and happy to see them.

The memory of the Wanted poster that resembled Tanner suddenly appeared before her eyes. She glanced between the two men and wondered what this could mean.

If he were a wanted man, wouldn't his brother know? Wouldn't he have seen the poster before Tanner came to town?

"I've been back in Fort Worth now about two years, and since that time I've been marshal." He glanced at her.

Tanner started to laugh, his voice nervous and edgy. "It's hard for me to imagine my baby brother being the marshal."

Tucker glanced at Tanner. "You've been gone a long time, Tanner."

They rode along, only the creaking wagon wheels and rattling of the wagon breaking the silence until Beth thought she would scream from the tension.

Tucker's smile was nice, his mannerisms gentlemanly, and while the thought of marrying a marshal was daunting, she hadn't seen any flaws that would have kept a man like him from marrying before now. So why did he need a mail-order bride?

"How far to your home?" Beth asked, clasping her hands nervously in her lap.

"Oh, it's about an hour's drive by wagon. We're not far from town, but far enough."

"Do you live out on the ranch?" Beth asked.

"No. I live in town. But I'm out here every few days checking on Mother, making sure that Travis hasn't tied her up and thrown her down the cellar."

Tanner smiled. "They still don't get along?"

"Oh, when father died, they got along real well until Mother decided it was time for Travis to take a wife. Then it was like putting two polecats in the henhouse."

Tucker eyed his older brother. "Just wait until she starts to plan your wedding."

Tanner grimaced, his mouth thinning into a tight line. His eyes met and held Beth's. "I'm never getting married."

Tucker laughed. "Don't let Mother hear you say that or she will take it as a personal challenge. All of her sons should be married. No one is spared the eternal vows."

"I will never marry," Tanner repeated.

"We'll see," Tucker said, tugging on the reins.

They rode along, only the creaking of the wagon wheels and the rattling of the buckboard breaking the silence. Two miles passed before Tanner spoke.

"Since Papa died and you're the new marshal, who's taking care of the ranch? Travis?" Tanner asked.

"Yeah, he's always loved this place, so he's taken over the running of the ranch. I just help out occasionally."

"You never were fond of cattle," Tanner said.

"Nope, and I'm still not."

They hit a rocky spot in the road, and Beth felt as if her insides were being rattled loose. Her shoulder had started to throb again, and she couldn't wait to get to the ranch and out from between the two men.

Suddenly, she felt herself lifted in the air. She had no handhold, and she grabbed for Tanner's arm just as her bottom slammed back down on the hard bench.

"Whoa, slow it down," Tanner called to his brother. "Beth's still hurt."

"Sorry, I always forget about that damn washout."

Beth let loose of Tanner, a blush creeping up her face. She should have reached for Tucker, not his brother. Yet she and Tanner had shared intimacies that left her feeling comfortable reaching for him. But they had to stop. No one could know of what had transpired between Tanner and herself.

That secret must go to her grave with her.

It was then that she noticed the white two-story house looming in the distance.

Tucker pulled the wagon to a halt and glanced over at his brother.

"It's been a long time, Tanner. We've put a couple of coats of paint on the house, had to build a new barn because of Travis's stupidity, but other than that, nothing much has changed. Except that Papa's gone and Mother—Well, Mother has gotten a little grayer, but she's more ornery now than since before you left."

Beth glanced over at Tanner and saw him swallow hard, his throat moving rapidly. He blinked several times and then cleared his throat.

She didn't know how long he'd been gone, but it was obvious that his unexpected homecoming had affected him deeply.

"Welcome home, brother. Giddyup," Tucker called to the horses, and the wagon rolled on to the house Tanner had called home.

Beth would also call the ranch home until she married Tucker. The man she was here to marry, the man who had paid her passage to Fort Worth, the brother of Tanner. How was she going to live with herself knowing that she had sex with Tanner, on her way to meet Tucker?

Ten

Beth walked out of the big house, striding across the long, covered veranda to the swing that hung from the eaves. She needed to escape for just a few moments from the happy reunion taking place inside. The day had brought about unexpected complications in her life, and she needed just a chance to collect her wits.

The moon was rising over the edge of the Texas prairie, and the lonesome cry of a coyote could be heard in the distance. The noise was eerie and haunting and filled her with a forlorn feeling that seemed fitting for such a day.

A soft southerly breeze teased wisps of curls around her face as she sat in the porch swing and gently rocked in the evening air.

The front door opened, and she glanced up to see Tucker stroll out to the edge of the porch. He struck a match in the dim light and lit a cigarillo.

"Nothing like a Texas evening filled with stars," he said, turning toward her in the darkness.

"I'm finding that out for myself," she said, gazing at his silhouette in the moonlight.

He took a drag on his smoke, and Beth watched the tip glow a bright red. Slowly, he blew a curl of smoke out into the night air, clearly enjoying the process.

"Tanner tells me he was the one who took care of you after you were shot," Tucker said, his body leaning against the rail as he gazed over the moonlit prairie.

She let her feet push against the porch, sending the swing to rocking. She was trying so desperately to remain angry at Tanner for the way he had treated her these last few days, still, it was hard when she remembered all that he'd done for her. And now they were here together, trying to deal with the situation life had dealt them.

"Yes, he took me to the doctor, but there was a cholera epidemic going on. So Tanner couldn't leave me as he'd planned. He spent the next several weeks nursing me. Not many men would have cared for a sick woman."

"Tanner is quite a man," Tucker said, his voice filled with respect.

"Yes, he's remarkable," she said, trying to merge the image of Tanner the nurse with the man who had greeted his family that afternoon. The least he could have done was told her his real last name. He could have saved them some major complications if only he'd been honest. And why had he kept his last name a secret?

The Wanted poster had said Jackson. But mainly she'd observed the face, that haunting picture of a dangerous man with dark eyes and furrowed brow that looked so much like Tanner. But was it the same man?

Beth cleared her throat, feeling uncomfortable with the conversation, but she tried to keep from showing her emotions in the dark. Instead, she swung nonchalantly, hoping she appeared at ease.

Would they be compatible? she wondered. Would it really matter if they weren't? After all, she was here, she had nowhere else to go, and she could only hope she would be accepted.

"Are you feeling better since the accident?" Tucker inquired.

"I'm healing. The shoulder is still tender, but it's better."

This was the man she was going to marry, and so far they had barely spoken, let alone touch one another. Though she hadn't expected much; after all, they had just met. But it was almost as if Tucker were holding back. She sensed reluctance from him and didn't know if it concerned her or something else.

"How long have you been the marshal?" she asked, trying to make small talk, knowing she must get to know this man. Aware that she had left Georgia with no expectation of anything more than someone to take care of her, she hoped that with marriage would come the feelings a wife has for her husband. But suddenly that didn't seem enough, and she realized she could blame Tanner for awakening these feelings that were demanding fulfillment.

"About two years," he said, and glanced at her in the darkness. "Before that I spent some time in Tombstone."

"Do you enjoy your work?" she asked.

"Very much," he acknowledged.

He took the last drag on his cigarillo, threw it on the porch, and ground it beneath his boot heel. When he was done, he walked across the wooden porch, his boots ringing soundly against the floor, and sat down next to her on the swing. He slid away from her, and she wondered suddenly if she should ever have come here or simply stayed in Georgia.

"So why did you leave Georgia?" he asked.

"As I said in my letter, there was nothing left for me after the war. I lost the plantation to taxes, my parents died, and I thought it was time for a new beginning. I wanted a new start in life, so here I am," she said, his nearness not eliciting any special emotions, only a deep sense of sadness about the ugly choices she'd been forced to make in life.

"What about you?" she asked. "Why have you never married?"

He shrugged. "Never had a reason to. Besides, I'm not one for staying in one place long."

He kicked at the floor with the toe of his boot. "So why's a pretty lady like yourself a mail-order bride? You must have had a dozen or more beaus or lost loves? Surely one of them asked you to marry him."

Beth gazed into his eyes in the silver moonlight and swallowed. No, there had never been the chance to fall in love with anyone. The war had broken out the year of her debut, and after that there had been the general.

And then there was Tanner.

She pushed the thought out of her mind. This man was her future; he had to be her focus.

"No. No lost loves. The war took care of any beaus."

For a moment the air was tense between them as they sat there in silence. Beth didn't know what else needed to be said. They would have a lifetime to find out about one another. A shiver passed through her at the thought.

Was she making a mistake? Could she learn to love this man, sleep with him and bear his children?

"Huh, your family seems nice. I enjoyed watching Travis and Rose at dinner tonight," she said, wanting to change the direction of the conversation and her thoughts.

Actually, she'd almost felt jealous to see the love they so easily expressed for one another.

He laughed. "Someday we'll have to tell you about their courtship. It was rather rocky, but in the end they managed to get together, though we lost a barn before they settled their differences."

"Your mother was so happy to see Tanner. It was nice to see such a happy reunion."

The reunion had been happy, but what if Tucker knew what she had done with his brother? She would cause a rift between the brothers that would be difficult to heal.

"God, I tried to convince Mother he was dead after all these years, but here he is. It's hard to believe he was alive and we never knew it."

"How long has it been?"

"Close to eleven years ago he snuck off to join the army. Travis and I, we envied him for his courage to just take off. We wanted to go fight so bad, but our father said it was a senseless battle and refused to let us go. Tanner had run off to join, but I couldn't leave without saying good-bye after watching Mother grieve and worry over Tanner. And Travis—well, he's always loved this ranch more than anything else. He wanted to go, but not bad enough to leave the ranch."

"Hmm, in Georgia every family lost at least one person, if not several, to the war."

She shivered from the cool night air, and Tucker glanced at her.

"Are you cold?" he asked.

"Just a little," she said, suddenly feeling anxious.

"You've had a long day, and you're still not over that bullet wound. I better get you in the house."

"It has been a long day, and I still tire very easily," she said, glancing at Tucker and feeling the need to escape their sitting so close to one another. It felt awkward, and a brief moment of sadness almost overwhelmed her. It should have been Tanner sitting here beside her, not his brother.

She brushed the feeling aside. It was late, she was tired, and tomorrow morning the whole world would look better. Yet somehow she was suddenly very afraid that Tucker's caresses could never eliminate the feelings and emotions his brother had stirred in her.

Tucker stood and pulled her from the swing, his hand gripping her small one in his. His hands were large and rough, just like his brother's, but they weren't the same. They didn't leave her wanting and needy the way a single touch from Tanner did.

Tucker walked her to the door and opened the wooden portal. "Good night, Beth," he said, ushering her inside.

"Good night," she whispered, wishing she felt more and that she didn't have this sinking feeling in the pit of her stomach. Wishing that Tanner were the brother she planned to wed.

The next morning found the sun just a faint blush on the eastern sky when Eugenia watched her troubled son come down the stairs, his eyes meeting hers in a surprised glance. The sensitive young boy had turned into a hardened man, his blue eyes cold and dangerous. Her mother's instincts warned her that the man was troubled.

But she was determined he would feel the healing love of his family and find his rightful place in the world.

His face bore the ravages of a painful youth, his eyes much older than his twenty-seven years.

"Good morning," he said awkwardly. "I didn't expect anyone would be up just yet."

She smiled. "You haven't changed all that much, Tanner. Even as a boy, you were always the first one up in the morning. You'd wake your father and me by slamming the door as you went out."

He glanced away as an anguished expression crossed his face. "Mother, I wish I could tell you that I'm that same boy, but I'm not."

She shrugged and tried to put him at ease. "Boys grow into men. Men face choices that we can never prepare them for, which change them forever. But a mother's love is for eternity."

"I'd like to believe that was true, but—"

"It's true, Tanner. No matter what, I still love you."

He stepped into the kitchen and poured himself a cup of coffee, not saying a word. His back was to her. "Tell me about Papa. What happened?"

Eugenia watched the son that she had always known was the most vulnerable of her three boys. He was the one that lovingly took care of a wounded bird, who bottle-fed an orphaned calf, who sobbed and insisted on a funeral for his pet rabbit. Of all her boys, he was the one she had known would face the toughest road in growing up. He was the son least prepared for the rigors of combat, yet he was the only one who had gone off to fight in the War Between the States.

She took a deep breath. "Even though the doctor warned your father he was working too hard, he refused to slow down. His heart couldn't take much more, but he worked right up until the day he collapsed."

"What about Travis and Tucker? Weren't they here to help?" Tanner questioned, his back still to his mother.

Eugenia sipped her coffee and tried to help Tanner understand. "The ranch was your father's life. Travis was beside him working every day, but your father didn't know the meaning of slow down."

He finally turned around, walked to the table, and sat down beside her. "Where was Tucker?"

"Tucker spent some time sowing his own wild oats.

Of the three of you, he's the least interested in working the ranch. And once again your father would not have listened to Tucker any more than the rest of you," Eugenia said matter-of-factly.

Tanner gripped his coffee cup until his knuckles turned white, his head bent low. "I should have been here."

"Why? He wouldn't have listened to you any more than he listened to Travis or me." She took a sip of coffee. "Besides, you were out finding your way in the world. I'm just grateful you finally found your way home."

Tanner turned and gazed at his mother. "Maybe so, but I could have said good-bye."

"Yes, that would have been nice, but it didn't happen."

They sipped on their coffee, the silence of the house broken only by the ticking of the clock.

"So why didn't you believe I was dead?"

"I just didn't. Mother's instinct, I guess—but there was no proof. Once the war was over, I didn't know where to turn to for help." Eugenia stared at her son. His stubbornness was so much like hers, but his quiet, observant ways reminded her of his father. "We were so scared that you were dead, but there was no evidence, no body. I refused to believe you had been killed until someone could prove it to me. And no one could. Finally, I hired an investigator, though he was of little help."

Tanner reached out to touch her. "I never meant to hurt you, Mother."

Eugenia patted his big man's hand with her own, remembering how she used to hold his small boy's clasp. This big, tough, dangerous-looking son of hers still hid a heart that was sensitive and loving. "I know you didn't. I'd really like to know where you've been these last ten years just so I could understand why you didn't come home."

Tanner stared at her. "The less you know about what my life has been like, the better. It's for the best if we just keep everything to the present."

Eugenia stared at him, fear causing her to shiver in the predawn light.

"As long as you understand that regardless of the past, I love you. You're my son."

He reached out and wrapped his arm around her and hugged her neck to his. "Thank you, Mother. It's not been an easy ten years."

"Will you tell me at least if you're married? Do you have any children?"

"There's no one, Mother. I'm alone." He paused, his voice halting. "I'm . . . sorry . . . for not contacting you before now. I was afraid . . . afraid that Father wouldn't welcome me back."

Tanner released Eugenia and sat back in his chair. He had always been so quiet, albeit sincere, when he spoke, which was completely opposite of what was expected from the man. The dangerous man who wore his guns like a professional, who was hardened and nervous, still spoke like the boy from long ago.

"Your father watched and waited for you right up to the day he died. He knew the two of you were at odds over the war, but he never thought you would actually run off to enlist. Tanner, I know he prayed for your safe return every night."

Tanner's face was a mixture of pain and sadness as he shook his head. "I was an idiot for fighting a war that could not be won. I've seen things and done things—"

Eugenia clasped her hands on top of his large leathery fingers. "Some lessons can only be learned through experience, and I think this was one you had to suffer through."

"You're right, Mother."

As if he had suddenly told her too much, he removed his hands from hers and picked up his coffee cup and took a sip. Slowly, he sat the cup down, taking a calming breath before he turned back to her.

"So what about Travis and Tucker. They've told me a little bit about themselves, but I'd like to hear your version."

She laughed, easing the atmosphere and enjoying her time alone with this son that she loved desperately. "Travis has followed in the ways of your father. He's stubborn to a fault, and I had to trick him to get him married. But now I think he's found a woman who will help him see that there is more to life besides this ranch. And he loves Rose so much."

"She's different. Not at all the kind of woman I expected Travis would marry."

"Yes, she's exactly who your brother needs. I can only hope that there will be grandchildren soon."

"And what about Tucker? He's the marshal?"

"Tucker left when he was eighteen, determined to make his own way in the world. He's always been a good shot, but he soon found he could outshoot just about anyone. He did all right until about three years ago in Tombstone, where he was almost killed. After that he came home to Texas, and now he's settled down, changed."

Tanner listened to his mother, nodding his head occasionally at her words. "My baby brother is the marshal. Great, just great."

Eugenia glanced at her son, confused by his sarcasm. "It is great, Tanner. It's the perfect job for Tucker."

He just shook his head.

"Now Beth has come. Soon she and Tucker will be married."

"Yeah."

"You'll be next, Tanner. We'll have to find you a nice girl to help you settle down."

"No, Mother." His voice was firm, sure. "I'll never marry. Don't even think about trying to set me up with anyone."

"All men say that. Your brother Travis said the same thing, and look, he's happily married now," Eugenia exclaimed.

"I'm different."

"You are no different from any other man. Stubborn as can be when it comes to settling down."

"But Tucker is going to marry Beth?" Tanner asked.

Eugenia gazed at her older son. "Well, Tucker hasn't sworn he'll marry her. Only that he will give it some time before making up his mind."

"What?" Tanner said, his voice rising. "He better damn sure marry her. He should be glad to be getting a woman as fine as Beth."

Eugenia watched the anger cross Tanner's face like a flash fire in a drought. He was furious, and she didn't understand. Had she missed something?

"She has no one. The war has taken everything from her. She has to marry," he said, the frost in his voice so noticeable that it surprised Eugenia.

She watched in interest. Tanner was tense; his eyes glared, but his words were sincere.

"We'll take care of Beth, Tanner. No matter what happens, I'd never turn someone out into the cold with no place to go."

* * *

Later that same morning, Tanner almost ran over Beth in the hallway outside her room. She was just coming out of her bedroom, her hair neatly in place. A dress, the golden brown of burnished autumn, brought out the color in her cheeks and made her hair glisten. God, he wanted to take her right here in his mother's house.

He glanced down the empty hall and grabbed Beth by the arm. She tensed and resisted him, but he managed to push her back into her room.

"What are you doing?" she hissed between clenched teeth.

Beth's room was across the hall and down two doors from Rose and Travis's room, but they were out riding this morning, and his mother was in the office taking care of business. They were upstairs alone.

"I'd like a word with you," he said, firmly shutting the door behind him and blocking any escape route.

"Are you crazy? If your mother or brother were to find us, we'd arouse suspicion. Get out, now!"

"Not until I've asked a few questions."

"Like what?" she said, jerking loose of his hold.

He stepped to within inches of her. "Like why in the hell you never told me that my brother was the man you were going to marry?"

"I would have loved to have shared that information with you, but Tanner and Tucker? How was I to know you were related," she said, sarcasm dripping from her words. "And you never asked for the name of the man who was going to marry me, remember."

"He's my brother, damn it!" Tanner said, his voice louder than he'd intended.

"Shh!" she said right back at him, her face inches from his. "How was I to know? The better question would be Why weren't you honest with me and give me your full name?"

"I didn't think it was information you needed."

"I'd say you were wrong." She took a deep breath, her chest rising with indignation. "If you had used Burnett just once, I would have known. Instead, I was as surprised as you!"

He wanted to reach out, smooth back her hair, touch her, taste her full lips until she was begging him to take her, but she belonged to his brother now, not him. She was strictly off limits.

He grabbed her by the arm, bringing her close to him. "My brother can never know what happened between us. You're going to marry him, just like before."

Her hazel-green eyes turned to emerald stones that glittered as cold as ice. "Why would I tell him? You've made it clear that our one night was a mistake. So why would I give up marrying the man I originally planned to for you?" She pushed him away. "Don't worry about me; I'm a survivor. No matter what, I'll be fine."

Tanner ran his hand through his hair, wanting to clear his thinking. He hadn't been honest with her. He hadn't told her his last name. He had made it clear that their night of passion was just that, a night, not a lifetime. But God, how could those simple decisions come back to haunt him, hurt him, as they were at this moment. Why did life always seem to be so complicated?

And no amount of reasoning could shake the awful feeling of frustration that seemed to overwhelm him at the thought that Beth belonged to his brother and not him.

"I don't like it any better than you, but what's happened is over and done with. From here on you're Tucker's woman, my future sister-in-law."

She glanced at him and swallowed hard. "Get out! Get out now before I scream and bring the entire house in here."

"You wouldn't."

"Don't test me. I'm angry enough to risk it all. Just get out and leave me alone," she said, her voice suddenly choking.

Tanner glanced at her and knew he had to leave. He had to go before one of them said something they would always regret, but bitterness choked him. It wasn't fair. Why this woman and his brother?

Quickly, he opened the door and peered outside. The hall was clear. He glanced back at Beth one last time, feeling that things would never be the same.

"I didn't mean to hurt you," he said before he quickly slipped out the door.

Beth watched him shut the door and wanted to scream, but tears were clogging her throat. He hadn't meant to hurt her? What had he meant, then? Just to teach her that sex could be truly beautiful between a man and a woman and then go his merry way as if nothing had happened?

Tears streamed down Beth's face, and she felt as if a chapter of her life had just closed along with that door— a brief moment of happiness that had left her reeling with the knowledge that she had betrayed the man she was supposed to marry, only to find out her deception had been with his brother.

It couldn't get any worse. Though she had never meant to hurt Tucker, she felt she had deceived him in the worst sort of way. How could she tell him that she had been with Tanner in a way that could convey the complex emotions behind what happened between them, that she had come to rely on Tanner's strength, his kindness, his compassion, and that he had appealed to her in a way no man ever had? Part of her wanted to forget about Tucker's letters and follow her heart to Tanner.

But Tanner didn't want her. He had apologized for having sex with her, and that had hurt her even more. The general had taken her, no apologies, no regrets, but sex with him had been a duty to fulfill. With Tanner, it had been so much more than a duty, and that was what frightened her most of all.

She could not marry Tanner. He had made it painfully clear that he wasn't interested in her, that he didn't care. Their brief night together was just that one night of great sex to him, though their lovemaking had seemed so much more. He'd bluntly told her he would show her just how bad he could be, and he had certainly fulfilled that promise.

Maybe the hired gun was not capable of showing his feelings or emotions. Maybe the war had permanently damaged him to the point that no matter what happened, he was unable to be with a woman on a permanent basis? All she knew was that he didn't want to be with her.

The tears came faster as she thought of what she had done. Unintentionally, she had cast a shadow of pain and doubt over her budding relationship with Tucker. And even worse, every time she looked at Tucker, the resemblance was just enough to remind her of Tanner.

She swiped at the tears that rolled unheeded down her face. She would get over Tanner. She would forget about him in time, and she would make her relationship with Tucker work. She had no choice.

For if she didn't marry Tucker, she had no idea what would become of her.

Eleven

Tanner was tempted to just keep on riding. Not to stop in Fort Worth but to continue riding until either he or his horse dropped from exhaustion. But the image of his mother's face, filled with joy when she'd seen him in the hotel restaurant yesterday morning, returned like a blow between the eyes.

And he knew he could never hurt her like that again.

No matter how much he wanted to run away from the problems of Beth, the Bass gang, and even his brother, the marshal, he could not leave town again without saying good-bye.

With his unexpected homecoming, he was enjoying the family he'd long since given up ever seeing again. He just didn't have the strength to say farewell right now. He'd missed his family, their oddities, the way they bickered among one another, and the way his mother still hovered over them. And he had missed being home when his father had died.

So many years had passed, yet they'd welcomed him back with open arms and even fewer questions. He'd never expected such a homecoming, and he wondered why he hadn't come home when he had the chance, before he lost everything.

At the time he hadn't thought, he'd only been running

from the horror of war, of men dying and the nightmare he was living, which plagued him even now in his sleep.

And then there was Beth. Sweet, beautiful Beth, whom he thought about way too much, who it seemed was engaged to his brother but had given him the most pleasurable night of his life. Images of Beth lingered, ever present on the fringes of his mind.

He had to give her up; she was Tucker's intended. He had no right to even think about her, let alone remember how she felt in his arms, the sweet smell of lavender on her neck, or her quiet strength and dignity. Somehow he had to abandon his memories of Beth and never forget she belonged with his brother.

If it hadn't been Tucker that Beth was to marry, it would have been some other faceless man, but never Tanner.

After the life he'd led, he had no right to be happy, to consider a woman coming into his life. Robbing banks had made his life transient. He was constantly on the move, leaving at a moment's notice. His was a life in which no permanent commitments were possible. He didn't deserve a good woman like Beth.

Yet Beth's mission had been to find a husband. And Tanner knew he had nothing to offer her. He could only give her heartache, and somehow he thought she might have had a life already filled with that terrible emotion. His brother at least had a job and a place to live, which was more than Tanner could provide.

Still, it hurt to think that Beth had not told him it was his own brother she was engaged to. He would never have intentionally slept with Tucker's woman. However, she hadn't known any more than he had. Now they had this moment in time that he and Beth shared, a night spent exploring each other's bodies and consuming each other's souls. That one night would forever haunt him in memory and guilt.

Their weeks together would be like a pleasant remembrance to take out and replay over and over as he sat around a lonely campfire. She would be safe in the arms of Tucker while he was wandering from town to town, solitary and cold, searching for his life.

How could he blame Beth for what had happened between them? He hadn't given her his last name. He hadn't told anyone his real last name in many years because he'd been afraid that somehow his family would find out he was alive. Now one tiny slip of a woman had done more damage to his exile in the weeks he'd known her than all the years he'd been missing.

The thought of turning her over to any man had been painful enough, but the thought of her with his own brother made him totally irrational—one night of pleasure exchanged for a lifetime of guilt and deceit.

Tanner spurred his horse into a full-blown gallop, dust rising from the horse's pounding hooves. Trees and bushes whipped by him at an uncontrolled speed. He was a fool. He didn't deserve the love of a good woman, the pleasure that one night had brought, being loved and cherished by any human being.

But somehow Beth had managed to break down all his barriers and had shaken him to his very core. And no amount of running was going to clear that fact from his mind.

Beth was beautiful. She was a strong woman who had endured and survived the War Between the States, which was more than he could say. Somehow he didn't feel as if he had survived, he had only lived through the battles, and now he just existed until his nightmares caught up with him and jerked him out of a sound sleep.

Tanner pulled on the reins, slowing the chestnut mare to a slow trot. It wasn't the horse's fault his life was in total disarray.

Regardless of the situation with Beth, he couldn't stay with his family for long or else they would be touched by his past, and he refused to soil them with his tainted history. However, leaving Beth behind with his brother was going to be the toughest thing he'd ever done.

Beth watched as Rose sat in a corner of the parlor and picked up a pair of knitting needles once again.

"I'm going to learn how to use these blasted things," she said, frustrated at her jerky movements. "If Eugenia can do this, I can, too."

She paused, looking at Beth expectantly. "Do you knit?"

"No, I occasionally embroider, but even that I haven't done in ages," Beth said, watching Rose clumsily work the needles.

"Travis wanted a lady for a wife, so I'm trying to learn a few of the finer arts in my spare time," Rose admitted.

"Oops! I think you just dropped a stitch," Beth warned as she watched a piece of yarn form a bubble in the middle of a row of neat pearl stitches.

"Drat! Now I'm going to have to pull these out," Rose said, her eyes never leaving the yarn. She flopped down the yarn and needles. "Practice, that's all it takes. I may not be much good at needlework, but I can read your palm; or give me a set of tarot cards and I'll give you a reading."

"You can read palms?" Beth questioned.

"That's how I used to earn my living." She laughed

and wiggled her brows. "I met Travis at a séance I was having. He came to warn me to stay away from Eugenia."

Beth smiled. "You two seem very happy."

"We are, but we didn't start out that way."

"Oh?" Beth said.

"No, Travis thought I was cheating his mother, and the Burnett men are very protective of Eugenia. No one gets away with mistreating Mama Burnett."

"I bet they had interesting childhoods, living here on the ranch, three boys growing up together," Beth said, the image of her own children playing out in front of the house a warm thought.

"I'm sure they did." Rose tilted her head and gazed at Beth. "So, what do you think of Tucker?"

Beth bit her lip, her gaze sliding to the door to make sure no one could overhear. "Tucker seems very nice. He appears to be a good, hardworking man. He's handsome, everything a girl could want in a husband."

Rose looked at her strangely. "But how do you feel about him? Does he make your heart pound, or do you get goose bumps when he touches you?"

No, but his brother makes me feel that way.

She had to bite her lip to keep from saying the words out loud. She was surprised they came so easily to her.

"I don't know. I haven't noticed. But we've only been alone once, and we didn't . . ."

"You mean he hasn't kissed you yet?"

"Oh, no. I mean it's not like we've had time to get to know each other." Beth fiddled with brushing a piece of lint from her skirt, feeling uncomfortable with Rose's questions.

She didn't know how she felt about Tucker Burnett yet. She was trying to remain open-minded, but he didn't appear very demonstrative of his feelings. Yet how many men really were.

"Did he hold your hand or put his arm around you?"

"He sat beside me in the swing the other night. We talked," Beth acknowledged, feeling anxious about confiding in Rose.

Rose frowned. "Hmm. What you two need is some time alone. Some time to figure out if you're meant to be together."

"I guess so," Beth answered, feeling extremely awkward speaking to Rose about Tucker.

"You just don't seem very excited about him," Rose observed.

"I . . . I like Tucker. I think he'll make an excellent husband," Beth said, suddenly afraid Rose would tell the others.

Rose shook her head. "But you're not tripping all over yourself to find a preacher."

Beth glanced at her future sister-in-law, trying to answer as honestly as she could without giving her thoughts away. "I think these things take time. I've only known him now for two days, and I hardly think that's enough time to bring a preacher into the picture."

"You're smart to wait." Rose leaned forward in her seat and gazed at Beth, her expression sincere but stern. "I didn't like Travis, but I felt such a physical attraction and an overwhelming need to be with him even when we were fighting."

"I don't want to rush into this and then both of us spend our lives regretting what we did." Beth looked anxiously at Rose. "Tell me more about how you knew that your husband was meant for you."

Rose laughed. "Those were tough days." She sat back. "All I knew was that when Travis kissed me, nothing else mattered. Whatever dreams or goals I'd had for the future went right out the window. I had planned on going to New York to become an actress, but Travis filled in the empty spaces in me. He made me realize I was reaching for someone else's dream, not my own. I don't regret marrying him in the least. Hopefully, I've loosened him up some and been a good mate for him, too."

Beth watched the young woman and marveled at how happy and at peace she seemed. She knew from watching her interact with Travis that the couple were desperately in love. But was Tucker the man that Beth was supposed to marry, really? Why did it feel as if she were choosing the wrong brother?

"Was there someone else that you cared about, that you left behind?" Rose asked.

"No. There was no one in Georgia. I've waited for a husband for a long time," Beth said. "I want to be married, to have a family. I've spent the last few years taking care of everyone but me. Now there's no one."

Rose nodded her head. "Did you leave your family behind?"

"My mother and father are both dead."

"I know that feeling. You're all alone in the world."

"Yes," Beth said.

Rose glanced at her, a quizzical expression on her face. "Well, take your time and get to know each other before you make a decision. Tucker is a very sweet man."

"Does Tucker want to marry me?" Beth asked, suddenly concerned about their future or lack of one.

"I'm sure he must be feeling anxious just like you are. The two of you need to spend some time alone, getting to know one another."

Beth glanced at Rose, feeling awkward but wanting information from her just the same.

"So you knew fairly soon you wanted to marry your husband?" Beth asked, going back to their earlier conversation.

Rose smiled. "I was all alone in the world except for a servant who had grown up with me. I ran a séance parlor and read palms on the side. I was trying to earn enough money to go to New York to become an actress when Travis entered my life in a sudden, unexpected way."

"Will you read my palm?" Beth questioned, looking for answers anywhere. She wasn't certain that marrying Tucker was the right thing, but she didn't see any other option. Maybe Rose could give her a clue.

"I'd love to."

Rose took Beth's right hand in her own; she grasped her palm and closed her eyes. Then she turned Beth's hand over and opened her eyes, staring at the lines that she saw on the inside of Beth's hand.

"Hmm. Your fate line shows you've had serious financial problems recently."

Beth laughed, the sound sarcastic and filled with pain.

Rose traced a line that ran beneath her index finger, across her palm. "This is your heart line. See how long and deep this line is etched into your hand? That shows you are passionate and loving."

If not for her night with Tanner, she would never have believed she was a loving woman. It was still odd to think of herself in such a manner, but maybe it was true.

"Your life line is strong and steady, so you should have a long life."

Rose turned her hand more closely to the light. "Your fate line is the one that concerns me, your life and heart lines are fine. But your fate line tells me you must be careful or you could make the wrong choices in life."

She traced the lines on the inside of her palm with her index finger. "Your youth was fraught with change, but then your life line indicates you will settle in for a long, happy life."

Beth stared at her hand, amazed at what Rose had told her. "Where did you learn how to do this?"

"One of my father's girlfriends."

"Is it true?"

Rose shrugged. "Can be if you believe it."

Beth pulled back her hand and glanced down at her palm as if looking for the answers to her questions.

"Tonight, after dinner, I'm going to try to arrange it so you and Tucker may have some time alone," Rose said with a smile. "I'll take my husband upstairs, and Eugenia will follow my lead once she realizes what I'm doing, since she's so anxious to marry her son off."

"Thanks. I would like to spend some time getting to know Tucker before I make my decision."

"As you should." Rose laughed, clearly pleased. "Tonight, then!"

Tanner rode down Main Street to the Palace Saloon, one of the many drinking establishments that lined the road. Noise spilled through the open doorways, some of them filled to capacity with raucous cowboys who were passing through town on a cattle drive.

He dreaded this meeting but knew it was inevitable. Though Tanner had left a message at the hotel for McCoy when they suddenly left San Antonio, somehow he knew that he'd not get away that easily. McCoy was known for his tenacity. He would follow Tanner here and demand that he rejoin the gang.

As if he had any other choice. He knew what his responsibilities were, he just hadn't been in a hurry to see them through. He knew he had obligations, but since Beth had been shot in the botched holdup, he had spent his time taking care of her. Now, because his family was back in his life, that could create more problems. Especially his brother, the marshal.

How was he going to explain that one to McCoy or Sam? Sorry, I forgot to tell you, my brother is the marshal of Fort Worth. Sam would take pleasure in killing him and sending his body back in pieces to his brother. McCoy could make his life a living hell.

He pulled his horse to a halt and swung his leg over the saddle horn and slid to the ground. He looped his reins over the post and walked into the saloon, his boots resounding on the wooden floor.

As he pushed open the door, McCoy sat there sipping a beer at the bar, his head bowed over the drink as if he were praying.

Tanner slid into the chair beside him. "Hello, McCoy. You're never far behind me, are you?"

"Nope." The man glanced up, and his dark eyes met and held Tanner's, his gaze cold and intense in a face that was rugged and weather-beaten. The man unfurled his body to his full six-foot height. Streaks of gray were dispersed among the black strands.

"About damn time, Jackson. I was beginning to think you'd run out on me for good."

"Nope. Been taking care of business." Tanner sipped his drink. "So what are our friends up to?"

"Actually, they're close by," McCoy said.

"What?"

"Sam Bass has family living up in Denton County. So you don't have far to go."

Tanner shrugged. "I don't want any part of this. Not here in Fort Worth."

"Why not?" the older man asked.

"Why be in such a hurry? It will only get you killed. Just give me a little time and then I'll go back. But I'm not willing to take a chance here in this town. The law knows me here."

Sitting across from Beth at dinner that night, Tucker observed the way the light of the candles radiated off her red hair, her eyes sparkled when she smiled.

Beth was a woman who seemed pleasant and sweet, but he wasn't attracted to her. He didn't feel a blinding sense of need, and though he wanted to help Beth, he didn't think marrying her was the answer.

Tucker didn't know what to do about Beth Anderson. So he decided that for now he was not going to do anything. He would just go along with his mother's plans and see if he could find some way to get out of this terrible mess without hurting Beth. But it was obvious he could never marry her.

Dinner was over; they pushed back from the table, and now Cook was preparing to clear the dishes away.

"All of you scoot on out of here; get out of my way," the cranky old man said, shooing them out of the dining room as he carried dishes into the kitchen.

The entire family went into the parlor, where they usually gathered.

"Tanner, tell us about your travels over these last few years. I'm sure you must have seen many different places?" Rose asked.

Tanner looked as if he were cornered, his discomfort

obvious on his face. "Not much to tell. I've been here and there, earning a living."

"But surely you've seen some sights that you can tell us about."

"Nothing that ladies should hear."

Rose, obviously disappointed, turned to Beth. "What about you, Beth? Tell us about your home in Georgia."

Beth swallowed hard, her eyes misting over. She coughed to clear her throat. "Jonesboro, Georgia, is where my family was from. Four generations of Andersons occupied that house until I had to sell it. During the war, we lost all the barns, the slave quarters, and every outbuilding, but somehow managed to keep the main house from being burned."

"How did you manage that?" Tanner questioned. "Every plantation I came across in Georgia had been ransacked and burned."

"I . . . I don't know. The Yankees used it as a military outpost for a while. At the end of the war, the taxes were high, but I managed to keep the house for a little while," Beth said, her voice quivering.

"You were damn lucky. Most Confederate families who kept their plantation homes were Yankee supporters or ones that donated something to the government's cause," Tanner said, watching her.

Beth's face turned ashen, and Tucker wondered at her loss of color, though the memory of losing her home must hurt. Being in Texas had kept most of the war at bay, and Tucker had been wet behind the ears when the war started.

"I managed to save our home, but it did me little good, as it's now in the hands of a carpetbagger."

Tucker had heard horror stories of people thrown out

of their homes by easterners who had come south looking for a quick bargain.

"And now you're here with us, away from all that," Eugenia said, her voice excited. "I think a celebration is called for, since Beth has joined us and Tanner has returned home. I was thinking that we needed to have a dance."

The men groaned.

"A dance to celebrate, and it would be an excellent opportunity, if Tucker and Beth are ready, to announce their engagement," Eugenia said, her face filled with enthusiasm. "We'll invite all of our friends and family. It will be fun."

"It's really not necessary," Beth said.

"A dance does sound like fun," Rose interjected. "I haven't danced in ages."

"Mother, do you want to go through all this work?" Tucker asked.

"Yes, I do." She glanced around at her sons. "We'll hold it in two weeks. That will give you boys a chance to build the dance floor, set up the pavilion, and butcher us a calf."

Travis shook his head. "You didn't do this for Rose and me when we got married."

"If you recall, you were barely speaking to me when the two of you tied the knot," Eugenia replied, giving her oldest son a sideways glance.

Rose took her husband by the arm and gave him a knowing glance. "Speaking of being a newlywed, I think it's time we retired for the night. I'm feeling sleepy." She yawned. "Eugenia, the dance sounds like fun. The three of us girls—we'll spend tomorrow planning the dance and barbeque."

Eugenia suddenly stood and said, "I think I'll make

an early night of it, too. Tanner, I'm going to need your help tomorrow, so you might want to turn in early also."

Tucker watched as Tanner glanced at Beth. For a moment it almost appeared that his glance was filled with longing, but Tucker wasn't certain.

"Yeah, I guess I better get to bed." Tanner paused, looking at Beth. "Good night, Beth. Good night, Tucker."

Tucker watched as his mother and Tanner disappeared out the doorway, along with Rose and Travis. "I think we're being left alone on purpose."

"I think you're right," Beth said with a nervous laugh. "Rose told me she'd take care of getting us by ourselves tonight, and I guess she did."

"Rose is a pretty remarkable woman. I like her a lot," Tucker said, walking around the room to stand closer to Beth.

"She's been very nice to me since I arrived," Beth said.

The room fell silent as they stood there suddenly feeling awkward and very aware that they were alone.

Beth took a seat on the loveseat, and Tucker felt like a fool standing. He sat down in his mother's rocker. God, he'd never had this problem with a woman before. Always before he'd been certain of how to act and what she expected. But this was his first mail-order bride, and well, he was like a young boy doing his first courting.

She clasped her hands in her lap, and he noticed they were shaking slightly. She was just as nervous as he was, and that made him feel more at ease. They both were anxious about the outcome of this meeting, and Tucker had the advantage. He knew the truth, that he had never sent those letters and that although she was here to marry him, the chances were slim they'd ever tie the knot.

"What do you think about the dance?" she asked.

He smiled. "I think that Tanner and Travis are going to have a hell of a lot of work getting ready for it. And then the three of us are going to complain about having to dance."

"Do you dislike dancing?" she asked.

"It's an unspoken rule of the male species. You're suppose to groan and moan when you're invited to a dance. You never let on that you like dancing, because that's for fops and fools."

Beth laughed, easing the tension just a little. It was so quiet in the house, Tucker could hear the ticking of the clock. She had a nice laugh, and he was sorry that he didn't feel anything for her. He'd wait until after the dance, and then he'd tell his mother and Beth he couldn't marry her.

"I'm sorry. I've never thought of men who danced as fools," Beth said, seeming to relax a little.

"A cowboy always has to swagger and act tough. You just haven't lived long enough in Texas to know that yet, ma'am," Tucker said, exaggerating his accent.

Beth giggled. "I thought my Georgia drawl was bad, but I must say you've outdone me."

"Why, thank you, ma'am."

The room fell silent as once again Tucker didn't know what to say. They sat across from one another, feeling uncomfortable, and he wondered again how he had let his mother put him in this position.

"What will you do to help your brothers get ready for the dance?" Beth finally asked.

"I'll stay out of their way. That's the best thing I can do for them," Tucker said. "You see, a hammer, nail, and I don't go together any more than a cow and I seem to get along. Some people are made for working on a ranch and are handy with their hands. Me, the world is a safer place when I'm chasing bad guys or patrolling the street. A hammer becomes a dangerous tool in my hands."

She laughed.

"When was the last time you were at a dance?" Tucker asked.

"My debut ball two months before the war broke out," she said, her eyes darkening to a deeper hazel.

"Oh, my, then you are long overdue for some dancing," Tucker said, wishing he could feel something for this nice woman.

"I don't think I even remember how," she said quietly, as if recalling the event.

She jumped up. "Will you practice with me?"

"Whoa, I don't know if that's such a good idea."

"Why not?" Then she smiled. "I've already forgotten. You're just groaning and moaning so I won't think you're a fop or a fool."

"Nothing to worry about there, ma'am. But I guess we could do a little practicing," Tucker said, feeling very uneasy about what they were about to do.

He pushed the loveseat, table, and rocker out of the way and cleared a big enough space for them to dance. Then he took Beth's hand and pulled her into position, trying to keep plenty of space between them. She stood awkwardly in his arms.

"The main thing to remember about dancing is that you're supposed to be having fun. So relax and let the music move your feet," he told her, knowing that at this moment he was about as relaxed as a grizzly bear that's been awakened from a long winter's nap.

"Are you sure we should be doing this tonight?" she questioned. "You said you didn't like dancing."

"Tonight's great. Besides, you're going to want to dance the night away. And I may not always be your partner. Nice women are a rarity around here." He thought for a moment. "Tell me what dances you've learned so far."

"I was taught the Virginia reel, the waltz, and a quadrille, but it's been so long, I don't know one from the other," she said.

"Okay, let's start with the easiest one, the waltz," he said, placing her hand in position. "Okay on my count, here we go. One-two-three. One-two-three."

Beth started laughing as she stepped all over his feet. "I'm sorry," she said.

He stopped. "It is rather hard without music, isn't it."

"Yes."

They stood there for a moment looking at each other. If Beth were any other woman, he would have kissed her by now, but he hadn't. He hadn't even thought about kissing her until just this moment, and even then it wasn't because he wanted to kiss her.

"Let's try again, and this time I'll hum a few bars."

He hummed, and she counted, and they struggled through the waltz. When they'd completed the dance, without Beth stepping on his toes, they stopped.

"I think you've got it."

"I think I do, too. Thank you," she said shyly.

"My pleasure."

"Look, I've really had a good time tonight, but I think I better retire," she said, glancing shyly up into his face.

"Yeah, it is getting rather late," he said.

She leaned forward and put her lips to his, taking him completely by surprise. It was a gentle kiss that should have been more, but somehow the spark just didn't ignite, and though Tucker wanted there to be more, it just didn't happen.

What did a man do when there was no fire, no flame, not even a spark?

They broke apart, and she opened her eyes and stared at him, her look questioning and thoughtful.

"I . . . I best be going upstairs now," she said.

"Good night, Beth. Sleep well," Tucker said, and watched as she disappeared out of the room.

He'd felt nothing but the sense of kissing a really nice woman.

Twelve

Tanner pounded the nail into the two-by-four, taking his frustrations out on the piece of iron. It felt good to be doing physical labor, to drive the demons from his soul.

He'd heard Tucker and Beth last night in the parlor, laughing and dancing, of all things. While he'd been lying in that big bed, struggling to forget that night in her arms, trying to remember that she was Tucker's woman.

"Tanner!" Travis barked.

He stopped hammering and glanced up at his older brother. "Yeah?"

"You still here with me?" Travis questioned. "You seem a hundred miles away. Let's take a five-minute break."

With the back of his arm, Tanner swiped the sweat from his brow. The rays from the Texas sun, which pummeled him were relentless. "Sounds good."

He walked over and sat down beside his brother on the back of the wagon and picked up his canteen of water. They'd spent the morning designing the makeshift dance floor, and now were actually building the platform from leftover lumber for the new barn.

"Mighty warm today," Travis observed, gazing up at the afternoon sun.

"Yeah," Tanner replied distantly, still thinking of Tucker and Beth dancing in the parlor, of his brother holding her in his arms. Tanner's stomach clenched in response to the vision of his younger brother's hands on Beth. The image was so vivid that he could hear the tinkling of her laughter and Tucker counting out the rhythm of the dance.

"So what do you think of Beth? Do you think she's the woman for Tucker?" Travis asked, turning his canteen up and letting the water trickle over his chest and down his back.

"Why wouldn't she be?" Tanner said, a strident note in his voice, which he failed to cover. He glanced quickly at his older brother. "Tucker should be glad he's getting her. Beth is an intelligent, beautiful woman. She has more social graces and manners than any woman I've ever met."

Travis stared at Tanner, perplexed. "How long have you known her?"

"Only since the stage holdup," Tanner said. "But she's a fine lady. And she needs a husband."

Travis raised his brows questioning. "Why does she need a husband?"

Tanner took a swig of water and washed it down his parched throat. "She left everything behind in Georgia to start again here in Texas. Tucker would be a fool not to marry her."

"Even if he loved someone else?" Travis asked.

"No one could compare to Beth," Tanner said, and tilted his canteen of water back, letting the water flow down the front of his open shirt, cooling off his heated chest.

"Oh," Travis said, watching Tanner. "You two must have gotten to know each other fairly well during the time you were together."

Tanner shrugged, thinking of how Beth had seen more than he hoped she ever told his family but also remembering the times he'd helped her from bed, the way she looked in the morning, the way a moonbeam looked on her naked skin.

He took a deep breath. He couldn't go any further with that thought.

They sat sipping their water, resting, watching white puffs of clouds drift across the clear Texas sky.

"It's been nice this past week having you here helping out on the ranch," Travis said, glancing out across the land. "You know there's plenty of work to keep the two of us busy on this ranch if you wanted to stay."

Tanner glanced at his older brother. "What are you saying?"

"I'm asking you to settle here and help me run the ranch," Travis said. "You could live at the house, or if you wanted more privacy, we could fix up one of the line shacks for you to use."

Tanner stood and walked around to the side of the wagon and leaned against the buckboard. "I can't do that. I'll come back to visit when I can, but I can't live here permanently."

"Why not?"

"I need to keep moving. I don't stay in one place very long," he said, unable to meet his brother's eyes.

Travis glanced down at his drink. "Mother's going to be disappointed. She was really planning on you staying here with us."

"I know. But I can't stay. I have some things I have to take care of," he said, taking a swig of water.

"You know, Mother told Tucker and me not to ask you about where you've been, but I have to, Tanner. Why didn't you come home after the war?" Travis asked his younger brother. "We kept waiting and worrying about you."

Tanner glanced at his older sibling and shrugged, not about to confide in his family why he hadn't come home from the war, why he really couldn't stay. "Time sort of got away from me. Then it seemed like I had been gone so long, and I hadn't left on very good terms. I just couldn't come home."

"So for ten years you've been wandering the country?" Travis asked, his voice rising. "Thinking that none of us cared about whether you lived or died? We hired investigators, held séances, and tried every way we knew of to find you."

"Séances?"

"Mother's idea, not mine," Travis, stated. "So you've just been traveling all this time?"

"More or less," Tanner said vaguely, not looking at his brother.

"Damn it, Tanner, you could have been more responsible. If not for Father, then at least for Mother."

Tanner looked at his brother, meeting his gaze. Travis was angry with him for being gone all these years. "Maybe I should have come home sooner, but I didn't know I would be welcome."

"Did you think to write, send a letter, a telegram, anything to let us know you were alive?" Travis stared at Tanner, his eyes cold with anger. "What finally brought you home? What changed that made you want to see all of us?"

Tanner picked up his hammer, intent on getting back to work and ending this conversation. How could he an-

swer that question? His family would still not know if
he were dead or alive except for his chance meeting with
Beth on that stagecoach.

"I . . ." He shrugged his shoulders. "I was here."

Travis stared at Tanner, his face turning even redder
than the tinting of sunburn on his dark skin. "You didn't
intend for us to see you that day, did you? You weren't
really coming home. You just got caught."

Tanner picked up his hammer and began to pound the
nail into the wood.

"Damn it, Tanner, you still don't care about us. You
got caught and can't even admit it."

Beth gazed down at the completed pavilion. Chinese
lanterns were strung gaily around the dance floor. Tables
and chairs were scattered across the lawn, with decorated
lanterns on each of the tables. One long buffet table was
situated close to the house, loaded with food. Wagonloads of guests were beginning to arrive.

Cook ran around dressed in his Sunday best, making
sure that the food and drinks were ready, Eugenia not
far from his heels.

Beth watched the preparation for the festivities from
her upper bedroom window. She glanced down at the
peach silk of her dress and its full flounced skirt. Fourteen years ago it had been the latest fashion, but now
the style was dated, to say the least. Bare shoulders and
full skirts were no longer the rage, but it was her only
party dress, and somehow it still fit.

She wrapped a lace shawl over her shoulders to protect
her from the evening breeze and wandering glances. Nervously, she twisted an end of the shawl over and over in

her hands. She kept looking out the window for Tanner and Tucker and had yet to see them.

A knock on the door startled her.

"Can I come in?" Rose called.

"Yes."

The door opened, and Rose hurried in and shut the door behind her, keeping her hand behind her back. A mischievous grin lit her face, like the glow from a bonfire.

"You look stunning. If you weren't nearly my sister-in-law, I'd be so jealous, but instead I'm excited." She thrust out her hand, a corsage gripped in her fingers. "This is for you."

Beth looked at her, stunned, as she accepted the arrangement of tiny peach roses made to wear around her wrist.

"How lovely. Did you make this for me?"

"Well, I made it, but at the request of a certain gentleman, who just happens to be one of my very handsome brothers-in-law," Rose said with a smile, her eyes twinkling with delight.

He'd sent her a corsage.

"Tanner asked you to make this for me?" Beth asked without thinking. She caught her slip almost immediately and tried to laugh it off. "How silly of me. I meant Tucker, of course."

Rose gazed at Beth, a quizzical expression on her face. She paused and then said, "Yes, Tucker. He asked that I give it to you, since he was busy downstairs."

"How thoughtful of both of you. It's very lovely."

"Here, tie it on for me," Beth asked, handing the corsage to Rose.

She tied the rose-and-ribbon corsage on Beth's wrist and proceeded to fluff the lace and bow into position.

When she was finished, Rose stood back and admired Beth.

"You look absolutely dazzling tonight."

"My dress . . . it's not too old?" Beth questioned.

"It's beautiful. All the ladies will be envious. Now, come on, I know that they're all waiting for us downstairs. Let's go."

Beth let her fingers trail over the flowers. "Thanks, Rose. You've been very kind to me."

Rose laughed gaily and took Beth by the hand. "Come on. This is going to be so much fun tonight."

She led Beth down the stairs to the waiting Burnett men and Eugenia. At the bottom of the stairs, Rose let go of her hand and went to stand beside her husband. Beth glanced into Tanner's brown eyes and watched as his gaze started at her head and trailed down her body, lingering over her curves.

A blush flamed her cheeks as he glanced back into her eyes and she felt the heat of his stare. She swallowed, trying to calm the racing of her pulse as she observed how handsome he looked tonight.

Tucker cleared his throat, and she turned toward him and smiled.

"You look fantastic," he said, and stepped up and offered her his arm.

She placed her hand on the inside of his arm, her skirt lapping around his feet. She glanced up at him; though his eyes were bright, his gaze didn't have the same effect on her as Tanner's heated looks. But they would. All she needed was some time, and then, whatever physical reaction she had to Tanner, she would feel for Tucker. She was certain of it. And she was determined to marry Tucker and forget about Tanner.

After all, Tanner didn't want her.

Eugenia swooped down on the couples, checking them out like a soldier inspecting the troops. "All of you look so nice. Come on, everyone, let's go greet our guests."

They walked out the front door, across the wooden porch, and down the steps to the waiting party.

Beth turned toward Tucker and gazed into his eyes. "Thank you for the corsage; it's lovely."

He brought her hand up to his mouth and kissed the back of it. "You're welcome. This is your party; enjoy it."

Beth wanted to feel something, anything at the touch of his lips to the back of her hand, but she felt only awkward—no rushing sensations, no welcoming response, only a trickle of unease that left her tense.

The two couples split at the pavilion and went their different ways, Tucker introducing Beth to their guests, Travis and Rose greeting old friends. Tanner and Eugenia wandered together through the gathering, Eugenia introducing him to newcomers and reacquainting him with ones that were here before he left.

Children ran through the crowd, playing chase or hide-and-seek, while the adults mingled, catching up on the latest gossip and renewing old friendships.

The smell of roasting calf drifted over the gathering, and the crowd soon congregated around the buffet table. Lines formed as the guests made their way down the table, which was loaded with food.

While the guests ate, the musicians warmed up their instruments beneath the star-studded sky. The food was good, and the people were friendly, but Beth kept looking around her, always searching for the man whose gaze she could almost feel upon her.

After dinner, Tucker left her side and joined a group

of men over by the barn. Beth sat at the table with Rose, who brought her up-to-date on the latest gossip.

"See that woman in the blue dress with the two young children," Rose whispered.

"Yes," Beth replied.

"She's married to the minister, who is standing over by Mr. Kincaid. He owns the El Paso Hotel. Personally, I think he has a thing for Eugenia, but she doesn't know it."

"What makes you say that?" Beth asked.

Rose raised her brows. "The way he looks at her, the way he laughs more when she's around."

"Do you think Eugenia would be interested in remarrying?"

"I don't know, but it's something to consider, given the fact that she is so involved with her son's lives."

"You aren't considering trying to get the two of them together, are you?" Beth asked.

"Why not? If she were married, she'd be less likely to be an interfering mother-in-law. Don't get me wrong, I love her to pieces, but she has a tendency to be too involved with her sons' lives. And that, dear friend, is a personal warning for you."

Beth smiled. "Surely it's not that bad."

"Just remember that you were warned," Rose said.

The musicians started to play in earnest, and suddenly couples were heading toward the dance floor. Travis came and grabbed Rose around the waist. "I think it's time I carried you off to the dance floor."

"Ooh, I love it when you become demanding," she said, gazing up at her husband adoringly as he twirled her off in the direction of the pavilion.

Beth watched as one by one the couples began to waltz. She watched Travis and Rose weave through the dancers. Eugenia passed by in the arms of Mr. Kincaid, and Beth had to bite her lip to keep from laughing.

One dance turned into two and then three as Beth sat and watched the couples on the floor. Suddenly, Tanner was standing in front of her.

"Where's Tucker?" he asked sharply.

She shrugged. "I don't know. Last I saw him, he went off toward the barn with some men. Why?"

"I thought he taught you to dance the other night?"

Tanner had heard them in the parlor that night when she had kissed Tucker, which had been a terrible mistake? She swallowed nervously.

"He did."

"Then why in the hell aren't you out there dancing with him? You two have a fight already?"

Beth stared at Tanner, amused at his brusqueness. "No, we are not fighting. I just thought he must be busy. So I've been watching."

He grabbed her by the hand. "Come on. You didn't come to watch."

Pulling her onto the dance floor, he took her in his arms. The musicians were playing a waltz again, and they glided into the steps. His hands felt rough, as a man's hands should feel. His palms were calloused from working around the ranch.

The touch of his skin against hers wreaked havoc on her senses.

"I thought you didn't know how to dance."

"No, I just hadn't danced in so long, I was afraid I had forgotten," Beth explained patiently.

"You're doing just fine. Not that my younger brother would notice."

"Thank you." She smiled at him. "So are you having a good time tonight?"

Tanner shrugged. "It's all right. So many of these people I don't know. They all moved here after I left. Mother keeps introducing me to all the marriageable young women. She wants me to settle down here."

"Are you going to stay?"

"No. I should have left already, but I haven't wanted to. I'll have to, though, soon."

Beth felt her stomach sink. He was leaving, and though it shouldn't matter, it did. She nodded her head as if to agree, hoping for some time to compose her unruly emotions, which were plummeting. She smiled, her mouth tight and stiff.

"Where will you go?"

He shrugged. "Don't know yet."

He spun her around, and she gasped. "You know you're not a bad dancer yourself."

"I get by."

The waltz ended, and he removed his hand from her waist, leaving her skin warm and tingling. He walked her back to the table, his steps brisk.

"I'm giving Tucker five minutes, and then he better show up," he said, glancing around for his brother.

"Tanner, I'm sure he's gotten busy somewhere and he'll return soon."

"This is your big night, your party. He should be here at your side," he said, his voice almost a growl.

"It's all right," she assured him.

Tucker walked up to Beth's side. "There you are. I saw you dancing with Tanner. I was in the barn talking."

"Why aren't you dancing with Beth?" Tanner asked.

Tucker glanced at him, surprise evident on his face. "I would have been, but you were dancing with her."

Beth stood up and put her hand on Tucker's arm, suddenly feeling the need to separate the two men. "Come on. You may dance with me now."

He took her by the hand and led her to the dance floor, leaving a flustered Tanner behind.

Tanner watched his brother put his hands on Beth and had to force himself to unclench his insides. If the sight of Tucker touching Beth bothered him now, how would he react when they kissed? When they were together as husband and wife? When she had a baby someday?

He turned and walked away, forcing his back to the sight of them dancing, their arms around one another. He had to get accustomed to the thought of them as a couple. He had to adjust or he could never be around them. He had to forget the memory of Beth naked and trembling with passion in his arms.

The musicians finished up one song and played another, and then they played another before Tanner forced himself to look back at the dance floor.

Beth was dancing, but not with Tucker. Now she was dancing with a young man named Mike that Tanner had met earlier in the evening. He glanced around the area for Tucker and found him dancing with a young girl whose beauty was no comparison to Beth's. But Tucker was laughing and having a good time, while Beth was putting up with some two-bit cowboy who had already stepped on her toes once while Tanner was watching.

Was Tucker out of his mind? How could he let some cowboy dance with the woman that was going to be his wife?

Beth stumbled back to the table, where she sat down and removed her foot from her slipper. Tanner ambled over and sat down beside her. He wanted to take her small foot in his hand and gently rub the limb and soothe away her pain, but he couldn't. It wouldn't be proper to massage her foot, though it was tempting.

"How are you holding up?" he asked.

"I'm fine, really," she said.

"How's the shoulder? It's not aching, is it?" he asked.

She grimaced. "A little bit."

"Maybe you should quit for the night."

"No. I'm having a good time."

He glanced at her; although she seemed anxious, almost depressed, she told him she was having fun.

What was wrong with his foolish brother?

She slid her foot back into her slipper. Another cowboy came up and asked Beth to dance, and she left Tanner sitting at the table alone. He watched as she glided around the floor with the young buck, and Tanner wanted to strangle his brother. Where was he?

Tucker came around the floor with a young girl in his arms that Tanner didn't know. He watched as his brother laughed at something the girl said and wondered why he was neglecting Beth. After all, even though Beth was the prettiest woman here tonight, Tucker had spent more time in other women's arms than in Beth's.

The band began to play a slow waltz once again, and Tanner saw Tucker make his way to Beth. He watched as his brother placed one hand on her waist and her other hand in his. He groaned as he saw Tucker pull her in closer than was really appropriate, and he had to look away when Beth smiled up at him.

She should be dancing with Tanner, smiling and laughing with him, gazing at him as if he were the most important man in her life. But he could never be that person in her life. That was his brother's job.

Tanner glanced up just in time to see the song end

and Tucker lean down and give Beth a chaste kiss on the lips.

It was more than he could bear. He had to get out of here now, tonight. He couldn't wait another minute, couldn't stand the sight of his brother with Beth another moment. For Tucker had not behaved toward Beth the way she deserved to be treated.

He whirled around and marched toward the barn, his legs carrying him as fast as he could walk, away from the sight of the two of them together. The wide-open spaces could never hurt as much as watching Beth and Tucker.

He slung open the barn door, strolled in, and began to saddle his horse. It would take only moments to gather his few belongings, but if his horse was saddled and ready, then he could slip into the house, get his things, say good-bye to his mother, and ride away before anyone noticed.

Tanner took the bridle down from the wall of the stall. He slipped the bit into the horse's mouth and threw his saddle blanket on its back, followed by his saddle. He began tightening the flank cinch and adjusted the foot stirrups. He'd be gone within the hour.

The door of the barn opened, and in walked Tucker.

"There you are," Tucker said, his mouth dropping open in surprise. "What are you doing?"

"I'm leaving," Tanner said without ever looking at his younger brother.

"Now?" Tucker said in surprise. "Does Mother know?"

"Nope. Just decided a few minutes ago."

"What in the hell is the matter with you?" Tucker said, his voice rising. "We have a yard filled with guests and you think now is the time to leave? Do you give a damn about how Mother is going to feel about this?"

Tanner stood and walked to within inches of Tucker. "Who the hell said it was any of your business what I do?"

"When you're about to break Mother's heart a second time, I make it my business."

"You're a fine one to talk! What about Beth? You've been out there dancing with every female within the last fifty miles and left her sitting alone." Tanner grabbed Tucker by the front of his shirt. "She doesn't deserve to be treated that way."

"Get your damn hands off of me—right now. I'm treating her just fine."

"The hell you are." Tanner threw the first punch, hitting his brother smack in the nose, popping his head back. A surprised look appeared on Tucker's face. "If you didn't want to marry her, why in the hell did you send for her? You don't deserve a woman like Beth."

"You bastard, you hit me!" Tucker charged his brother, knocking him to the ground.

Tanner felt his body slam into the earth along with a fist to his rib cage. They were throwing punches, scuffling on the ground trying to get the advantage, when the barn door opened and Travis walked in.

"What in the hell is going on here?" he questioned.

He pulled Tanner off Tucker and held him at bay. "Why are you two trying to kill one another?"

Tucker stood and brushed the dirt off his pants, sending his older brother a glare. "Ask him. He's been acting strange all night. Then I came in here and caught him saddling a horse, leaving again."

Travis glanced at Tanner. "Is that true? You were going to sneak off again?"

"I wasn't sneaking off, I was riding out tonight."

"In the middle of the party that Mother threw for your homecoming and welcoming Beth you were going to leave?" Travis asked in disbelief.

"Yeah, I was," Tanner said, shaking loose from his older brother.

"Your timing is lousy, Tanner," Travis spat.

"Well, my baby brother doesn't know how to take care of a woman. He's been dancing all night with everyone else but Beth." Tanner's voice rose. "Why in the hell did you send for her if you didn't want to marry her?"

Tucker picked up his hat and dusted it off. "You explain it to him, Travis. I've got to go before I beat the shit out of him again."

Thirteen

Tanner felt the blood trickling from his nose and put a hand up to wipe it away. He couldn't remember the last time he'd gotten into a scuffle with one of his brothers. But sometime while Tanner was gone, Tucker had certainly learned how to throw a punch.

"Come into the tack room. We need to clean you up before you go off anywhere," Travis said, carrying the lantern into a small room off to the left.

Tanner felt like a boy again as he obediently followed Travis, the memory of other fights returning with a pang to his bruised ego, times when Travis had patched him up when he'd gotten into a fray with either his brother or another kid.

The room was filled with reins, bridles, and cinches hung from the wall. In the center of the room was a worktable with a couple of chairs scattered about.

Travis pulled out a chair. "Sit," he commanded.

Tanner sat in the chair, watching his brother, tilting his head back to keep the blood from dripping. He wanted to get on his horse and ride as fast and as far away as possible. He wanted to run from the sight of Beth and Tucker together, to escape from the jealousy that was eating away at him inside.

Tucker had what Tanner wanted, and there was nothing he could do to change the situation.

Travis sat the lantern down on the table and reached up into a cabinet. He pulled out a bowl, a small tin of salve and some bandages, and laid them on the table.

From a metal bucket sitting nearby, he poured a small amount of water into the bowl. "Wash the dust from your face."

"My damn nose is bleeding. I can't."

Pulling out the other chair, Travis sat down at the table. He dipped a rag into the water and handed it to his younger brother. "Here, hold this against your nose."

Tanner took the rag and held it to his bloody nose.

"So, you're leaving tonight?" Travis asked.

"Yes," Tanner said suspiciously. His brother was going to try to talk him out of leaving, but there was nothing Travis could do to stop him. He was leaving, he had to get away.

"Why so suddenly?" Travis asked, sitting across from Tanner. He leaned back and propped his ankle on top of his knee.

"Just felt it was time to go," Tanner said, handing the bloody rag back to his brother.

Travis shrugged, as if it meant nothing that Tanner was leaving.

"Well, you're a man. It's not like the last time you snuck off, when you weren't old enough to make that decision. This time you can come and go when you please. You might want to wipe your face down; it still looks streaked." Travis handed him another wet rag. "So, will we ever see you again?"

Tanner glanced at his older brother, surprised by the question. "Yes, I'll come home occasionally."

"When you admitted you hadn't intended to come

home this time, I wondered if, when you left, you would ever return," Travis explained, leaning his chair back and gazing at his brother.

"I'll be back."

Tanner sensed that his brother's brown eyes were fixed on him and felt as if he were being examined.

"What? Why are you staring at me?"

"Nothing," Travis said. "You've changed. I knew the war would change you, but I never realized how much. I guess we're different, too, but you're not the same kid that left."

"I'm ten years older. I've seen a lot of things . . ."

"Yeah, I'm sure you've seen things you probably never want to remember. You're different, and I guess we're all still adjusting to the changes."

He handed Tanner some salve. "Here, put this on your knuckles. You scratched them up pretty bad."

"You and Tucker are different, too," Tanner said, taking the salve and smoothing it over the back of his hand.

Travis shrugged. "I'm sure we are. Mother's older."

"Nothing has remained the same," Tanner said, his voice rough.

"No. I guess it hasn't," Travis said. "We all grew up while you were gone."

An uncomfortable silence stretched between the brothers; there was so much that needed to be said, that Tanner knew he couldn't say.

Tanner glanced down at his red knuckles. "I better be going."

"Be sure to tell Mother good-bye before you leave. I know she's going to be upset."

"Of course. And I'll try to send you a message every so often," Tanner said brusquely. "Let you know where I'm at."

"That would be good. Mother wouldn't worry quite as much. Also, if something should happen to her, I'd have a way of finding you. She is getting up in years, you know."

Tanner glanced at his older brother. Did he keep mentioning their mother so he'd feel guilty leaving them all behind once again?

"Look, I realize I'm different. But I didn't have much choice in changing."

"Yeah, I guess war does that to a man." Travis stared across the table at him. "But I can't help but wonder what besides the war has caused you to change? Where have you been these last ten years besides fighting for the Confederate army? What kept you from returning to us, before now?"

Tanner resisted the urge to put his head in his hands. He wanted to confide in his brother, tell him all the things he'd done, but he couldn't. His past was his own to deal with, and he wasn't about to inform his family of what had happened or the ugliness he'd taken part in.

He shrugged nonchalantly as if it meant nothing when actually it meant everything. "I couldn't return."

"You know, Tanner, we all worried when you didn't come home. We didn't know what to do, whether we should have a funeral or just keep hoping for the day that you came home." Travis dusted some dirt from his pants and then glanced back up at Tanner. "But now you're back, and we're damn happy that you're here with us, regardless that you're different. You're safe, you're alive, and you've come home."

"I . . .I've been surprised you all welcomed me back," Tanner said, his voice soft.

"Why? You're still a member of this family."

"I didn't think you would want to see me again."

"We all prayed that you would come home safe and sound." Travis shook his head. "We'll still be here if and when you ever decide to rejoin us."

Tanner swallowed. It was true they had accepted him with open arms and he was the one holding back. But he was still an outlaw, and sooner or later it was going to catch up with him. And then there was Beth. How much more of watching her and Tucker could he take?

Travis took a deep breath. "Whether you decide to stay or go is up to you." He paused and stood up, stretching. "I'm going back out and join the crowd. I hope you'll stay at least until the morning, when we can give you a decent sendoff."

Tanner watched as his brother put his hat on.

"Now, I'm going to go find my wife and make her dance with me again." Travis extended his hand and gripped his younger brother's in a handshake. "Goodbye."

He walked out of the barn, leaving Tanner to make the decision of whether to stay or go.

Damn it! Travis still had this effect on him. He'd always made Tanner feel as if he were misbehaving whenever he was considering doing something questionable. Though Travis was different than when they were younger, he still could make you think twice. He still could make you feel irresponsible.

Tanner threw out the bowl of dirty water. He guessed he did owe Tucker an apology. But the oddest thing was, he really didn't want to leave. Somehow tonight, sitting here with Travis and even fighting with Tucker, had made him feel as if he'd come home.

It was the damnedest thing, but suddenly he knew this was where he was meant to be, where he belonged, and he didn't want to leave.

Still, there was the situation with Beth and Tucker. How much longer could he watch the two of them, without saying something? How much longer could he keep his hands off his brother's intended?

Beth lay curled up in a ball in the middle of the bed, facing the window. The sliver of the moon peeked in through the glass panes, and she watched as the breeze lifted the curtains in the open window.

She couldn't sleep. Tonight's events had left her restless and worried as she'd watched Tanner and Tucker—and compared the two men without intending to. And now sleep was as distant as the Georgia shoreline from the Texas plains.

The party had broken up sometime after midnight, and even now a group of people were camped out on the edge of the front yard, sleeping in their wagons, waiting for dawn to take them home.

She'd had a good time until Tanner had announced he would soon be leaving. Though she knew she shouldn't be thinking about him, he refused to disappear from her mind. She kept telling herself it would be for the best if he were gone. She could concentrate on Tucker and try to forget the way Tanner made her feel.

But her mind refused to let him go. She should be glad; instead, she only felt miserable.

That one night in his arms had made her feel things she'd never thought were possible. She hadn't planned on experiencing passion, she'd never dreamed of feeling complete, of being totally satisfied, after a man's possession of her body.

She'd planned only on getting married to a faceless man whom she'd never met, with no passion, no excitement, nothing but the security he could provide her. Now Tanner had completely ruined her safe situation, engaging emotions she had never believed in until he came into her life.

The thought of sharing a bed with Tucker was not what she had anticipated, and she could only blame that on Tanner. If he had not shown her passion, she wouldn't be missing it now. She wouldn't have expectations that she feared Tucker could never fulfill or desire feelings for the man she was to marry that were not possible.

If she had met Tucker first and he had awakened her passion, they might have had a congenial marriage. Beth didn't know, but she wasn't drawn to Tucker as she was to Tanner; there was no urgency to be near him, no restlessness when he was around.

Only with Tanner did she have such feelings, and they were wrong. Tanner was not her intended; he was not the man she was going to marry; she'd already experienced being with him in the flesh.

She sighed. Tucker wanted a wife, a mother for his children. She was going to be that woman, that person who would be by his side, caring for his children, taking care of his home. She would be all that and nothing more.

But suddenly the thought of spending the rest of her life with a man she didn't have at least some feelings for seemed so cold, so lonely. She sighed and rolled over, punching her pillow.

She was crazy to even think these thoughts. Her life, her very livelihood, depended on her marrying. For if she didn't, she would be forced to find a job, and they were few and far between for a woman like herself.

This was not how she'd imagined her life when she'd left Georgia; it was not what she'd expected. But now the thought of marriage to a man who didn't love her, didn't want her or even desire her, seemed so cold. But, that was exactly what she'd expected when she'd left her home behind.

Tucker had not been the most attentive suitor tonight. In fact, since she had arrived, she'd never felt any sense of personal closeness from him. But she kept reminding herself that she shouldn't expect any tender emotions from him. They were just marrying because it was convenient to each of them. So why was she suddenly having trouble accepting the way they felt about one another?

Because his kiss, compared to Tanner's, left her unexcited. Because when he'd put his lips to hers this evening while they were dancing, she'd felt absolutely nothing.

And the worst part: He was a perfectly nice man who probably had turned the heads of many women tonight. But for Beth there was nothing but the feel of his lips against hers, two body parts rubbing against one another that had failed to create any sort of pleasure. And somehow Beth felt as if she were the one at fault.

Though it was summer, she shivered and tugged the covers up higher.

Why had she expected to feel anything? Their relationship was based on an agreement, nothing emotional or physical, just a few letters they had exchanged, an ad placed in the paper she had responded to in the hopes that marrying would solve her financial situation.

God, she was so tired of everything in life, of it being so difficult and of the many choices that seemed so irreversible.

Tanner was leaving soon, and Tucker's kisses had failed to move her. What had she done? Promised herself to a man when all she really wanted was his brother.

* * *

A heavy morning mist hung over the cemetery like a blanket, covering the headstones. It was early, first light to be exact, but Tanner had walked up the small hill to pay his respects to the man buried there.

It wasn't as if he believed he was actually there on the plot of land, but it was the only place he felt comfortable in talking to a dead man, even though the man had been his father.

He found the grave among other friends and family who were buried in the small cemetery. Vines grew thick covering the graves, shielding them from the hot Texas sun.

Gazing at the date chiseled on the marker, a sense of futility overwhelmed him. The years had sped by, and his father had been dead for over two years. Tanner could have come home and seen him, could have been reunited with his family. But he had let his fear and shame, not to mention his stubborn pride, keep him away from the people who loved him. He had refused to face his father and admit that he had been right; there was nothing heroic about killing. War was hell.

The sun peeked over the eastern horizon, casting its rays on the layers of mist, chasing them away like ghostly wood nymphs. Soon the heat from the sun would clear the haze away, but the graves would remain protected by the tall oaks and the entwining vines.

His hat was in his hands as he stared at the tombstone, the words he so badly needed to say lodged in his throat. Even though his father was dead, it was so terribly hard to admit that he'd made a huge mistake and had paid dearly with the complications in his life.

He cleared his throat. "Hi, Papa. I've come home."

Only the sound of the wind answered him as a breeze blew through the leaves of the oak trees. "I'm sorry I didn't come earlier, when you were still alive. Guess I didn't think you'd want to see me." He lifted his eyes to the trees above and swallowed hard. "Guess I thought you'd always be here."

A bird began to trill a song in a nearby oak, and for a moment Tanner was tempted to walk away. This was crazy, talking to a tombstone. Someone would think he'd gone absolutely mad if they saw or heard him.

But he didn't leave. He simply stood there, listening to the wind stirring on the hillside. "You know, Papa, sometimes it's hard to admit when we're wrong, when we've made a mistake."

His throat clogged up with tears as he thought of the morning he and Carter snuck off to go to war. So much like this morning, when he was considering leaving again. "You were right about the war, Papa. It was hell. There was nothing heroic about killing men like myself and watching people you know die."

A tear splashed on his hand, and he raised his eyes to the sky, hoping it was rain he felt falling on his cheeks. But the blue sky shone brightly on him as he glanced up.

"It's just me now. Carter—he didn't come home with me. War can do so many things to your mind, to your soul. You tried to warn me, but I refused to listen."

Tanner dropped to one knee beside the grave and hung his head. His shoulders shook as he let the tears roll down his cheeks. "You see, I should be there with you, and Carter should be here. He was the brave one, the decent one, and now he's gone."

The wet ground penetrated his clothing, but he didn't care. He barely felt the moisture. "It was my fault, Papa. Carter wouldn't have died if it hadn't been for me."

Tanner stared at the stone marker and wished it were

gone and that his father were here, giving him hell for the things he'd done since he left home so many years ago. Instead, a squirrel scampered across the graves and up the nearest tree, where it chattered at Tanner as if he were an intruder.

And he was.

Death had claimed this land, and regardless of how much Tanner wished he were dead, he was still a very living, breathing human being.

He swallowed his tears and took a deep breath. "I never meant to hurt you and Mother. I just didn't feel like you would want me to come home after the way I left. I assumed you would think I was dead. But Mother says she's been waiting years for my return. And Travis and Tucker have welcomed me back. It's as if they were happy to see me."

Tears rolled unbidden down his cheeks. He twisted his hat in his hands. "I wonder if you would have welcomed me home. Mother tells me you looked for me; she said you died awaiting my return. I should have come home earlier. I'm sorry, Papa."

"My life is not something I'm proud of. I've done a lot of things I regret. Now I'm home, but I'm afraid my past is going to catch up with me. I don't want to go, but I feel like I should keep on the move."

He paused. "I'm tired of fighting and running. I'm tired of always looking over my shoulder."

Tanner stood and swiped the dreaded tears from his face. He hadn't cried since Carter died.

He walked around the edge of the grave and picked a fallen leaf off the gray weathered stone. "What do I do, Papa, leave again or stay and take a chance on my past catching up with me? Do I stay and watch Tucker marry Beth, wishing it were me?"

The wind picked up in the trees, rustling the leaves, disturbing the stillness, vanishing the last of the early-morning mist. Tanner glanced down below and saw the family gathering on the porch. Even from here Beth's auburn hair shone like a beacon. Could he watch his brother make her his wife?

The time to decide had come. And suddenly he knew what he wanted to do.

Tanner was going to stay and take a chance that someone from his past would find him. Suddenly, he didn't care if they found him. His family had welcomed him home, he'd found acceptance and love within their welcome embrace, and he wanted to remain here with them as long as possible.

Their love had given him more peace than he'd felt for many years, and he wasn't ready to leave again. But staying would mean he would have to accept the fact that Tucker and Beth would be married. Beth belonged to his brother and regardless of how hard giving her up would be, he would do the honorable thing and not interfere in their relationship.

But he would have to learn to live with the knowledge that he'd slept with his brother's fiancée. No matter what happened between Beth and Tucker, he had come home and found his family once again.

Tanner put his hat on his head. "Good-bye, Papa."

Beth watched as Tanner walked from the cemetery on the hill toward the house. Suddenly, she knew the moment was upon them to say good-bye, and she didn't know if she could do it without crying.

He was leaving. And she couldn't stand the thought of saying good-bye. She wanted to go back into the house, but they were loading up the wagon to attend church this morning. If she ran back into the house, it was going to look suspicious.

Tucker took her hand and helped her into the wagon. He'd spent the night at the ranch instead of returning to town. Several of the guests from last night's party were loading up their wagons also, with the intention of following them into town and on to church. But first they had to say good-bye to Tanner.

She stared at him walking across the open yard, memorizing every detail, every nuance: the swagger to his walk, the way his brown eyes looked, the way he wore his hat low on his forehead, the dark stubble of his beard.

Travis helped Rose up into the wagon just as Tanner reached the house. "Guess you'll be leaving this morning," Travis said.

Beth held her breath as Tanner glanced at his older brother, a bemused expression on his face. "Not yet. I've decided to stay a little longer, that is if you can put up with me the way I am and if Tucker doesn't mind me staying."

Beth released a sigh of relief. He was staying, and her heart felt as if it were going to pound out of her chest. Part of her was relieved, and part of her was anxious. If he stayed, there could never be anything between them, but she didn't want him to go.

Rose glanced at her sharply. "You okay?"

"I'm fine," she lied, feeling relieved.

Tucker smiled at Tanner. "As long as you don't decide to try to kick my ass again."

Tanner grinned sheepishly, shrugged, and glanced at Beth. "Not anytime soon."

She wondered at the remark and then noticed the way Tanner's knuckles were scuffed. Had they fought?

Eugenia stepped out onto the porch from inside the house, unaware of what had been going on. She smiled. "Looks like we're all ready. Let's get going."

The women were seated in the wagon, with Travis handling the reins, while Tucker and Tanner rode their horses. After all the dancing and partying late the night before, the group was quiet as they made their way to Fort Worth and the little church nestled on the edge of town.

All in all, there were three wagonloads of people who had spent the night and then followed them to church this morning. The ride was uneventful except for the way Beth's eyes constantly strayed to Tanner. She couldn't help but stare at the way he sat a horse, how the sun bounced off his black hat, the way her heart seemed to flutter at the sight of him.

She took a deep breath, determined to cast him from her mind. Tucker was riding alongside him, and he sat a horse just as well as his brother. But it wasn't the same, and she knew it.

They pulled up in front of the little white chapel, and Travis set the brake on the wagon. He jumped down and unloaded first his wife, then his mother. Tucker helped Beth out of the wagon, and then they all proceeded into the chapel.

Beth couldn't remember the last time she had been in a church. She took a seat next to Tucker, with Tanner on her left. She glanced around the chapel at the people who were greeting one another and felt as if she shouldn't be here.

The people who attended church seemed to be nice people in the community. They appeared to be well dressed, conservative, and friendly. Yet Beth felt out of place. As a child, she remembered weekly visits to church.

This was not the place a woman with her past was welcome, where she would feel comfortable.

Eugenia brought the pastor over. "Reverend, you remember my son Tanner, don't you? He's the one who went off and joined the army."

"Yes, Mrs. Burnett, I do. It's been many years, though."

"Nice to see you again, Reverend," Tanner replied.

"And this is Miss Beth Anderson. She's a guest in our home, but we hope that she will eventually join the family."

"Nice to have you, Miss Anderson."

Beth felt like a hypocrite. She was sitting in a church surrounded by people who had never confronted the choices she'd faced in her life. No, she wasn't happy about what she'd done, she never would be, but the alternatives had not been acceptable.

The service started, and Beth felt even more uncomfortable at the first prayer. Not only had she made some very difficult decisions that bothered her; she'd also been intimate with Tanner. And part of her didn't regret being with him. They had shared wonderful, passionate sex that had shocked her with the intensity of how good it had been.

And now she was sitting beside his brother, waiting for the time when he would ask her to marry him.

It wasn't fair. One man made her feel alive, one man needed a wife, and she needed a husband.

The reverend approached the pulpit and began to preach on sins of the flesh, and Beth felt as if her face were flaming with shame. She couldn't meet the man's eyes. Church was not a place where she belonged, and this chapel was just not somewhere she fit in, especially sitting between the man she was to marry and the man she wanted to make love with, again.

She glanced at Tanner from beneath her eyelashes. Yes, she wanted to touch him again, and that surprised her. If he made the slightest overture, she would give up everything for that moment in his arms again.

And that realization suddenly frightened her. What was she thinking?

She was sitting in church beside the man she was going to marry, dreaming of the way his brother's hands made her feel, the way his kiss aroused her. Worse, she felt absolutely nothing when Tucker's lips touched hers.

Church was a place where forgiveness could be found, but suddenly she didn't want to find redemption. She wanted only to experience the passion that Tanner seemed to arouse. Only with this man had desire completely swept her away, and somehow she wanted to experience their union again.

Suddenly, the air seemed oppressive. She should never have come here. The walls felt as if they were closing in on her. The preacher's voice droned on from the pulpit; she couldn't breathe, and she couldn't take another minute sitting inside this chapel.

She felt faint. She stood, only knowing that she had to get out of there. She had to escape the confines of this room, these people, and the sins that weighed heavy upon her soul.

Beth eased her way out of the pew and walked rapidly down the aisle and out the door. Closing the door quietly behind her, she stopped on the porch of the small building and breathed deeply of the fresh air, willing herself to relax. With each breath she slowly began to unwind.

The door opened, and Tanner strode out onto the porch beside her, his face filled with concern. She wanted to moan but didn't. Why had he followed her?

"Are you okay?"

She took a deep breath. "I think so. I had to get out of there." She glanced uneasily at him. "I got too warm, I thought I was going to faint."

He stared at her, concern evident on his face and in his voice. "You didn't overtire yourself last night, did you?"

"I had some trouble getting to sleep." It seemed awkward to be standing on the steps of a church talking quietly. His brown eyes were red-rimmed and tired. "It looks like I wasn't the only one who stayed up way past bedtime last night."

"Yeah, I guess we all stayed awake late last night." He gazed at her. "Are you sure that's all that's bothering you?"

What could she say? That it was that final thought of wanting to experience passion with him again, of not having any desire for his brother, that had finally driven her from church. The thought of her past and the choices she'd made had screamed sinner. Coupled with the preacher's sermon, it had driven her from the building and sent her fleeing.

"I'm sure," she reassured him, knowing it was a lie but unwilling to confess the real problem. "It was just so stuffy in there."

"Then come on. Why don't we sit out the rest of the sermon in the wagon. I'm sure the good Lord will understand."

Beth smiled and couldn't agree more. She couldn't stand the thought of going back into that building. Yet she also felt anxious about sitting outside with Tanner.

Since she still wanted him, being alone, just the two of them, was only going to add fuel to the fire that she needed to extinguish.

He led her over to their wagon and helped her up onto the bench, then climbed in beside her.

"We'll wait for the others out here."

She nodded her head, unable to look at him right now. All she could think about while she'd sat in between him and Tucker was the way his hands felt on her flesh, how she wanted to make love with him again.

"What's wrong, Beth? You seem troubled," he asked.

She knew confiding the truth to him, about her feelings for Tucker, would send Tanner fleeing. She also knew he was too perceptive to believe any evasion or falsehood. So she told him partially what was bothering her.

"I don't belong in a church," she said, her voice barely above a whisper.

"Why not?"

"Several reasons."

"Like what?"

She gazed at him, unsure of how he was going to take her next statement but suddenly needing to tell him. "One reason is because of what we've done."

Tanner cleared his throat, his eyes glancing away. "That wasn't all your fault."

"No, but I could have refused you, and I didn't," she said, gripping her reticule tightly in her gloved hands. "I liked what we did together."

Tanner bowed his head and turned his hat over and over in his hands. When he spoke, his voice was gruff. "But that was before I found out you were intended for my brother."

"You're right. But if I wasn't going to marry Tucker, would it have been any different?"

"I can't answer that, Beth," he said, not looking at her.

She sighed. "I've made some bad choices in the past. I want to make sure this time that I'm making the right one."

Tanner frowned. Beth knew he was going to ask more questions, but at that moment the front doors opened, and the crowd began spilling out.

Beth sighed a breath of relief. She'd almost told him too much. She'd almost revealed her darkest secret, and she wasn't ready to share that with anyone, not even Tanner.

Fourteen

Tucker glanced around his mother's kitchen, not really noticing the fixtures but staring off into the distance, his mind replaying that morning at church.

Beth had jumped up from the pew during the service and all but ran outside. Her face had been pale, her eyes wide and lost-looking. When he'd asked her about leaving, she'd shrugged and said she became overheated in the small room. Although the chapel had been stuffy, her excuse had seemed prepared, something he would have said to his mother when he'd been caught playing hooky from school.

Oftentimes he'd seen an almost fearful look in Beth's eyes, which he'd always attributed to her new surroundings. But maybe it was more. What could trouble her enough to send her fleeing from church?

Travis came into the room, his boots clunking on the wooden floor.

"Where is everybody?" he asked.

Tucker shrugged. "The women are upstairs resting. Tanner's out in the barn, rubbing down that horse of his."

Travis went to the wooden stove and poured himself a cup of coffee from the pot that sat on top of the cast-iron stove.

"What are you drinking?" Travis asked, holding up the pot of black brew.

"Water."

Though it was probably close to a hundred degrees outside, coffee always seemed to be Travis's drink of choice.

"Should have known," Travis muttered, setting the pot back down on the stove. He took two steps and pulled out a chair from the table and sat across from his brother. "You and Beth seem to be getting along pretty well."

Tucker glanced at him as he twirled his glass in his hand, wishing it were something stronger than water.

"Actually, I don't know what to do about Beth," Tucker said with a sigh. "Beth's easy to get along with, she's nice. I could do a lot worse, but I don't love her. I'm not even attracted to her."

"That's a problem."

"Yeah, I know."

"So what are you going to do?" Travis asked.

Tucker shrugged. "Don't know. I keep hoping that something will happen, that somehow everything will work out without my having to hurt her. Though I don't know what kind of miracle I'm looking for."

Travis stared across the table. "Have you noticed anything unusual about Tanner?"

"What do you mean?" Tucker asked.

"He's not like the way I remember him," Travis said.

"He was a kid when he left, Travis. Now he's a man."

"No, there's more to it than that."

"Tanner is quiet, more withdrawn. But the thing I noticed was the way he wears his guns," Tucker said. "Loose and within reach. It's a good thing he's my brother; otherwise, I'd be watching him real close."

Travis frowned. "Yeah, I noticed. Has he told you anything about where he's been for the last ten years?"

"Nope."

"Has he said anything about what he was doing during all that time?"

"Nope."

"Did he say where he's lived or traveled?"

"He's told me nothing about his past. Not even about the war," Tucker acknowledged.

"That's my point. He's been so closed-lipped about what he's done for the last ten years. I wonder about what's going on inside him."

"What do you think it means?"

"Don't know." Travis glanced upstairs and then leaned closer. "He let it slip that he'd had no intention of seeing us while he was in Fort Worth. If you hadn't heard him that morning, we would never have known he was here."

Tucker frowned. "You mean, he would have come to Fort Worth without seeing Mother? Or us?"

"Yes," Travis said, then quickly added, "Mother doesn't know."

"Let's keep it that way," Tucker said. "If she ever found out, she'd be hurt."

Tucker silently contemplated what Tanner could have been doing for the last ten years. His thoughts wandered back to what he himself had been doing ten years ago, and instantly his mind saw the image of a young boy, fascinated with guns, shooting at targets almost every day.

"So why would a man hide his past?" Travis asked.

Tucker took a moment and thought of all the criminals he'd arrested since he'd become marshal.

"In my mind there's only two reasons, shame or trouble," Travis said, glancing at Tucker. "Could be something happened during the war, but could be he has a reason to hide."

"You think Tanner was in some kind of trouble with the law and that's why he's keeping quiet about his past?" Tucker asked, speaking his thoughts out loud.

"Don't know. That's your area, not mine."

"True. But you'd think he'd talk about the war, what he saw, what he did. You'd think he'd slip up just once if he was wanted."

"I know. He hasn't said a word," Travis replied, then leaned toward his younger brother. "It just seems odd to me. He's a lot quieter than when he was a kid. Maybe he doesn't trust us enough to tell us whatever it is that he's hiding."

"Maybe he's not hiding his past; maybe he can't talk about it," Tucker said. "I mean, maybe the war was so bad, he doesn't talk about the things he saw. You know, that kid he ran off with died."

"I'd forgotten about that. What was his name? Carter?"

"Yeah. I remember him. Real fun-loving kid. They used to be inseparable. Has he even mentioned him?"

"Not at all." Travis took a sip of his coffee. "He shocked me this morning when he said he was going to stay. I was really dreading telling Mother he was leaving."

Tucker cocked his head, a sudden thought entering his mind. "Could this be about Beth somehow? After all, they were together for several weeks while she healed in that hotel room. Do you think in taking care of her he formed some kind of attachment? She is a damn good-looking woman. Could that possibly be the reason he's acting so different?"

"Nah, I don't think so," Travis replied. "I don't think they knew one another until Beth's accident."

"You're right. I remember Tanner saying they were on the same stagecoach."

"Besides, you know how women talk. I'm sure Beth told Tanner all about you, so he would never become interested in his brother's girl."

Tucker tilted his head and rubbed his chin thoughtfully. The scrap of whiskers sounded loud in the room. "But you said he didn't intend to see us while he was in Fort Worth."

"Do you think that Tanner knew Beth was on her way to become your wife?" Travis asked, questioning.

"I'm not marrying her. But it does seem odd. Why would he think he could keep from seeing us if he'd known that Beth was coming here at my supposed invitation?"

"Hmm, makes me think maybe he didn't know," Travis said.

Rose appeared in the doorway, interrupting the conversation. "Why wasn't I invited to this meeting? Is it just for the men of the family?"

Travis held out his hand, and she walked from the doorway and joined him at the table. She stood behind him, and he took her hand and held it against his chest. "You're always welcome, sweetheart. Did you rest?"

She leaned down and kissed him on the forehead. "Yes, I did, and I'm feeling better."

Tucker frowned. "Are you sick, Rose?"

"I've just been a little tired, but I think it's the heat." She stared across the table at Tucker. "I heard what you said about your brother. It would be hard when you're dependent on someone to take care of you not to grow close to one another. I think Beth and Tanner became really good friends."

"So they're friends. Why would he think that he could bring her to town and just leave her without seeing us?" Travis asked, glancing back at his wife.

She shrugged. "I don't know. But I've been watching them, and whenever they're in the same room, they try not to look at one another unless they know the other one is not watching."

Travis shrugged. "I hadn't noticed."

"Me, neither," Tucker said.

"And last night, when I went up with the corsage, she asked if Tanner had sent it," Rose said.

"Well, he might have," Travis insisted.

"Why would she expect it from him when she's Tucker's intended?" Rose insisted.

"She's not my intended," he fairly hissed. "I'm not going to marry her."

"Then you need to tell her."

"I'm waiting for the right moment. She's nice, and I feel bad that she's traveled all this way and I'm the one who supposedly sent for her."

Rose shook her head at Tucker, then came around and sat down in a chair beside her husband. "I think Beth and Tanner are both trying very hard not to notice one another because they don't want to hurt you, Tucker."

"God, please hurt me!" he cried. "I like Beth, but I don't want to marry her or any other woman."

Rose smiled. "Marriage isn't bad, is it, Travis?"

Travis returned his wife's smile with a wicked grin. "Don't ruin it for him, honey. Let him believe the worst right up until the moment he gets snatched away by love."

She laughed and patted her husband on the knee. "Were you snatched, dear?"

He smiled and gazed into his wife's eyes. "Not snatched, sweetheart. I was yanked kicking and screaming all the way. And God, am I grateful."

She leaned toward him and whispered just loud enough for his ears, "Come upstairs and I'll let you show me just how grateful you really are."

"Gotta go, Tucker," Travis said, jumping up, and grabbing his wife's hand, he pulled her from the chair. His feet moved faster than Rose could keep up with as he pulled her toward the stairs.

Tucker shook his head and groaned. "Oh, God. I think I'm going to be ill. My brother is besotted."

Later that night, Beth couldn't sleep. She'd lain there tossing and turning, hoping she would eventually relax and tiredness would overcome her. Instead, her mind had replayed the scene in the little chapel over and over until she'd wanted to scream.

She'd jumped up and almost ran out of that small church, embarrassing herself and probably the family. Somehow she'd managed to lie and say that it was the heat. In actuality, it wasn't the high temperature that had sent her fleeing; rather, it was sitting between the two brothers, the preacher's sermon, and her past.

Neither man had any suspicions about what had sent her running from Jonesboro, Georgia, and she wasn't about to tell them.

Both men she felt gratified to know for different reasons. Tanner for his caring, protective ways and Tucker for the fact that he was willing to marry her and give her a home. Yet she felt so torn sitting between them, thinking of sharing a bed with the man who had nursed her while she planned to marry the man who had promised to take care of her.

She shouldn't be having these feelings for Tanner. After all, she was engaged to his brother. But the emotions were there, and no matter how much she tried to push them away, they refused to retreat.

A noise interrupted her speculation. It sounded like a moan. The groan came again, and she scrambled to a sitting position in the bed, listening. It was then she heard another cry, a deep, mournful sound that tugged at her heart.

Was that Tanner? The sound came again, sending a shiver down her back, and she realized it was louder.

It had to be Tanner.

He was having a nightmare, and she had to get to him, comfort him, before he woke the whole household up with his cries.

However, it was none of her business, and she didn't belong in Tanner's room in the middle of the night. His family would help him, they would wake him from his nightmare.

The sound came again, along with the image of Tanner thrashing in the midst of his dreams, trembling in fear. The thought of his enduring another torturous nightmare had her scrambling out of bed. She had to help him.

Beth threw back the covers and jumped from the bed. She grabbed her wrapper from the top of her trunk and yanked it on, covering herself. She opened the door to her room and peeked down the hall. No one was awake. The sound came again, and this time she could hear Tanner flailing about in his bed.

She hurried down the hall, opening and closing the door to his room quietly, before rushing to his side.

Beth gazed at the sleeping man and was overcome by a rush of protectiveness. She watched as he pitched about in the throes of the dream that seemed to plague him. Leaning over the bed, she laid her hand on his shoulder and shook him hard.

"Tanner, wake up." She bent over closer, her whisper louder. "You're safe, Tanner. Wake up."

The shaking only seemed to agitate him more, and she leaned still closer, hoping he'd hear her tense whispers.

"It's a dream, Tanner. Wake up," she pleaded.

Suddenly, he reached up and pulled her into bed with him. She almost let out a scream as he turned her, splaying her beneath him on the bed.

If they were found, there would be hell to pay, and Travis and Rose were just across the hall. She was surprised they hadn't already been awakened by his moans.

How would she ever explain being in his room? In his bed?

"Wake up, Tanner," she said, doubling up her fist and pounding his shoulder and back. She had to stop him before he did something they both would regret. "Wake up!"

She took a deep breath, the musky scent of Tanner causing her pulse to accelerate. How could just the smell of him cause her body to react with such desire? How could the feel of him, all of him, make her forget his brother?

Beth realized he was awake when she felt his erection stiffen and grow. He raised his head and gazed at her, their eyes met in the darkness, and a shiver passed through her at the desire that radiated from his gaze.

She wanted him as much, if not more, than the passion she saw reflected in his eyes.

Trembling with anticipation, she watched as his mouth

descended, covering her lips in a kiss that was more savage than gentle. He stretched his body full length against her, letting her feel every hard muscle. His hands molded her soft curves against his muscular frame until they were meshed together, muscled thigh to hardened chest. His mouth caressed hers, coaxed her until she relaxed, her arms slowly winding about him, all thoughts of discovery momentarily forgotten.

It was a kiss of torture, filled with secret desires and dreams that haunted him in the night, and she reveled under the assault of his lips. This was what she had thought of constantly since that night in San Antonio. It was what she wanted. She pulled him to her tighter, as if to protect him, shield him, from the dreams that disturbed him.

His tongue entered her mouth, sweeping the inside of her lips, leaving her gasping and needy. She pressed her body against his, seeking the hardened flesh of him between her thighs, yearning only to satiate the desire Tanner created within her.

God, how she wanted him—hard and filling the empty holes in her soul, the places only Tanner could fill.

The sound of a coyote howling at the moon sent an eerie chill up Beth's spine. As she lay beneath Tanner in his bed, only her wrapper and nightgown separated her and disaster. She shouldn't be kissing him, she shouldn't be here in his bed, but a sense of rightness overwhelmed her.

This was where she belonged, where she was meant to be.

His hungry lips coaxed her, pervading her body with delight until she no longer heard the voice of reason inside her head. She only wanted this mind-numbing satisfaction to possess her, fill her, until her soul was brimming with Tanner. For only he seemed to incite this storm of sensation in her body and leave her disintegrated and shattered with pleasure.

His hands shoved her burdensome wrapper and nightgown off her shoulder, out of the way, seeking access to her skin. His mouth trailed a string of kisses down her cheek, under her chin, along her neck to her shoulder. Her breathing sounded raspy and harsh in her ears, and she gasped at each new sensation. Whereas her hands once were pounding against his back, they now caressed, stroking him like a cherished lover.

"Oh, Beth, sweet temptation," he whispered against her neck.

She shuddered, his words thrilling her. He continued his path down her neck, to the top of her shoulder, his tongue lingering in the sensitive curve of her nape. His lips and warm breath sent shudders rippling through her.

He raised his head and gazed into her eyes, his look scorching her with its intensity. She watched as he lowered his mouth toward her. Eagerly, she rose up to meet him.

Slanting his lips across her mouth, he kissed her deeply and thoroughly, as if to mark her as his own. Beth wanted to cry out, to push him away, but she needed him so desperately that she clung to him.

As his hands reached the neckline of her nightgown, he grasped the material in his fist and yanked. Rending the material, he pulled it down out of his way, exposing her flesh to his hungry gaze.

She gasped at the feel of the cool night air on her naked flesh; her nipples hardened with excited pleasure. He pulled the offending garment off her shoulders and from around her hips. He tossed the ruined gown onto the floor. Next he tackled her drawers until they, too, lay in a heap on the floor. Soon she lay beneath him, naked and vulnerable, quivering with desire for him, only him.

There was no turning back. No second thoughts, nothing but a sweet sensation that this was right. This moment in time belonged to the two of them.

He shed his own drawers, his only piece of clothing, and tossed them aside. Greedily, he placed his lips on her breast, his tongue laving attention on her nipple. She arched her back, giving him more access to her breast, her hands clutching the hair on the top of his head. She was insistent and caressing all at the same time, and she yearned for more of Tanner.

His body molded to the contours of her skin, and she reveled in the feel of his muscular thighs and hard chest, firm and solid against her. For every place their skin touched, she rejoiced in the way his flesh seemed to warm her with a heat that burned from within.

His hand skimmed down her rib cage, over her stomach, lower, until he felt her wiry curls against his fingertips. He went still lower, seeking the silky folds between her legs. Searching and finding her very center, he delved his fingers into her hot, moist core.

Gently, he teased and stroked the tender petals as Beth gripped the tangled sheets, clutching them in her fists. Never had she experienced the frenzied passion that Tanner incited within her. Never had she enjoyed joining with a man until him.

Just the touch of his hand to her velvety folds left her hungry and shivering with need. She glanced up at him in the darkness and stared into his eyes as she cried out, disintegrating beneath his hand, quivering with her release.

She lay spent, her heart still racing, her breathing jag-

ged as she clung to Tanner, his broad shoulders hovering
above her.

He kissed her temple, her eyelids, and her nose. She
could feel him rigid and hard against her leg, waiting
patiently for her to catch her breath.

Only with this man had she experienced passion; only
Tanner made her feel like a woman, sheltered and protected. He made her heart feel emotions she had long
since given up on ever experiencing.

Tanner made her feel, made her hunger for desire, and
that knowledge just increased her passion. She wanted
to return the same feelings to him that he was giving to
her. She wanted to know that he hungered for her, as she
did for him.

"Beth," he whispered huskily in the dark. "I need you.
Love me."

She whimpered at his words, the thought of his needing her astonishing. Did he mean physically or emotion-
ally? Or both?

He bent his head and suckled her breast, her nipple
hardening into a pointed kernel. With trepidation, she
reached down until she located the proof of his desire
between his legs. She touched him, wrapped her fingers
around his shaft, and lovingly stroked him. She gazed
into his passion-filled brown eyes, his face a grimace of
pleasure and pain.

"Oh, God, Beth," he moaned. "You're turning me into
liquid fire."

The feel of him, hot and smooth, was intoxicating; she
felt his blood pulsating through him. She drew the tip of
his shaft between her fingers and skimmed her palm over
the top.

He grabbed her hand, his breathing jagged. She
glanced up into his eyes, staring at the desire shimmering

within his gaze. With her free hand, she reached up and cupped his chin and pulled his mouth down to hers.

God, how she needed him. How she wanted only him. And the pure joy she felt at that thought thrilled her. Gentle, tough Tanner, who had cared for her, protected her, and battled for her. No one had ever sheltered her as he had. No one had ever cared quite like him. This sweet, gentle man who hid his true nature, seldom letting anyone in past his guard, had won her heart and her soul.

His lips caressed hers, teasing and sweeping her mouth with an urgency that gripped her, holding her captive with his kiss. Her moans of pleasure were muffled as he took her hand and guided him into her center. She shifted to accommodate him, lifting her hips to meet his. She arched her back, her hips rotating slightly to give him deeper access into her center.

He plunged deeper into her, and she welcomed him with a sense of homecoming. This was her destiny, her fate. They were meant to be together. And no two people could ever have shared such a sense of happiness that being with Tanner brought Beth.

He filled her with a sweetness she'd never experienced as he thrust into her over and over until she thought she would go mad with ecstasy. She gave herself to him, risking it all for a man she'd trusted with her life, the very man she was giving her heart to.

With every driving stroke, she matched him, she met him, she loved him.

Passion burst forth like a shower of sparks, scorching her with its intensity as he rhythmically pushed her toward the flame.

She felt as if she were burning, and she glanced up into his gaze for one final soul-scorching look and felt as if she'd been pushed over the edge into the fire.

Beth was falling, tumbling, end over end, over a cliff, until she landed fractured and shattered in Tanner's arms.

With a shuddered cry, he reached his own release, and together they lay helpless, sweating and completely undone by what had just transpired.

Beth ran a hand across his forehead. He was her safety line, her love, and she could only lie in his arms recovering, trying to pull herself slowly back together.

He was her beginning, he was the start of something brand-new that was wonderful and exciting, yet she was promised to his brother. Surely there was some way that they could find a way to be together, that the two of them could heal each other's wounded hearts with a love that could last a lifetime.

She breathed a heavy sigh. "Dear God, what do we do now?"

Fifteen

Beth couldn't believe she had voiced her thoughts out loud. At this moment in time she didn't want to think about what tomorrow would bring. She only sought to enjoy tonight and the feel of Tanner's arms around her.

"What made you come to my room?" he asked, ignoring her previous question.

"I heard you having another nightmare and couldn't stand the thought of you suffering." She sighed. "I had to wake you. I couldn't bear to hear you moan."

He wrapped his arms around her and pulled her in tight against him, her breasts crushed against his chest.

"What do you dream about?" she asked. "Your face is always so tense and frightened that I'm scared for you."

At first, she didn't think he was going to respond as he lay there beside her, his body stiffening, his voice silent. Finally, after minutes had passed, he spoke.

"When I was a kid, I had a friend that I went everywhere with. He was like a brother to me." Tanner took a deep breath and sighed as if it were too painful to remember. "When the war broke out, we both wanted to enlist right away, but our families refused to let us go. We were too young, they told us. But we were boys, and we dreamed of being heroes. We didn't understand the realities of war."

Tanner rubbed her arm, his absentminded touch somehow soothing as he spoke. "My father and I argued over which side was correct. He said both sides were at fault and that it was a senseless war. I was young and naive, and so damned arrogant. We clashed often and loudly over my wish to join the South. I can still hear Papa saying that the North would prevail, that the North had the factories, the resources, while the South had only its honor."

He paused, his mouth so close to hers as they lay on their sides, facing one another, their legs entwined. She ran her toe along his muscled calf. "So what did you do?"

"I was already sixteen, so on Carter's sixteenth birthday we left early one morning, before anyone could stop us. We traveled across country until we reached the Confederate troops. By this time the army would take any able body they could find, and we saw our first action within days. I remember feeling so excited that I was finally going to get to fight the Yankees. God, I was so stupid and naive."

Tanner took a deep breath and exhaled slowly, his body tense, his voice quivering. "That battle was my first lesson in what war is really about."

She ran her fingers down his arm until she found his trembling hand and grasped it in her own, mesmerized by the story of Tanner as a hopeful young boy going into battle. Quietly, she asked, "What happened?"

He laughed, the sound hollow and filled with pain. "Very quickly you learn the rules of survival. You become immune to the blood, the broken bodies of men you care about. You learn it's better not to be concerned about the people around you because they may not be there tomorrow. You remember the faces of the ones closest to your own age. You die a little inside each time you take a life."

He shuddered at the memories, and her heart ached for him.

"So what happened?"

She watched as Tanner tensed and shrugged his shoulders, the motion an attempt to make his words less revealing. "Not much. We fought every day; we were constantly on the move. We walked until we wore holes in our boots, and the nights we went to bed without food were too many to count. Our clothing became filthy and our hair, full of lice."

He shuddered at the memory. "I can still feel those nasty bugs crawling on my body. But the worst was the shortage of guns and ammunition. It's hard to fight if you don't have the gunpowder. Soon I realized my father was right. The army was short on supplies. The South didn't have the factories necessary to win the war, and I could lose my life because of my own stubborn insistence on being a part of the carnage."

Beth reached up and kissed him on the lips tenderly, a loving reminder that he was here in the present, that he had survived.

She waited for several minutes, but he didn't say anything more, yet she knew that couldn't be all.

"So what happened to Carter?" she finally asked, dreading his answer. "Did he come home?"

His body stiffened, and through the moonlight shadows she could see something painful in his expression.

"By July of 1864 we were sick of the war and were in the midst of the battle for Atlanta. It was July, it was hot, and Sherman had been bombarding the city for damn near a month. Dysentery was raging through the troops, we were weak, tired, and all I wanted to do was go home."

"Why didn't you?" she asked.

"Pride, mostly. Couldn't go home and face Papa as a loser. Like a fool, I wanted to come home the war hero."

His hand stroked her naked skin, but his touch wasn't a caress. His eyes looked hollow, vacant, his touch somehow rigid.

"What happened to Carter?" she asked again.

"The federal army was advancing on Atlanta. That afternoon, we were trying to cut through their flank. Carter had been sick, but we all had been ill. Our division had been combined with William Walker's, but we were to try to take Bald Hill." He hung his head and then raised his eyes to gaze into hers and even the darkness could not hide the pain she saw reflected in his eyes.

"We always fought together, looked out for one another. Carter was protecting my back. There was smoke everywhere, and screams kept renting the air. A cry caused me to glance behind me, and Carter was down on his knees, too weak to stand any longer, still trying to defend my back. When I ran to help him, a Yankee charged me."

Tanner took a deep breath. "I was defending myself when a second soldier charged me. Carter rose from his knees and fought the attacker, but he was weak. I was supposed to be helping him, but I was still fighting off the first soldier boy. I killed the guy, then turned around in time to see Carter step between me and the second soldier's attack. The man ran him through with his saber, intending to kill me, but Carter took the blow instead."

Tanner was silent for several minutes as he gathered himself. "He gave his life for mine."

His voice had dropped almost to a whisper, and by the moonlight streaming through the window, the tears were visibly rolling down his cheeks.

"I held him in my lap, trying to stop the bleeding. But there was nothing I could do. His wounds were fatal, and all I could do was hold him while he died. My best friend died in my arms. I held him, knowing it should have been me lying there instead of him." Tanner swallowed. "Seventeen years old and one of the best people I had ever known, my friend, and he bled to death in my arms."

Silence filled the darkened room. Beth wanted to wrap her arms around Tanner and hold him until he was finished; instead, she held his hand in hers.

His voice sounded tight and choked. "The army doc tried to tell me there was nothing I could have done to save him, but I knew I'd turned my back on him for a moment and he'd saved my life. I was alive because he had sacrificed his own life, and I didn't deserve to live."

Beth reached up and stroked the side of his face. His cheek was wet with tears. She didn't say anything; rather, she gathered him in her arms, stroking him, giving him comfort.

After several minutes he cleared his throat. "Eight thousand men lost their lives that day. Me, I threw down my gun and walked away. I couldn't fight anymore. I couldn't kill any more innocent men or boys.

"It should have been me, Beth," he cried. "It should have been me."

For several minutes she just held him, and then she whispered, "Shh. He wanted you to live. He loved you, and if your places had been reversed, you would have done the same for him."

"No. I'm not a hero like Carter was. He was a good man."

Beth didn't know what to say. In her heart she believed Tanner was just as much of a hero, but he didn't want to hear that now, and she knew it was useless to try to convince him otherwise. She let it go.

"That was ten years ago. What did you do after that?"

"I went to Louisiana. I hid in the swamps and drank until the war was over. I stayed there until I made the decision to get even with the Yankees for what they had done to me and for Carter's death. That's when I started my next career. I began robbing Yankee-owned banks."

Beth felt her heart plunge to her knees. It was true. "Oh, Tanner, that was your face on that Wanted poster. You are a wanted man."

"That was me. I was uncertain as to whether you recognized me or not," he said, his voice not bragging, just stating a fact. "At first, I enjoyed taking the money. It was a way to get even. I also thought it would be a way to die. I prayed I would get shot during a holdup, but somehow I was always spared."

Dear God, he had been trying to kill himself. She could understand feeling the desire to end it all, the wish to die. Thank God he'd never been successful.

"And then one day, during a robbery, I shot an innocent man. Not intentionally; he came in at the wrong time and startled me. I didn't kill him, but later I found out that he had a wife and children. Why should he have to pay for my sins with his life?"

He shifted in her arms and rolled to his back and stared at the ceiling.

"So what happened?"

"I decided I wanted to make a clean start. I knew I was wanted, so I couldn't come home. I planned to leave, go to California." He paused. "But I never made it. A man who had been in my unit of the army caught me in south Texas. He recognized me and knew I was wanted. He turned me in for the reward money."

"But I don't understand. If you were wanted, how did you get released?" she asked, unable to keep quiet any longer.

"I didn't."

He rolled over and wrapped his arms around her, suddenly pulling her naked body up against him. His lips descended onto hers with fierceness, like the life-and-death struggles he'd experienced, very effectively shutting her up. He pushed her back, rolling her until his body was slanted over hers. His lips consumed hers, and his rough hands stroked her with fevered abandon.

She wanted to stop him; she wanted to push him away. She had so many questions, but his caresses were insistent, and she was caught up in the passion Tanner's touch created.

Soon she didn't want to stop him; she wanted only to comfort him, give him the love he had long been denied. She longed to ease his pain and somehow help him, though she had no idea where to begin except to give, during this small moment of time, the only thing she possessed: her body and her heart.

Though Beth wished it were different, she could no longer deny that her heart was involved with Tanner. Somewhere she knew she had fallen for the handsome outlaw and his rough, caring ways. She had probably fallen in love with him back in that hotel room in San Antonio but had just refused to acknowledge her feelings for the man. And now she had traveled all this way to marry his brother, only to realize she loved Tanner.

* * *

Much later, Tanner pulled Beth spoon fashion into his embrace and lay his head in the curve of her shoulder, breathing in her sweet womanly fragrance. He should have sent her running back to her room, but instead he had allowed himself the luxury of holding her in his arms, of letting his own wicked ways influence her.

And now he'd committed the worst crime of his entire life. When he and Beth had been together in San Antonio, it'd been different. He hadn't known who Beth was, but this time he'd sunk to his lowest level ever.

He'd slept with his brother's intended right under his very nose.

For this was Tucker's home more than Tanner's, and somehow he'd been unable to resist the chance of being with Beth once again. When she'd come to his room and awakened him from the nightmare, he'd been unable to resist the lure of her arms.

She would always be a temptation to him, be the one woman he'd want above all others. But there was no way for them to be together. He was not worthy of her. Beth needed a husband, and Tanner could not be that man, but his brother could marry her, provide for her and take care of her. At least he would know that in Tucker's hands Beth was well taken care of. But he could never stand to come back to them, to be around the couple, to watch them together.

His hand slipped down to her naked waist, and she sighed with pleasure. How could he ever look at Beth again and not remember the times he'd spent with her? How could he ever think of her in his brother's embrace? She had to wed Tucker, since Tanner could never marry. Yet he'd coerced her into his bed the first time and hadn't resisted her tonight. He'd ruined Beth's life as much as he'd damaged his own.

One more evil deed against his already tarnished soul. She had no money, no place to go. Beth needed a husband; she needed his family to take care of her.

But Tanner knew he could never marry her, never offer her the kind of life Tucker could provide.

Tanner's past would haunt him for the rest of his days, and his future looked bleak. He could never wed and burden another person with the deeds of his youth and with a future that held no promise.

He would leave before daylight.

"So how do I explain to your brother I can't marry him?" Beth asked, breaking the silence.

Tanner was jerked out of his reverie by Beth's comment. "Why would you tell him that you couldn't marry him?"

Beth glanced up at him, an odd expression on her face. "Because of you and me."

He ran his hand through his hair, wondering how she was going to take it when he said that he would not be marrying her, that Tucker was still the man she needed to marry.

"Beth, this is not going to work," he said with a sigh. "I'm wanted by the law; I've done so many bad things in my life. You deserve a man who's worthy and good, someone you can respect, who can settle down with you and give you a whole passel of kids. I could never be that man."

"Why don't you think you're worthy enough to deserve happiness? Do you think that you're the only man who found out that war wasn't about being a hero? You were sixteen years old when you ran away, you're not the same man anymore," she said, her voice rising.

"You're just saying these things to make me feel better.

You're trying to convince me to marry you. I don't deserve you, Beth."

"Why? You deserve to be happy just like the rest of us. What makes you so different besides the fact that you did some stupid things when you were young? Do you think you're the only one who wouldn't go back and change some of the decisions they made when they were young and naive? Do you really think you're the only one the war affected?"

"I know the war affected many people, but most people didn't start robbing banks to get even with the Yankees." He sighed. "There are too many things I've done and seen that could hurt you, Beth, and you don't deserve that kind of life."

"Why do you think that my life was so perfect? I'm not a saint by any means. You said it yourself. How did my family keep from losing their plantation? Let me tell you how I saved my family home. How I kept a roof over our heads." She paused and took a deep breath. "I—I became a general's mistress. A Yankee general."

He watched as she faced him, her eyes flashing. "You see, I, too, was affected by the war, though I didn't go off to fight a battle. I fought much closer to my home and to my heart. I struggled to keep my family together with a roof over our heads. And I fear that you will think badly of me once I tell you what happened."

He took his hand and ran it down her arm, stroking her gently. "I could never think badly of you."

There was a moment of silence, and then she spoke, her voice shaking. "Jonesboro was not far from Atlanta. Though our family home wasn't a huge plantation, we had enough land and slaves to live comfortably. Then the war broke out. Since I was an only child and my parents were elderly, the war didn't really affect us until the battle came to our doorstep."

She shuddered and took a deep breath. "General Green was a Yankee officer who ordered that the house be burned. We had no place to go; my father was sick, and my mother was frail. So I begged and pleaded with the general not to burn the house."

She took a deep breath. "He agreed on two conditions. Pinewood became headquarters for the Yankee officers. They moved in, and we were relegated to the servants' sleeping quarters. Second, General Green became my— he came to my bed."

Beth swallowed and took a deep breath, then released it slowly. Tanner could feel the tension radiating from her body.

"I . . . I didn't realize that the decision I made that day, to keep my family together, with a roof over our heads, would affect me for the rest of my life."

"What do you mean?" Tanner asked, fearing her response.

"The tiny community that we lived in soon found out what I had done. I was no longer accepted, though I had managed to keep my elderly parents in the home they had lived in all their lives. My own reputation was completely and irreversibly damaged. Friends I had known since childhood snubbed me on the street. But worse, even my parents were ostracized."

She shifted in his arms until her eyes met his. "My father died before the end of the war. I know he knew what I had done, but we never spoke of it. He never acknowledged my shame."

"I'm sorry," Tanner said.

She shrugged. "My mother was humiliated. Her only child had saved her from living in a tent, but she only acknowledged the disgrace I had brought upon the family. She would rather have become a beggar than for me to sleep with the enemy. When she died, she was a bitter old woman."

"What happened after the war ended?" Tanner asked, knowing she must have lost the plantation if she had come west.

"After the war, the general was transferred. I had no one left to work in the fields. I had no one to help me pay the taxes."

She sighed and glanced up into his eyes. "Four years after the war ended, I lost it all. I sold everything I could, and we lived in a little house in town until my mother died six months ago. With her death, I had absolutely nothing left and no reason to stay in a town where acquaintances no longer looked me in the face. A town where no eligible man would take a second glance at me unless he thought there was a chance of getting into my bed. Then I saw your brother's ad in the *Atlanta Gazette,* and I sent a reply."

Tanner took a deep breath. Her story made him feel sad. The war had taken so much from both of them. It had stolen their youth, changed them into people they had never had any intention of becoming. He'd never meant to turn into an outlaw or dreamed he would spend part of his life running from the law. And Beth had never intended to become a man's mistress; rather, a wife and a mother. She was an innocent who had done what she had to do to save her family.

"I'm no different from you, Tanner. I've done things that I'm not proud of, but I had no choice. I guess part of me left Georgia hoping to escape what I had done, but no matter how far I run, it'll always be a part of me. No matter what I do, I will be a soiled woman, a woman no man would ever want to marry, including your brother."

"No. You're wrong. You did what you had to do to save your family. What would have become of you if you'd let them burn down your home? What would have become of your parents? They were too elderly to work."

A tear slipped down her cheek. "You and I both know that most people would have rather we starved to death or even had to sleep in a tent before I let a Yankee touch me. As ridiculous as it sounds, the people in town despised me because I had managed to keep my family together. And when I lost the plantation to taxes, they laughed. I had finally gotten what I was due."

"No, you did what you had to do. Give yourself a chance," Tanner said.

"Then why can't you give us a chance? You're wanted by the law. Do you think that would matter? We'd be together."

"It would matter to me. Sooner or later you'd regret being with me. You'd think you should have married Tucker. You'd start to hate me . . ." His voice trailed off.

"No. I could never hate you." A tear rolled down her cheek, and she swiped it angrily away. "So what do we do now?"

"We enjoy tonight and wait to see what the dawn brings." Tanner held her in his arms, soothing her until she fell asleep.

Tanner lay beside Beth, watching her sleep. Her face was peaceful and relaxed in slumber, her breathing steady and even. Her skin was as smooth as silk, and when her eyes were open, they were warm and inviting. He glanced down her graceful neck and strong shoul-

ders to her uplifted breasts, so full and round, so tempting
and pleasing to his sight. His eyes continued down to
the curve of her waist, and he imagined his hands span-
ning her small frame. His gaze went still lower to where
her legs joined her body in graceful abandonment. In
sleep her limbs were pulled up as she lay on her side,
facing him.

She was breathtakingly beautiful, and his heart ached
with the knowledge that he must leave her. For neither
one of them had the willpower to stay away from each
other, and somehow Beth needed a man who was up-
standing and good. She deserved someone who had lived
a life she could be proud of, who could prove to her she
had done the honorable thing by sacrificing herself for
her family. She needed a man who could remain by her
side and give her a lifetime of love and children, a man
like his brother. She should marry Tucker.

His heart swelled with pain at the thought of her and
his brother together. But what could he do? He was
wanted by the law for a crime he readily admitted com-
mitting. He was haunted by his past, and his future, yet
to be determined, looked bleak.

Tucker was a lawman; he could give a woman a future,
a home. He could offer Beth everything that Tanner could
not, and she ought to have a chance at happiness. She
deserved a man like Tucker.

Just as Beth had done the honorable thing by sacrificing herself for her family, it was time Tanner did something respectable in his life. God knew he had done so
little good in his life before now. But doing the admirable
thing was also going to be painful.

She was the most courageous woman he'd ever met,
but he couldn't have her. She deserved a principled man,

one who could love her and show her she had done what was important at that terrible time in her life.

But if Tanner stayed, he knew Beth would only continue to seek him out, as he sought her. Therefore, eventually they would get caught, and his brother would be hurt. He had to leave. That he confronted his past was long overdue. It was time he settled once and for all what he had done and put the war and its effects behind him.

Until he faced the past, he could never have a future.

Tanner glanced out the window. It was maybe an hour before dawn, an hour before the family started to rise and greet the new day. If he left now, he could get away and hopefully redeem his past before anyone had knowledge of what he had done. It was his last chance to clear his name. Then he would go far away until Tucker and Beth were safely married. Once they were married, he could never be with her again, but if he didn't leave now, that marriage would never take place. And that wouldn't be good for Beth.

Rising from the bed, he dressed and packed his meager belongings. In less than ten minutes he was ready to go, though, in his heart he wanted to stay longer. He knew he had to leave now or forever regret his decision this day.

And though he'd snuck off in the night once before, this time he was doing it for an honorable reason. This time he had to go, intent on giving his brother a most precious gift. He was leaving so that Tucker could marry Beth and heal her wounded soul.

He'd write his mother a brief note once he was settled and ask for her forgiveness one more time, but he had to leave, and he couldn't stand the thought of a long good-bye.

He carried the sleeping Beth down the hall to her own

room and tucked her into bed. He glanced down at her once more and felt the urge to hold her one last time, but he knew that if he did, he would probably never let her go. For her own good, it was time he stepped out of her life and sorted out his own troubled past.

His soul ached with the thought of leaving her, and her smooth cheek was a temptation he could not resist. He leaned down and brushed his lips against her soft skin one last time, trying to memorize the vision of her sleeping. With determination he turned his back on her and walked to the door.

It was time to resolve his past once and for all.

Sixteen

Tanner swung his leg up and over the saddle, mounting his horse. He took one long, loving glance at the old homestead and then turned his mount toward the gate. The image of Carter waiting for him at the edge of the pasture, waving his arms excitedly, rose before him like a ghost from the past. They'd left on a morning much like this one, when the dawn had been a promise in the eastern sky—two young boys leaving on a grand adventure, with dreams of being heroes.

He squeezed his eyes shut and let the pain wash over him in waves of sadness. The only way he was going to get over the past was to let himself grieve for his friend, to experience the pain instead of shutting away his feelings. But his emotions were raw after last night's discussion. And somehow he wondered if he would ever get over missing Carter, of wanting to talk to him, only to confirm that he was gone forever.

Tanner took a deep breath and kicked his mount forward. But today was different from when he'd left home with Carter. He wasn't running any longer, he was going to face his past and see if he had a future. Today would find him facing his toughest challenge and meeting it head-on, instead of running from the pain that had haunted him for so very long.

Though he was leaving behind the family that had welcomed him back into their midst with few questions, this time he wasn't running away from them. Their strength and love had encouraged him to exorcise the demons that plagued his soul.

But his biggest source of strength and encouragement had come from Beth. They had talked and loved each other up until the moment he had carried the sleeping woman back to her room and to her bed. And though he hated leaving her, he knew in his heart he was sacrificing the life he could give her for a far better one with his brother. He was leaving Beth to Tucker, who could offer her so much more than a life scarred by the past, an uncertain future, and a man who didn't deserve her. Tucker was worthy of Beth; Tanner wasn't.

Just as Carter had given up his life for Tanner, he was giving up Beth for her sake. Maybe it was a twisted sense of honor, but Tucker was a good man who could help Beth find her sense of self-worth and honor again. He could redeem her and prove to her the value of her sacrifice. He could heal her inner wounds as she had somehow helped to cauterize Tanner's.

Birds were beginning to stir as the first rays of dawn lit the sky. A rabbit scampered across the path in front of him, and he couldn't help but think that this could be his last day on earth. Somehow he'd managed to survive the war, only to risk being gunned down by a man who was known for his cold-blooded killing.

It didn't matter anymore. If he was meant to die, then he would have at least made his peace with himself and the people who meant something to him. Yet even if he were to succeed in clearing his name, he still would not be worthy of Beth.

Main Street was deserted as he rode into town, the

sun just beginning to peek over the horizon. It was the time of morning when the fish bite the best, and Tanner suddenly had an urge to do what he'd done as a boy. The need to experience joy in life instead of constant sadness overwhelmed him, and he promised himself, if he survived, he'd do some fishing. Life didn't appear quite as bleak as it had before.

Tanner halted his horse in front of the El Paso Hotel and wondered about the man he was going to see. He hadn't heard from him in several weeks, and he suddenly feared the man was no longer there.

He swung his leg over the horse and slid to the ground. Looping the reins over the hitching post, Tanner glanced one last time down the street before he entered the hotel. It was an old habit of checking to see who was watching him before he went in.

Tanner opened the door of the establishment and stepped into the lobby. Few people wandered about the lobby at this hour of the morning; in fact, the area was deserted except for a desk clerk. He went into the café to get a cup of coffee before he took care of his business.

Walking through the door of the small hotel's dining room, he was comforted by memories of the day Tucker had recognized him. He had never intended to come back, but now he was grateful for the time with his family. He could almost smell Beth standing beside him, the scent of lilacs present, as his brother had exclaimed over him while he tried to recover his wits.

He cleared his mind and glanced into the room; he couldn't dwell on that memory. Tanner spotted the man he was looking for sitting at a table, alone, reading the paper.

As Tanner stepped up to the table, the man glanced up at him in surprise and then slowly laid his paper aside.

"Good morning," Tanner said, suddenly feeling nervous. What if the man had given up on him? "Mind if I sit down? We need to talk."

The man only glared at him. He didn't say a word at first, but picked up his knife and fork and began to eat his eggs.

"Sit."

A waitress came to the table before Tanner had a chance to say anything. "Would you like a cup of coffee?"

"Yes," Tanner said.

"How about our breakfast special?" she questioned. Tanner wanted her just to go away.

"Sure," he said, and she hurried away to the next group of people who had just walked through the door.

Tanner took a deep breath and glanced again at the man sitting across the table from him. His face was an unreadable mask, and Tanner suddenly feared he'd waited too long.

"You know that job you've been after me for months now to get done."

He only nodded his head and continued to eat his breakfast.

"I'm ready now. I promise you this time that there won't be any more delays."

The gray-haired man's face was lined and weathered, he seldom smiled or showed any emotion. The man finished chewing the last bite he'd taken and dabbed the corner of his mouth with his napkin.

The waitress walked back to the table and poured Tanner a cup of coffee, dragging out the suspense even longer.

They both watched her saunter away. Finally, the man

turned to Tanner. "You're too late. Sam Bass has already left town. You lost your chance."

"Where did he go?" Tanner asked. "I'll go after him."

The man shrugged. "How the hell would I know. I'm just the unlucky son of a bitch who's spent the last six months following him."

Tanner glanced around the room to see if anyone had noticed his outburst. "Did he mention the hill country?"

"Well, since we didn't exactly have a conversation about where he was going, I couldn't answer that. I did overhear him say something about going back to some-place that sounded like Rural Rock."

"Round Rock. He's going to Round Rock. That's not far from where he likes to hole up. I bet he's going there," Tanner said.

"How do I know this time you're really going to fol-low him? How do I know this time you'll bring him in?"

Tanner frowned, but he couldn't blame the man for his skepticism. "You don't. But I have a favor to ask of you, and maybe after you've heard it, then you'll know I'm serious this time."

The waitress returned, filled their coffee cups, and put a plate of eggs in front of Tanner. He knew he should eat something, but somehow food wasn't very appealing right now.

"You and I both know that I may not live through this. Sam is damn good with a gun, and he's going to be angry with me for not showing up like I promised," Tanner said, pushing his eggs around on his plate.

"Well, it's good to know you played him for the fool, too."

"Look, I had some unfinished business, and now it's been taken care of," Tanner said.

"Wouldn't have anything to do with Beth Anderson, would it?" the man asked.

He shrugged and took a bite of his eggs, chewing slowly. They tasted like sawdust, though it wasn't the cook's fault, but his own lack of appetite. "If I get shot and killed, I'm asking that you let my family know."

"And where does your family reside?" he questioned.

Tanner smiled, knowing his next words would be a surprise. "My brother is Marshal Tucker Burnett, right here in town."

"Your brother is the local law and you never told me?"

Tanner shrugged and smiled. "Don't worry. He doesn't know about you, either."

"What else, Jackson? I can feel there's something else," the man said, frowning.

"My oldest brother, Travis, and my mother, Eugenia, live here also. Make sure my mother gets this note."

He reached into his pocket and pulled out the note he had penned to his mother that morning.

Marshal McCoy took the note from Tanner. "Your family lives here, your brother is a lawman, and you hadn't said a word?"

"Sort of figured you either knew or you didn't, and I wasn't going to inform you." He took a sip of his coffee. "After all, I hadn't planned on coming to Fort Worth. I didn't plan on seeing them ever again. But I have now, and I'm glad. So if something should happen to me, I'm asking you to let my brother know. He'll take care of the rest."

"Oh, and by the way, you might want to start calling me Tanner Burnett, since that's my real name."

* * *

Early-morning sunlight streamed through the window, and Beth stretched, not wanting to leave the comfort of the bed. She snuggled under the covers and listened to the sound of the windmill churning, pumping water from the ground. It was such a pleasant, rhythmic noise, and it filled her with peace.

Memories of sleeping in Tanner's arms, of being carried back to her room, were distant images. The rest of the night had been a blur of emotional responses that had left her filled with hope for the coming day. Sometime last night she realized she loved Tanner, had loved him since he'd taken care of her bullet wound in that hotel room in San Antonio.

She loved him in spite of the fact that the law wanted him, that the war had done considerable damage to his soul. She loved him for the man that he was, for having reassured her how courageous she was to have sacrificed her virtue for her family.

She loved him for his caring nature and for being the man she knew he would eventually be. For Tanner had a sensitive soul that he hid behind gruff mannerisms, hoping no one would notice.

Yet Beth also knew being wanted by the law was no laughing matter, but if he went off to prison, she would wait for him. For surely he wouldn't hang for his crimes, would he?

There was so much to discuss about the future, about their pasts, that had now somehow become interwoven. They shared a painful history that they would overcome together.

She would speak with Tucker today and tell him that she could no longer consider marrying him, that she loved Tanner. And though he had paid her way to come to Fort Worth, she would reimburse him for his trouble, somehow.

But she didn't think Tucker would mind being released from his marital obligations, for he'd never appeared the eager groom.

Beth jumped out of bed, anxious to greet the new day, face the challenges that last night had brought, and find Tanner. She wanted to gaze into his brown eyes in the morning light and revel in the feel of his arms around her once again—and maybe even steal a kiss or two.

Hurriedly, she dressed, putting on her best blue muslin. She splashed her face with cool water and then gazed out the window at the morning sky. It was a breathtakingly beautiful morning, and she couldn't stand the thought of being away from Tanner for another moment.

She opened her door and glanced up and down the hall before she hurried to his bedroom. Travis and Rose's room was directly across the hall from Tanner's, and she wondered why they had not awakened last night during Tanner's nightmare.

Beth knocked softly on Tanner's door. There was no response. She tapped again; still no response. Finally, fearful of being caught standing in the hall outside his room, she pushed open the door and went inside.

She stood frozen, looking into the room as her eyes took in the emptiness. His clothes were gone, his toiletries had disappeared, the bed was made, and the room was tidy. Everything of Tanner's was missing.

Her hands began to shake as she walked into the room and sank down on the bed. She took a deep breath, trying to still the trembling that rocked through her. A niggling sense of doubt told her to run and check the house, the barns, everywhere he might have gone to, but somehow she knew instinctively that he'd left.

Probably not long after he'd carried her back to her room, he'd stolen away in the night.

A tear ran down her face, then another one, until they were streaming down her cheeks. She sat on the bed, remembering the night before, the feel of him, the sharing of their tainted pasts. Last night had been a joining of their minds and bodies, and yet the morning light found him gone. Her heart felt as if it would burst from the pain.

Why would he leave after everything they'd shared? Why would he go? She didn't understand. She put her face in her hands and cried. Once again she was alone.

For several minutes she let the tears flow down her cheeks, releasing the heartbreak that threatened to overwhelm her. Everything had changed in the space of twenty-four hours. Still, she could not marry Tucker, but now she had no future, no place to go.

This time she'd made the worst mistake of her life. She'd fallen in love with a man who was wanted by the law, who had been missing to his family for years. This time she'd chosen a man who could never return her love, never marry her and give her the home and family she so desperately wanted.

She'd made some lousy decisions in her life, and suddenly, for the first time, she decided to take control of her destiny. Yes, she'd come west looking for a husband, but she was no longer going to depend on a man for her future. She was going to make it on her own. She had a little money from the sale of her jewels in San Antonio. She would take that and find her own way in the world, and without the aid of a husband or a father.

The sound of the door pushing open startled her. She glanced up, only to find Travis standing in the door. He didn't appear surprised to find her in Tanner's room.

"Where's Tanner?" he questioned.

She sniffed and wiped the tears with the back of her hand. "He's gone."

"Gone? Where?"

"I don't know. But his things are missing, and I haven't seen him," she said, sobbing.

Travis cursed and walked through the room in shock. He glanced at Beth, suspicion darkening his eyes. "Are you all right?"

"Yes. What's wrong? Why are you looking for him?" Beth asked, sniffing.

"Rose is sick, and I wanted to see if he would go into town and get the doctor."

"What's wrong? Is she going to be okay?" Beth asked.

"If it's what I think, she'll be fine in about seven months," he said with a smile.

"Oh, my God, how exciting," Beth said, trying to ignore her tattered feelings for just a moment. Being part of this family felt so natural, so right, yet she had to give it up.

"Don't say anything just yet. We don't want to tell Mother until we're sure. She will be so disappointed if it's something else."

"Congratulations! I'm so happy for you both." Beth smiled up at him through her tears. "Travis, I need to speak with Tucker this morning, and then I'll need a ride into town. We can contact the doctor and ask him to come out to see you and Rose."

"Thanks. Uh, I think I know what you're going to say to Tucker, and Beth, I'm sorry for what's happened."

"Thanks, Travis." She shrugged, trying hard not to start crying again. "I better go find him so that we can get started."

* * *

Tucker was sitting downstairs in the kitchen, sipping a cup of coffee, when Travis and Beth came down the stairs together. He had stayed the night before and was going back to town this morning. One glance at the look on their faces and he knew something was wrong.

"Good morning," he said, hoping to receive some kind of reaction that would alert him.

They both glanced at him, and then Travis went to the cupboard and took out two mugs. He walked to the stove and poured them each a cup of coffee, then handed Beth her cup.

"Everyone is up early this morning," Tucker said, trying to ease the tension he could feel permeating the room.

"Tanner's gone," Travis announced.

"What?" Tucker said. "When did he leave?"

"Early this morning," Beth said.

Her eyes were red and puffy. She looked as though she'd been crying.

"Is he coming back?" Tucker asked.

"No one knows," Travis said. "He left without telling anyone good-bye."

"Well, hell, I didn't think he would do this to us a second time," Tucker said, clearly angry. "Have you told Mother?"

"Not yet. Rose is feeling poorly, and I was going to see if, when you went into town, you'd have the doctor come out."

"What's wrong with Rose?"

"Well . . ." Travis grinned. "Don't say anything to Mother, but I think we're about to make you an uncle."

Tucker smiled and reached over, clasping his brother's hand. "Congratulations. Now maybe Mother will get off my back for a while."

Tucker quickly glanced over at Beth, suddenly aware of what he had just said.

She glanced at him, a rueful expression on her face.

Travis suddenly headed for the door. "I better get back to Rose; she's having a rough morning."

He hurried out the door, and they heard his boots clumping up the stairs to the room he shared with Rose.

Beth sat staring out the window, her coffee cup in her hand. "Tucker, there's something I need to tell you."

Tucker stared at the woman, her voice was uneven, and she kept blinking her eyes as if she were trying to hold back tears.

She turned to face him and sipped from her coffee. "I know that you and I had agreed I would come to Texas and if we got along, we'd get married. But I can't marry you, Tucker."

He stared at her and sighed, relief filling him like a breath of fresh air. He smiled. "I know."

"You're a nice man. You wrote beautiful letters, and at the time I thought it could work out. But now it just doesn't feel right."

It was all he could do to act saddened when all he felt was relief. "I understand. But what will you do?"

"I don't know yet, but I can't stay here."

"Stay here until you know what you want to do, where you want to go."

"I can't stay. Look, I never meant to hurt you. But it was almost if after we met, we didn't belong together. The letters that you wrote didn't seem to fit you."

Tucker took a deep breath. He had to tell Beth or feel guilty the rest of his life regarding her.

"I didn't write those letters," he said, watching her eyes widen in surprise.

She swallowed, then looked at him, astounded.

"What do you mean, you didn't write them? Who did?"

Tucker grimaced, afraid of Beth's reaction when she learned the truth. "At the time, she didn't think that Rose and Travis would ever get together. So she started trying to find someone for me. Mother wrote the letters."

"What? Your mother wrote to me and signed your name?" she said, her voice rising. "I left my home, sold all my possessions, and traveled all this way because of your mother's letters?"

He didn't know what to say. "She wants her sons married. And she'll do whatever it takes to get them hitched."

"How could she lie to me like that? I came here because of what was in those letters." Her voice rose, and her pale face was suddenly flushed.

"Sometimes Mother doesn't think things through. She doesn't mean to hurt people, it's just that her children are the most important people in her life, and she'd do just about anything to see them happy." He rushed his words, trying to quell the anger he could see rapidly filling Beth's face. "To her way of thinking, nothing could be better for you than marrying one of her sons."

"But what about my feelings? I traveled here to marry a man who I thought wanted me." Her eyes suddenly lit up. "You didn't want to marry me, did you? That's why you've been so distant. I didn't understand why you seemed so detached, so unapproachable. I couldn't understand why you didn't want to kiss me. Now I do. You didn't want to marry me!"

Tucker suddenly felt ashamed, though he knew he hadn't meant to be a part of this fiasco. "I . . . I didn't want to hurt you, Beth. You're nice, but I'm just not the marrying kind. We just weren't right for one another."

"You're so right. We were never meant for one another,

and I would have known that if you had written the letters."

She stood up, her hands gripping the back of the chair. "I sold everything in the house that I could. I left everyone I knew behind to come out west and start again. Now I have nothing. I would have been better off if I'd stayed in Georgia."

"I'm sorry," he said, but his apology seemed weak compared to the huge injustice that had been done to Beth. "What are you going to do?"

"Just take me into town. I can't stay here any longer," she said, her voice choking.

Tucker watched as she left the room, her skirts swishing as she walked out the door.

She was right. They had done Beth a terrible disservice.

Seventeen

Hot tears pricked Beth's eyelids as she ran up the stairs. She had to get away before she broke down completely in front of Tucker. Eugenia had sent the letters that were so warm and touching. She'd written anecdotes about the family and the ranch that made Beth think this was where she belonged, that here, in this family, she could find happiness once again and that the man who would be her husband would welcome her with open arms. Instead, the man she was to marry didn't even want her.

Everything had been a lie. Eugenia had purposefully tricked Beth into coming to Texas to marry her unwilling son, though Tucker didn't want to marry. No wonder he'd seemed so cold.

But even worse, she'd fallen in love with Tanner, not Tucker, and he didn't want her, either.

Beth had hoped for a new start in life, only to find out that even here she wasn't wanted. There was no place in this world where she was welcome, where she felt wanted and needed. And no one cared whether or not she took her next breath.

Tanner had left her without a word this morning. The dreams she'd spun about them the night before were just fabricated lies that lovers whisper in the night. Tanner obviously hadn't even been able to face her in the pre-dawn light and tell her good-bye. He'd simply vanished, leaving her behind to face the day.

Tucker didn't want to marry her; he'd only been acting on his mother's wishes, and even then he'd had no intention of following through. While part of her realized she should be grateful, part of her was angry and felt that she'd been tricked.

Then there was her past. She'd sacrificed herself in order to preserve the family home, only to be scorned and rejected by her parents and the rest of her meager family, who had been ashamed of her efforts to save their home.

No one wanted her. She had no place to go.

Tears ran unchecked down her face as she threw her clothes into her valise, not caring whether they would wrinkle. A sob escaped her, and she fell to the bed and cried heart-wrenching sobs. She was completely alone, with barely enough money to get herself out of town. She had fallen in love with a man who was wanted by the law, who had left her to marry his brother.

Beth was determined to get out of Fort Worth and leave the Burnett family behind. To stay and face them day after day, to be reminded that she was not wanted, would be impossible. Tears flowed unchecked down her cheeks, soaking the bed with the evidence of her pain. She cried heartrending sobs for the man who had ridden off and left her.

Finally, after several minutes, the tears ceased, and she lay there realizing nothing had changed. Only her eyes and nose were now red and swollen, and her heart felt lighter, though still fractured.

She sat up and dried her eyes. She had survived the war, the public humiliation of her friends snubbing her, the death of her parents, and the end of her dreams. She would survive this, too.

A husband had been a means to fix her financial situation, to change her reputation, but maybe she just needed to be alone, to go somewhere and start new, with no connections, no ties to the past.

She took a deep breath, went to the basin, poured some water into the bowl, rinsed her face, and dried it on a towel that lay nearby. The sooner she left the ranch and all the memories and reminders of Tanner, the better she'd feel. She couldn't look at Travis and Tucker without thinking of Tanner.

Quickly, before she lost her resolve, she finished packing the rest of her clothes into her trunk and valise. With a last glance she checked the room and then picked up her bag and walked out the door.

She squared her shoulders, tilted her chin up, and made her way down the stairs. She could survive without her mail-order husband, Tucker, but Tanner, whom she'd given her heart to, would be harder to get over.

As her foot touched the bottom of the stairs, she glanced up to see almost the entire clan waiting for her and felt her heart rise up in her throat. Only Rose was missing, and she was ill.

"Tucker, would you please take me to town? My things are all packed, and I just need my trunk loaded," she said, a determined note in her voice.

Travis cleared his throat. "I'll bring it down for you."

He went up the stairs and disappeared into the bedroom.

Eugenia stepped forward and took both of Beth's hands in her own. "I'm so sorry, Beth. I was wrong to write those letters and sign my son's name to them. I love my children so much, and sometimes I do things I shouldn't trying to help them."

Beth felt the tears well up inside, but she bit her lip, trying hard to keep them at bay. Eugenia's apology, while heartfelt, was premature; Beth was far too angry about the wrong that had been done her.

Eugenia squeezed her hands as if to try to reach her, and it was all Beth could do to keep from yanking her hands away.

"Please, Beth, stay here with us. Don't go. You can stay here as long as you need."

Beth shook her head. "I can't. I need to put this all behind me." She needed a fresh start, without the memories and the pain.

"You're too upset right now. Stay here and take some time before you make any hasty decisions," Eugenia pleaded. "I promise no one will try to influence you in any way. Just stay for a while longer."

"No. I can't stay here and watch for—I've got to go, now," Beth whispered, knowing she had to get away or break down and start crying again. She released Eugenia's hands.

Just then, Travis came back down the stairs carrying her trunk in his hands. "I told Rose I was going to go with you, Tucker."

"Okay," he said, looking at Beth. "Are you sure this is what you want to do?"

She took a step toward the door. "Yes, let's go."

He cleared his throat and then grabbed his hat off the rack on the inside of the door. " 'Bye, Mother."

Eugenia sighed. "You're always welcome here, Beth."

"Good-bye," she said, hurrying before she started to cry again. She stepped through the door, wishing somehow she could leave behind her broken heart.

The two men helped her onto the wagon and then piled in beside her on its seat, tying Tucker's horse to the back of the wagon. Travis would bring the rig home later that day.

With a flick of the reins, Tucker had the wagon rolling out of the yard of the large white ranch house, through the open gate, and down the lane that led to the road to town.

Beth glanced back behind her, taking one long, last look at the place she'd hoped to call home, where she thought she had found the family she wished could replace her lost one, when she'd realized how much she loved the thief.

She swallowed the tears that threatened to fall once more and glanced ahead. Once again, she'd taken the wrong road in search of her dreams. Once again, she was on the road to a new life, but this time she wasn't going to search for a man to take care of her. She wasn't going to look for a family to replace her own.

She was going to find a job, make her own home, her own life. She would take care of herself and not entrust her destiny to someone else.

The wagon bounced along, the silence tense as they sat rigid on the seat, bouncing on the wooden bench.

Tucker leaned forward and asked his brother, "What time do you think Tanner left this morning?"

Travis glanced at Beth. "I don't know. What time do you think he left, Beth?"

"Before dawn. I went to his room early, and he had already left," she said, her voice sounding dull even to her own ears.

Tucker frowned, the look on his face questioning. "Why did you go to his room?"

She shrugged, knowing that Travis wondered why she

was in Tanner's room this morning, unwilling to tell him why. "I went to his room early this morning to talk, and like you said, his things were all gone."

No one said anything for a few moments as the horses clopped along on the rough road. Travis was staring at Beth as if he were trying to understand. "There's more to this, isn't there, Beth?"

A warm early-morning breeze teased wisps of hair around her face. She brushed back her auburn locks. The day would be a hot one before noon.

"You were crying when I found you," Travis said softly.

Beth glanced at the man who looked like Tanner and felt her heart almost break. She was reluctant to talk about this with them. She didn't want them to interfere in Tanner's decision, but she could not deny that she loved him.

"I . . . I went because I had to tell Tanner that I could not marry Tucker. I could not deny my love for Tanner anymore, and I didn't think it was fair to Tucker." She sighed. "But he was already gone."

She watched the two men exchange glances, but she didn't care. It was out in the open: She loved Tanner, and she didn't care who knew the reasons for her tears.

"Why did he leave?" Tucker asked.

"He doesn't feel like he's worthy of me. That's all I know. When you find him, you ask him why he left. But me, I'll be gone."

"Stay in town for a couple of days, Beth. Let us try to find him before you leave. What if he loves you?" Travis said. "The Burnett men are a pretty stubborn bunch when it comes to saying those three little words."

"No. I've got to go; he doesn't love me or he would

never have left without saying good-bye. He wouldn't have left me behind."

Tucker glanced at her quickly before returning his attention to the team of horses. "Did he mention anyplace he was going, where he'd been? Can you think of anything that would help us to find him if he's not still in town."

Beth shook her head; she knew more, but nothing that could help them find Tanner, that would help them get back the brother they were missing, the lover who had left her behind.

They were on the edge of town. Soon it would be time for them to part company. They would take her to the stage office, where she could catch the next coach out of town. She would leave the Burnetts and their problems here in Fort Worth and try to get her own life in some kind of order.

"So what are we going to do, Travis?" Tucker asked his older brother.

"After we find out when the next stage leaves and get Beth settled, you go check in at your office. I'm going to locate the doctor and see about him going out to the ranch. Tanner is a grown man. Something's been bothering him since he came back, and he's just not ready to talk about it yet. I hope that wherever he's gone, he'll come back when he's ready."

"You're right. But it's damn selfish that he couldn't at least say good-bye. If he's decided to take off again, that's fine. But he could have the decency to tell us he's leaving."

"Tanner knows where we're at. If he wants to be with us, he'll come home," Travis said.

Beth sat in silence thinking of Tanner, her heart fractured and hurting, knowing the exact issue he was dealing with. The death of his best friend, and his father and the fact that the law wanted him were enough to send most people to the loony bin. No wonder he'd run, but still it hurt. Tucker was right in asking why he couldn't say good-bye? Why couldn't he have told her he had to go, asked her to wait for him, told her he loved her?

Because he didn't love her or he wouldn't have left her.

She bit the inside of her lip. God, it hurt so much, but she loved him, had wanted him enough to risk it all.

They turned onto Main Street, traveling past the brothels, the saloons, and the shops. The wagon rolled down the street, passing horses tethered outside busy shops. It was another typical day in the frontier town, and Beth was oblivious to her surroundings.

She knew her time was just about up. The dream was rapidly coming to a close, and she was going to leave behind the very people who could have the most contact with Tanner. God, how his very name made her want to cry.

They pulled up in front of the El Paso Hotel, and Travis jumped from the wagon. "I'll go check on the next stage."

Beth twisted the strings of her reticule in her hands. Tension gripped her, and she told herself to hold on just a little longer.

"I'm sorry things didn't work out, Beth. I hope you don't hate me for going along with my mother's deception," Tucker said, looking at her as if she were a fragile piece of china that would splinter at the slightest bump.

"No. I don't hate you. In fact, I'm grateful you didn't marry me out of obligation. You're a nice man, Tucker; you just weren't meant for me," she said, her eyes swimming with tears once again. But they were tears for Tanner not Tucker.

"So what are you going to do now?" he asked.

"I don't know. I just want to get out of this city as quickly as possible. After that, I'm not sure."

"Stay in town a few days. Don't rush off without thinking this through."

"I can't. I need to get out of town as soon as possible," she said.

Travis walked back up to the wagon, interrupting their conversation. "Stage has already left for today, and the next one won't be until Saturday."

"But that's almost a week away. Is there nothing else?" Beth asked, her voice anxious. God, she felt so desperate to get out of this town, away from the Burnetts.

"Not until Saturday," Travis replied.

"We'll get you settled into the El Paso until then," Tucker said, setting the brake on the wagon and climbing down.

"But that hotel seems so expensive. Isn't there something cheaper?" Beth asked, thinking of the scarce amount of cash she had left.

Tucker smiled. "Not that I'm going to let you stay in. This stay is on my mother; after all, she owes you."

Travis spoke up. "We insist. Then, on Saturday, you can catch the stage and save your money for when you get to your new home."

Beth glanced at the two brothers. "I don't want your mother's money."

"We know. But we insist," Travis said. "Believe me, you are not the first person to experience my mother's matchmaking."

* * *

Tucker went to the jail after he'd checked Beth into the hotel, while Travis searched out the doctor for Rose. So far, between the scene with Beth this morning and then bringing her into town to catch the stage, it had been a hell of a day. He'd hated telling her the truth, that he hadn't wanted to marry her.

He sat behind his desk, going over some paperwork, checking to see what had happened while he'd been out at the ranch, wondering where his brother had gone. What had caused Tanner to leave this time?

"Marshal, there's someone here to see you," the deputy said, interrupting his thoughts.

Tucker glanced up from his paperwork and saw a man who looked somewhat familiar.

He stood, and the man grasped his hand. "Marshal Tucker Burnett?"

"Yes."

"My name is Federal Marshal McCoy."

"Have a seat. What brings you to Fort Worth?"

"Your brother Tanner."

Tucker stared at the man, his heart plunging to his feet. "What about my brother?"

Tucker eased back down into his chair, his mind rapidly contemplating all of the possibilities as to what this man wanted with Tanner, none of them good.

"I spoke with your brother this morning. Until then I didn't know anything about you or I would have come to see you sooner."

"You spoke with Tanner this morning?"

"Yes, right before he left town."

Tucker nodded. "Where did he go?"

"That's why I've come to see you. I think he needs your help."

Tucker gazed at the man. "What makes you think Tanner needs my help?"

The man stared at Tucker oddly. "You don't know, do you?"

"Know what? My brother just came back after being missing for ten years. We thought he was dead, and then, several weeks ago, I saw him at the El Paso Hotel with Beth Anderson."

"Yes, Miss Anderson."

"That was the first time we'd seen Tanner in ten years. We thought he was dead."

"Tanner has spent the years since the end of the war robbing banks." The man paused, letting Tucker absorb the shock.

"Tanner Burnett? Why didn't I hear about it? I would have known who he was," Tucker said, disbelief evident in his tone. "I would have seen his Wanted picture."

"Ever heard the name Jackson Carter?"

"Yeah, he's the bandit who only stole from Yankee-owned banks," Tucker said. "Are you saying that my brother Tanner has been the famed Dixie Bank Robber, known for robbing Yankee banks?"

Tucker leaned back and shook his head, completely stunned that his brother had become a bank robber. Tucker had even said that if he weren't his own brother, he would have been watching him closely.

The marshal nodded his head. "Yes, Tanner. I didn't even know that was his real name until today."

"But I thought he was caught over a year ago?" Tucker asked.

"He was. When we found out Tanner knew Sam Bass, we offered him a deal to keep from sending him to prison. He joined the Bass gang and has been working with me to bring them in, though he's hardly been co-operative until today."

A trickle of fear crept down Tucker's spine. The Bass gang was one of the most notorious, cold-blooded gangs in Texas history.

"Today I noticed some changes in Tanner that haven't been there before. He suddenly wanted to get this job done."

"So where has Tanner gone now?" Tucker asked, suddenly very afraid.

"He's gone alone after Sam Bass and his gang. If he were my brother, I'd be going after him to help him."

Tucker couldn't get out the door fast enough after the marshal left. He pulled some extra guns out of the cabinet behind his desk and loaded down his saddle pouch with ammunition. Unlocking a drawer, he pulled out the guns he had put away since he'd become a law-abiding citizen and took out the six-shooters he'd had made during his gun fighting days. These were the ones he had used when he'd been down in Tombstone, trying to prove he was faster than fast, when he'd thought his life would end with the next man who met him in the street.

He strapped on the holster and checked the weight of the guns. They still felt good—lightweight, balanced, smooth, and with a trigger as quick as greased lightning.

Slamming the door, he turned the lock in the cabinet and grabbed his saddlebags, along with the two rifles.

Thirty minutes later, he was scouring the town to find his brother Travis. Whether or not Travis went with him didn't matter. Tucker could not let Tanner face Sam Bass alone.

No matter what he'd done, this was Tanner's chance

to get his life back, and Tucker could not turn his back on him now.

Tucker pulled his horse to a halt in front of the doctor's office and jumped down. The wagon from the ranch sat out in front of the doctor's house. He wrapped the reins of his horse around the hitching post and bolted up the steps to the door.

He pounded on the man's front door, wishing he'd hurry. A servant opened the door, and Tucker strode through the open door.

"Is Travis Burnett here?"

"Just a minute, sir."

"Travis?" Tucker called, not waiting for the servant.

The rap of boots sounded on the wooden floor, and then suddenly Travis stood before him. "What's wrong?"

"It's Tanner. We've got to go help him."

"What's the matter? Where is he?"

"I'll tell you on the way, but he needs our help. He's about to face Sam Bass and his gang alone. We need to help him."

Travis frowned. He turned to look behind him, and the doctor had followed him. "Doc, would you go check on Rose and tell her I'll be home as soon as possible."

The old doctor nodded. "I'll go out to the ranch and see her. You boys be careful going after that Bass character. He's done more than his share of killing in this area."

Tucker walked out the door, Travis following him. "I brought you a horse. Doc can take our wagon home, or we'll get it later."

"Thanks!" Travis said.

"I also took the liberty of bringing these along for you." He handed his oldest brother a holster with two six-shooters fully loaded and ready to go. "I know you aren't one for wearing guns, Travis, but this time we're going to need all the firepower we can get."

Travis strapped on the holsters and then approached his horse. He swung a leg up and over the saddle, mounting the Appaloosa. The doctor came out on the porch and watched the preparations.

"You boys be careful."

"Doc, make sure my wife is okay, and tell her I wouldn't let anything keep me away from her and our baby."

"Don't worry, son. She'll be just fine."

Tucker vaulted up on his horse, and the two of them rode for the edge of town.

"So why in the hell is Tanner going after the Bass gang?" Travis questioned.

"Our brother is the Dixie Bank Robber who was caught about a year ago. When they found out he knew Sam Bass, they told him the charges would be dropped if he helped bring in Sam."

"Why in the hell didn't he tell us?"

"Because he's stubborn as a mule, like you," Tucker said.

Travis glared at Tucker. "No, he's sneaky like Mother."

Tanner lay in the darkness, trying to sleep, knowing that he needed his rest. It had taken him only two days to catch up with the Bass gang. He'd ridden his horse hard, he'd slept little, and now he'd found them. He lay on his back, looking up at the stars in the night sky, thinking of Beth and the fact that he'd left her.

Was she angry that he'd gone without saying goodbye? He knew that if he had to say farewell, he never would have left, so he'd snuck out in the middle of the night like a thief. Damn it, she was better off without him. He had to remember that with Tucker she had a future, a home and a family that would love her.

She would also have a husband who could help her realize she was a good, courageous woman, who was worthy of her, who wasn't wanted by the law and could be by her side without looking over his shoulder, expecting to be taken away at any moment.

The snap of a twig had him reaching for his gun. He listened again and heard a horse snort, the sound muffled but not far off. He pulled his gun out of its holster, cocked the hammer back, and waited, pretending to be asleep.

Crunching leaves alerted him that someone was near.

"I ought to kick your butt like I did when you were a kid, you son of a bitch!" his brother Travis said in the darkness.

Tanner immediately recognized his voice and sat straight up just as his two brothers walked into camp. His bedroll slipped, and the two revolvers were still in his hand, though they were pointed downward.

"What for?"

"For leaving without a word."

Tanner shrugged and put his guns back in their holsters. "I got an urge to leave, so I left."

"Bullshit!" Travis exclaimed.

"We know everything, Tanner. We know why you're here," Tucker said.

Tanner glanced up at them and studied their faces closely. "What is it you think you know?"

"Federal Marshal McCoy came to my office the morning you left. He told me everything."

"Remind me to kick his ass the next time I see him," Tanner said.

"Not me. That could get me jail time," Travis exclaimed.

"So what are you doing here?" Tanner asked.

"Well, usually brothers help each other out. You know, watch your back and all that blood-related stuff," Travis said. "Otherwise, I'd be home with my sick wife."

Tanner ran his hand through his hair. "It's not worth one of you getting hurt for my mistakes."

"Nobody asked your opinion," Travis said.

"Look, we're here to help. You can either do it with our assistance or we'll tie you up and let you watch us take care of them," Tucker said.

Tanner shook his head. "I appreciate the help, but I doubt very seriously I'll survive this shootout, and Mother doesn't deserve to lose all of her sons."

Tucker looked at Travis. "I guess that's one way to avoid Mother's matchmaking tendencies from now on."

"Nah, she'd follow you to the grave and pick out an angel for you," Travis replied.

"Look, I'm serious. Sam is an excellent marksman. I'm going in alone," Tanner insisted.

Travis looked at Tucker. "See, I told you. He's like Mother. Stubborn to a fault."

Tucker shrugged. "Could be." He glanced at Tanner. "So, tell us what is the plan. What are we going to do to bring the Bass gang to justice?"

"You're going home, and I'm going to rejoin them in the morning," Tanner replied.

"I don't think so. How many men does he have?"

"I'm serious. Mother needs someone to take care of her."

Travis and Tucker burst out laughing.

"You've been gone way too long. Our mother is quite

capable of taking care of herself. It's the rest of the world we need to warn about that woman," Tucker said.

"But Travis has Rose, and you have Beth. I don't want to be responsible for your death and possibly making your wives widows."

"Well, Tanner, Beth is getting ready to leave town, so I'm all alone. Now, Travis we need to watch over carefully because he's about to become a daddy."

"What do you mean, Beth is leaving town?" Tanner exclaimed.

Tucker smiled and glanced at his older brother. "Should we tell him? I mean, after all, he's the one who left her."

Tanner's heart just about stopped. Had something happened to Beth? "Tell me what? What's wrong with Beth?"

"Beth came to me the morning you left and told me she couldn't marry me. Which I was glad to hear, since Mother was the one who arranged the marriage, not me. Travis and I took her to town just before we found out about you and your problems. She's catching the next stage out of town."

"She's leaving town? She has no place to go. I've half a mind to finish what we started the other night in the barn," Tanner said, clearly agitated.

Tucker smiled. "Hey, she doesn't want me. She ended the arrangement, not me."

Travis smiled. "If you let us help you, maybe we can get you back to town before she leaves. That way you two can settle your differences, and you can quit looking at her like she's naked."

Tanner frowned at his older brother. "I don't."

Travis smiled. "You do."

"Well, Tucker was supposed to marry her," Tanner replied hotly.

"Sorry, big brother, but she doesn't want me."

Tanner ran his hand over his face. "I left her for you, Tucker. She has no place to go. She has no one."

Travis smiled. "Not anymore she doesn't. She has you, just as soon as we can settle this problem with the Bass gang."

"She doesn't want me, Tanner, and I'm glad," Tucker replied.

"You don't love Beth?" Tanner asked Tucker.

Tucker laughed. "No! She's a beautiful, very nice woman, but Mother wrote those damn letters, not me."

"So where is Beth?"

"She's at the El Paso Hotel, waiting for the next stage. So we need to get this problem of yours taken care of and get back to town. I have my own situation brewing," Travis said.

A sense of relief filled Tanner. Tucker didn't want to marry Beth, the Bass gang was down the road, and his brothers had come to help him.

Tanner smiled. "I don't know what to say, guys. I'd forgotten what it felt like to have brothers who stood by you. Thanks!"

"You're welcome. Now are you going to congratulate me on being a daddy, or am I going to have to kick your butt?" Travis asked.

Eighteen

Tanner rode into Round Rock with Sam Bass and his gang of outlaws, intent on robbing the bank of the small town. He glanced around, looking for Travis and Tucker, knowing that they were waiting for the gang. Sam and his boys had spent the previous weeks robbing every stage between here and Fort Worth. When Tanner had caught up with them, their saddlebags were filled with twenty-dollar gold pieces that had been destined for Wells Fargo and a New York Bank.

Now they were on their way to Mexico and a life of ease, according to Sam. But first they had received word of one more gold shipment that had been destined for a small bank in the town of Round Rock—one last bank, before they headed for the border.

Alone, Tanner had joined up with the group of outlaws, determined to discover their plans and then leave word for his brothers. He'd managed to leave a note in Belton and Georgetown for them regarding Sam's intentions. And now, as they rode into Round Rock, Tanner scanned the street, looking for his brothers.

The street was quiet, with few people strolling on the wooden sidewalks and even fewer businesses open to customers. They were expected, and his brothers had seen to it that the town was prepared.

"Where the hell is everybody?" Sam said as they rode into town, their horses' hooves stirring up a small cloud of dust on the main street.

There were five outlaws, counting Tanner, and he knew the odds were against his surviving. Even with the sheriff's help, they were outnumbered. He could die, without ever seeing Beth again, a wanted man with little chance of ever clearing his name.

"Maybe it's a holiday of some sort," Seaborn Barnes said, riding next to Sam.

"It's too damn quiet," Sam stated, glancing up and down the street as they halted their horses in front of the local saloon.

The outlaw glanced suspiciously at Tanner. When he'd joined them in Waco, there had been a reluctant welcome from the members of the gang, and Tanner knew he was looked upon with distrust. After all, he'd been missing well over a month while they had continued their robbery spree.

Sam swung a leg over his horse and dropped to the ground. "Let's get a drink, and then we'll head over to the bank either this afternoon or tomorrow. But for now let's lay low and find out what's going on."

The rest of the men dismounted and tied the reins of their horses to a hitching post out in front of the drinking establishment.

Just as they moved to enter the door of the saloon, a voice commanded them, "Halt right there! Reach your hands to the sky or I'll shoot you where you're standing."

Tanner raised his hands and slowly pivoted to see the small-town sheriff coming down the wooden sidewalk toward them, his rifle pointed at the group. Tanner quickly scanned the street, looking for his brothers.

Travis was on top of the bank, and Tucker was coming around the side of the building, his guns drawn.

The sheriff had one shot and five men. What the hell was the man thinking? Where was his backup beside the other Burnett brothers?

Tanner glanced at Sam and watched him lick his lips anxiously, his eyes never wavering from the lawman.

"What's wrong, Sheriff?" the outlaw asked.

"I've seen your face before. You're Sam Bass." The sheriff appeared determined, but his gun was shaking, he was so nervous.

Tanner slowly eased himself away and to the side of the outlaw. He needed to get a better shot at the man whose surrender would mean his freedom. He watched Sam and knew he was going to go for his gun.

"Don't do it, Sam," he said, his voice low enough just for the outlaw's ears.

"Why not. It's an easy shot," the outlaw said. "The man's scared enough he'd miss a tree."

"Because I'd have to kill you," Tanner said. "And I really don't want to."

The outlaw glanced at him and laughed. "You turned us in, didn't you, Tanner? That's why this town is so damn quiet; they knew we were coming. I'm not going to jail."

Tanner never took his eyes off Sam as he watched the man's eyes and knew the exact moment he went for his gun. Sam's eyes flickered once, and then Tanner saw the outlaw's fingers reach for his Colt Navy revolver.

The next few seconds were a whirl of motion as Sam fired first at the sheriff, striking him in the shoulder, and then pivoted to fire on Tanner. But his shot went wide, and Tanner had pulled his revolver at the same time. He shot Bass just below his heart, knocking him to his knees.

The outlaws on either side of Bass dropped to the ground, dead.

The sheriff was lying in the street, trying to reload with one hand as Bass lifted his revolver and pointed it at Tanner. On his knees, he took aim.

At that instant, Tanner was certain he was going to die. He would never see Beth again or hold her in his arms, and his heart swelled with regret and sadness. Damn, he'd wanted a second chance with Beth. He'd wanted to be the man she married. The man she loved. He wanted to show Beth that because of her love, he was a decent man. She had given him a second chance at being a worthy man, but now he'd never have a chance to tell her he loved her.

At the flash of gunpowder from Sam's gun, Tanner pulled the trigger on his own gun. The bullet knocked Tanner down to the ground just as a flurry of shots sounded in the small town, ricocheting off the walls of the buildings that lined Main Street.

Tanner thought he was dying as he fell to the ground, his head bursting with pain, his last thoughts of Beth before he lost consciousness.

Eugenia pulled the wagon to a halt and set the brake in front of the El Paso Hotel. She glanced over at her daughter-in-law, Rose, who was looking a bit peaked. "Are you all right?"

"The heat really seems to be bothering me today, but I think once I get in out of the sun, I'll be fine," she said, fanning herself with a lace fan.

"Well, then, come on, let's get in the hotel and see if we can talk some sense into this girl before she catches the next stage out of town," Eugenia said, tying the reins to the brake.

Eugenia climbed down from the wagon, her team of horses somewhat nervous standing in the blistering sun. She patted the nearest horse on the neck. "Be back soon."

They walked into the lobby of the grand old hotel and stopped just inside the door, enjoying the cooler breeze. The lobby had a stately, if sparse, decor and a staircase in the middle that led to the guest rooms and another door that led to the dining room and bar, where the locals collected to discuss the latest cattle stock prices.

Rose laid her hand on Eugenia's arm. "You know, maybe it would be best if I were to go and talk to her first. I could see how she's feeling about the situation and then bring her back downstairs, where we could all have tea in the café."

Eugenia glanced at Rose and frowned. "That might not be a bad idea. She might still be upset with me."

"You were wrong, Eugenia," Rose admonished.

"Yes, I know. But honestly, I meant well. I just want my sons to be happy."

"They'd be ecstatic if you would quit playing match-maker," Rose said. "But I know in my own situation that your matchmaking was the best thing that's ever happened to me."

"Why, thank you, Rose. That was sweet of you," Eugenia said, smiling. Eugenia twisted her purse strings. "I don't understand why they get upset. All I do is introduce my sons, and the rest is up to them."

Rose shook her head, smiling at the older woman. "It's more, but I don't have time to argue with you. I'll go up to her room, then, and see if I can persuade her to stay. You wait here for me."

"Okay, take your time," Eugenia told her as she watched Rose hurry up the stairs to Beth.

Eugenia took a seat in the lobby, watching as people hurried in and out of the hotel, wondering where her sons were. The note from Travis had been brief, and she couldn't help but wonder about her boys.

Tanner's leaving the second time had hurt even more than the first. He'd left without saying good-bye again, after he'd promised he'd never do that again. Yet he had.

So once again she had one son who was married, one who had disappeared, and one she'd almost set up with the wrong woman. Tucker needed a hometown girl, someone from around here who knew him.

Old Doc Wilson came down the stairs and went to the desk clerk. "Here's my bill. Mr. Kincaid said to give it to you."

"Thanks, Doc, for coming out. Is he feeling better?"

"Yeah. Now I'm going home to rest. I'm getting way too old to be making house calls anymore."

Eugenia stood and stepped right into the doctor's path. "Hello, Doc."

"Mrs. Burnett. It's a pleasure to see you."

"Thanks. So Mr. Kincaid is sick?" she questioned.

"He's got a nasty summer cold. A man his age can't afford not to take care of his symptoms right away. He just needs some bed rest and fluids."

"I've ordered the kitchen to prepare him soup," the desk clerk said.

Just then the waitress came out of the kitchen with a tray laden with soup and bread in her hands. Eugenia took the tray right out of the girl's arms.

"I'll take it in to him," Eugenia said. "He could probably use some cheering up, and I'll make sure he eats well."

The old man had always been kind to Eugenia, and making sure he was feeling better was the least she could do while she waited for Rose.

She carried the tray up the stairs and down the hall to the last door. Balancing the tray with one hand, she rapped on the door with the knuckles of her right hand.

"Yoo-hoo, Mr. Kincaid, I have some soup for you."

Eugenia didn't wait for an answer but pushed open the door. The man was lying in bed, his back turned toward her. He rolled over and quickly pulled the sheet up to his chest.

Eugenia caught a glimpse of a nightshirt pulled up to expose a long masculine leg. She smiled and pretended not to notice. She laid the tray on a small table next to the bed. "Sorry if I surprised you, but I wanted to check and make sure you were all right."

"I . . . I just wasn't expecting you," he said, and smiled at her, though the luster that usually sparkled from his blue eyes was gone. He looked tired.

She reached behind him and grabbed his pillow, beating it until the feathers were more down than substance. She shoved the plump pillow back behind his back.

"Ready for a little soup?" she asked.

He sat up in bed and glanced at her. "You don't have to do this. I can feed myself."

"No, no. You're the patient. Just pretend I'm your nurse."

He glanced at Eugenia with a raised brow. "I've never received such special attention from a nurse before. Thank you."

"So how long have you been sick?" Eugenia asked.

"It came on me pretty sudden this time. I've been meaning to send you a note and tell you how much I enjoyed your party the other night. I hadn't danced like that in years. It was fun."

"Glad you enjoyed yourself. I guess, though, I was a little premature in wanting to announce at that party that Tucker was getting married. Seems that Miss Anderson has decided to leave town." Eugenia shook her head. "And Tanner, bless his soul, is running from something. I just don't know what yet."

Mr. Kincaid swallowed a spoonful of soup. "I noticed that Miss Anderson was back at the hotel, alone. She's hardly come down at all. Just to buy the latest newspapers is all."

"Yeah, Rose is talking with her now, trying to convince her not to leave just yet." She sighed. "I'm afraid my son has taken off for good, and Miss Anderson is about to hightail it out of here."

Phillip had a fit of coughing, and Eugenia handed him his handkerchief. "I wish I'd get over this stuff. If Sarah were here, she would have told me it was because I let myself become run-down." He sighed. "I sure do miss that girl."

"How is she doing?" Eugenia asked. "I haven't seen her since she went off to medical school."

"She's fine. There's a recent tintype of her over on the dresser, along with my great-grandson, Lucas, whom I've yet to meet. It's a shame about her husband passing away before the baby was born."

Putting the spoon of broth back in the soup bowl, Eugenia stood and walked over to the dresser and looked at the young woman. The girl had always been lovely, but the last few years had changed her into a beauty.

Eugenia picked up the picture and stared at the woman. She was a young widow with a child to raise. Why hadn't she come back to Fort Worth? Why hadn't she returned home to practice medicine? Why hadn't she remarried?

The idea came to Eugenia so quickly, it just about knocked her off her feet. Doc Wilson was getting up in years, and Fort Worth would need a younger doctor. Eugenia needed a woman for Tucker, and Sarah needed a father for her baby. If the young woman came to town, Fort Worth would get a doctor; Eugenia would have someone new to interest Tucker, and little Lucas could possibly get a father.

And best of all, she was a hometown girl.

Eugenia's conscience twinged for just a moment. She shouldn't involve herself in bringing Sarah home. She was not going to get caught up in her sons' lives anymore. But this was the perfect situation, and everyone's needs would be met. It was ideal!

She glanced at the older man in bed. He was getting up there in years, at least in his mid-sixties, and he needed his granddaughter. "How old is Sarah?"

"She's twenty-four, and my great-grandson is almost two."

Eugenia sat the picture down and came back to the bed. "She went to school with Tucker, didn't she?"

"Yes, I remember them attending at the same time," Phillip said.

The man turned his head to the side and coughed, his chest sounding raspy.

"So where is Sarah now?" Eugenia asked, spooning the hot broth into his mouth.

"She's still in Tombstone," he said, glancing at Eugenia. "I keep thinking about going for a visit but just haven't made the time."

"Why didn't she come back here to practice medicine?"

"Sarah originally had planned on being a missionary doctor to the Indians, but that didn't work out as planned. Instead, she found she was needed in Tombstone, so she stayed there." He sighed. "But I do wish she would come home, especially since she now has a son of her own."

It was meant to be. Sarah was destined to come home, and Eugenia knew just what would bring her running. And it wasn't a complete lie. She was just going to stretch the truth a little.

Eugenia smiled and lifted the spoon to Phillip's mouth. "Well, maybe someday she will."

The girl obviously had no way of knowing her grandfather was ill. Eugenia had heard the words from the doctor himself. An illness at his age could be very serious.

"You never know what will bring a person home," Eugenia said with a smile. "Open wide."

Beth heard the knock at the door and wondered what the maid had forgotten. She opened the door and was astonished to see Rose Burnett standing there.

"Can I come in?" Rose asked, her face filled with concern.

"Of course. Come in; the stage doesn't leave until one o'clock."

Rose stepped into the room, and Beth pulled over a chair from a table in the corner. The room was smaller than the one she had shared with Tanner. Besides a washstand, the bed, and a table with two chairs, it had little if any furniture. Yet it was plenty spacious for one lonely person to pace the area for days, trying to decide which road in life to take. It felt like a monastery when her memory kept returning to the hotel room she'd shared with Tanner.

"I'd offer you something to drink, but all I have is water. And we'd have to go downstairs for anything else," Beth said, hesitating. "I've sort of avoided being down there."

Rose reached out and touched Beth's arm. "I'm sorry that Eugenia sent those letters to you instead of Tucker. I tried to warn you that she sometimes gets a little carried away. She means well; she just wants her children to be happy."

"I've never met a mother quite like her," Beth said, her voice soft.

Rose gave a short little laugh. "Eugenia is unique, and I'm worried what kind of grandmother she's going to be. But we'll talk about that some other time. Right now I came because I think more is involved than your being upset about Tucker. In fact, I deliberately didn't bring Eugenia up with me so that I could talk to you about Tanner."

Beth sighed. She couldn't be too upset with Eugenia. After all, she'd deceived the Burnetts, too, by sleeping with Tanner and not telling anyone about her sin. She could have told Tucker, then asked for his decision, if she were really honest. But for her purposes she didn't. It was roughly the same thing.

"You're right. I can't be too upset with Eugenia, because without her interfering I wouldn't have met the man I love. It's just that I don't love Tucker. I love Tanner."

Rose smiled. "I thought so. I guess you fell in love with him before you met Tucker."

"I didn't intend to fall in love with Tanner, it just happened." Her voice rose. "And now I find out that he's a wanted man. And he's disappeared."

Rose reached across the small table and grabbed Beth's hands. "How do you know he's a wanted man?"

"He told me. I think that's one of the reasons he left."

Beth felt like crying, but her eyes were dry. She'd cried more tears since Travis and Tucker had dropped her off at the hotel days ago, and now she only felt numb and hurt.

"I think Tanner cares about you, but because of his brother, he hasn't said anything. And Travis and Tucker have gone after Tanner," Rose said in a rush. "The doctor brought me word from Travis not to worry, that he'd soon return with Tanner. Stay just a little longer, Beth. Wait until Tanner returns and then decide whether to go or stay."

"What will Tanner do when he returns? He's wanted by the law; he has a brother who is a marshal. He's not coming back, Rose. And even being wanted by the law would not have kept me from him, but he chose not to be with me. He left without a word, a reason, or even a simple good-bye."

"We'll find a way to help Tanner. Just give it a little more time," Rose pleaded. "Miracles don't happen overnight, and besides, where are you going to go?"

"Away from this place, where I've been hurt so badly."

"You know, Beth, I was a lot like you. I was pretty much alone in the world, trying to survive and make a living the best I could," Rose said, her voice sympathetic and kind.

"But now you have Travis."

"Yes, now I do have Travis, but I can't say that in the beginning it was easy. There was a time I was prepared to leave him and walk away to a new life." Rose paused. "But Travis came around, and I have to thank Eugenia for her meddling or we wouldn't be together."

"I can't stay here and be a part of this family and watch Tanner from a distance. It would hurt way too much, knowing that I loved him and that he's unwilling to love me." She took a deep breath, willing the pain to go away. "I'm leaving on the next stage heading west."

Beth glanced at the watch pinned to her dress. "I'm sorry to rush you, but my stage is due to leave in thirty minutes."

"I don't think he's unwilling, Beth. Stay at least until they get back," Rose implored. "Or at least tell me what your plans are so that I won't worry about you."

"I'll tell you only because he'll never follow me." Beth sighed. "I'm heading west. I'm going to try to find a governess job or a teaching position. Surely someone will hire me with the education I have."

Beth stood and walked over to the trunk that was lying on the bed. "I'm sorry, Rose, but I really need to finish packing and get my trunk downstairs. It's time for me to leave. I've got to be on this stage and put all this behind me. Tanner doesn't love me. He left without telling me good-bye, without even a loving kiss. I'm not waiting on his return so he can break my heart a second time."

Tanner awoke in a darkened room, anxious voices surrounding him. He squinched up his face, trying to concentrate on what they were saying. At first, the words sounded distant and distorted, but finally he recognized his brother Travis.

"It was just a scratch, Doc. Why isn't he coming around?" Travis asked.

"Give it some time. It's only been a couple of hours. He could remain like this for days, or even weeks. Why don't you boys go get a bite to eat while I finish working on the sheriff? After all, the group of you have kept me busy today."

Tanner tried to speak, but his lips were dry, and his voice didn't want to work. "No . . . not without me."

The sound of boots scurrying across the floor ricocheted in Tanner's head, and he felt as if he'd been drinking but knew that was impossible.

"He's awake," Tucker exclaimed.

"I see that," the doc said, grabbing ahold of Tanner's chin and gazing at his eyes. "How you feeling?"

"Like I've been on a two-week drunk. Make them be quiet or I'm going to throw up."

Travis chuckled. "Did that bullet knock any sense in that dense skull of yours?"

"Is that what happened?" Tanner sighed, feeling tired but anxious to hear about the shooting.

"You were grazed by one of Sam Bass's bullets, but you got him. Bass and two others are dead, and the fourth guy managed to escape. The sheriff was wounded, but he's going to be okay."

"How bad is it, Doc?"

"Just a scratch that probably gave you a concussion. You should be okay in a day or two."

"Not a day or two, tomorrow. I'll stay tonight only because I feel so bad, but tomorrow morning we're heading to Fort Worth. I have some unfinished business to take care of," Tanner insisted.

"That head of yours can't take another fall. I'd wait a couple of days at least," the doctor cautioned.

"If you're in a hurry to meet with Marshal McCoy, put it out of your mind," Tucker informed him.

"Why?" Tanner asked, fearing suddenly that everything he'd done to help catch Sam Bass had been for naught. What if they didn't clear his name? What if he'd almost been killed just for the state to put him behind bars?

Suddenly, the marshal's face was before him. "Because I'm right here and you're a free man, Tanner. With the demise of the Bass gang and the return of the gold, you've more than fulfilled your duties. The governor has already agreed to sign your pardon. You can go anytime."

Tanner sighed and felt an overwhelming sense of relief. He was a free man, he could come and go just like everyone else and wouldn't have to be constantly looking over his shoulder for the next lawman to haul him in. He was free to live the life of any normal citizen, to go home and be with his family without bringing shame upon them, to settle down, marry, and raise a family. To love Beth.

The memory of Beth, her head thrown back in passion, caught his breath. The thought of her smiling at him, encouraging him to stay, filled his heart. The image of her staying in that hotel room, all alone, waiting to catch the next stage out of town, suddenly overwhelmed him.

"Thanks, Marshal. I can't thank you enough for what you've done."

"Sure you can. Stay out of trouble."

"Not a problem!"

Marshal McCoy reached over and shook Tanner's hand. "Take care of yourself, Tanner."

Tanner returned his grip and then watched him walk out the door of the makeshift hospital. He turned and glanced at his two brothers. "We've got to get back to Fort Worth. I've got to find Beth."

Tucker smiled and nodded.

"If you're feeling okay, we'll leave at first light," Travis said.

"I'll be fine. You be ready to go. Now get out of here so that I can rest. I need my strength."

Nineteen

Tanner rode back into Fort Worth a free man ten days after the morning he'd left, determined never to return until he'd cleared his name. His thoughts were centered on finding the one person who had changed him, helped him realize he was a good man.

They rode up to the El Paso Hotel, and Tanner was anxious to find Beth and tell her how much he'd thought of her and missed her, that his only regret, when he thought his life was over, was not making sure she was safe and secure. He loved her even if he wasn't worthy of marrying her.

He'd thought about it all the way back to Fort Worth and realized that life had given him a second chance, an opportunity to correct his mistakes and decide his fate. And this time he wanted Beth, though he doubted that she would want to marry him.

After all, what decent woman would want a man who'd spent the last ten years of his life running away from the law and the dreams of a war that plagued him?

Travis pulled on the reins of his Appaloosa, the big steed coming to a halt.

"I'm going to head for home. I'm kind of anxious to see Rose," Travis said, turning his horse in a westerly direction. He glanced at Tanner. "I'll tell Mother that you'll come see her once you get everything settled. I know she'll want to talk to you."

"After I've spoken with Beth, then I'll come see her," Tanner promised.

"Good luck." Travis spurred his horse and rode off with an anxious gallop.

"I guess I better go over to the jail and see how things are going there," Tucker said. He reached over and offered his hand to Tanner.

"I enjoyed this trip. It felt good to be in a fight together with my brothers."

"Yeah, it did," Tanner agreed, enjoying the firm grip of his brother. "I notice you aren't any slouch with those guns, either. Last thing I remember before that bullet knocked me down was watching you fire off those revolvers of yours. Sometime you'll have to tell me how you became so good at using those guns of yours."

Tucker shrugged. "Once I was a stupid kid, just like you were, only I managed to realize my stupidity before I got killed."

"You were lucky."

"You want me to go in with you?" Tucker asked. "I could try to explain to her about our mother."

"No. Now it's up to me to work things out with Beth."

"Okay, but if you need me, you know where I am."

"Thanks, Tucker."

"Anytime." He turned his horse up the street toward the jail.

Tanner glanced at the El Paso Hotel as a flurry of butterflies filled his stomach. It was barely past noon, and he was anxious to find Beth and persuade her to stay here in Fort Worth with him.

Ever since that bullet had almost ended his life, he'd felt an urgency to be with Beth.

He swung his leg over the side of his horse and dropped to the ground. He dusted off his clothes, knowing he must look a sight after being on the trail for the last several days, but he hadn't wanted to stop and get cleaned up. He'd only wanted to come home to Beth, to tell her how much he needed her in his life.

With a quick twist of the reins, he wrapped them around the hitching post and then proceeded into the hotel. He opened the door and walked to the desk clerk, who immediately recognized him.

"Mr. Burnett, nice to see you again."

"Can you tell me what room Miss Anderson is in?"

"Miss Anderson?"

"Yes, you know the girl I brought with me the first time I came here. Auburn hair, large hazel eyes."

"She's gone."

Tanner felt his heart stop. "Gone?"

"She checked out several days ago."

"Did she say where she was going?" Tanner asked.

"No, but she caught the stage to Abilene, and from there it goes to El Paso."

"Thanks," Tanner said, bolting out the door.

He untied the reins of his horse and jumped up on its back. His head throbbed, reminding him he was still injured. He reached up beneath his hat and touched the bandage wrapped around his forehead.

Spurring his horse, he turned it in the direction of the city jail. He was going to tell Tucker his destination, and then he would be on the road, pursuing Beth.

He turned his horse up Third Street and then left onto Rusk to Belknap Street, where the jail sat, across from the courthouse.

Pulling his mount to a halt, he jumped down, ignoring

the throbbing pain in his head, and hurried up the steps into the building. He went directly to Tucker's office.

Tanner rushed in, not bothering to knock. "I just dropped by to tell you that I'm going after Beth. She took the Abilene stage several days ago, and I'm going to stop them."

"Slow down," Tucker said, glancing up from the paperwork that littered his desk.

"I want to get on the road."

"Look, I know you want to stop this stagecoach, but you look like a robber with that bandage wrapped around your forehead. If you go riding up on a stage, they may think you want something besides just Beth."

Tanner frowned. "I'll make it clear I'm not robbing them."

"With your past I think it would be better if we were clear you're no longer in the business of robbing stagecoaches."

Tucker reached into a drawer and pulled out a tin star, much like the one he wore.

"Why don't I just deputize you, real quick like, and that way you'll have no problem stopping them?"

Tanner smiled. "I like that idea. For once I'll be wearing the badge. But only until I find Beth."

Beth leaned her head back and closed her eyes, but every time she shut them, her mind played tricks on her. The rocking of the wheels and the creaking of the coach were identical to the time before. An older woman had chattered beside her, and she couldn't help but ignore the banker who sat directly across from her.

She felt as if she had somehow gone back in time and was headed to Fort Worth instead of Abilene. Only this time, Tanner didn't sit across from her. And now she was returning with a broken heart instead of a pocketful of dreams.

The desolation of the land they rode through was similar to her emotions. It seemed as if she could go for miles and miles and no one would care. No one would know that once again the belle of Jonesboro, Georgia, was without even a place to call home. No one would know that she had given up on marriage and intended to live alone.

Once again, she was on a stagecoach, but this time there were no moments of anticipation, no chills of excitement. This time she knew she was no longer the same woman who had traveled miles to meet the man she hoped to marry.

Now there was only a feeling of anger that had been kindling since she'd left Fort Worth. How could Tanner walk away when everything had seemed so right? How could he have made love to her so passionately, only to sneak away in the night?

She didn't understand. He'd said that he was wanted and told her about Carter. They'd shared so much that night, and now she couldn't help but wonder if he'd just been telling lies.

The carriage hit a rut in the well-traveled road and caused them all to bounce. Beth laid her head back and tried to sleep, but the image of Tanner kept intruding, which only seemed to fuel her anger.

The man had made love to her and encouraged her, then walked out before the dawn. He assured her that the past didn't matter, he'd said she had to sacrifice herself for her family, and then he'd left her without so much as a good-bye. His sweet-talking words had only been lies that had left her alone, broke, and so in love with him, she wished she'd die of heartache.

A shot rang out in the distance, and Beth peered out the window. Surely she wasn't so unlucky as to be robbed a second time.

She saw a rider spurring his horse faster, trying to catch the coach, which had suddenly picked up speed.

The man fired his gun a second time, and the older woman looked shaken. "Was that gunfire I just heard?"

"Yes, ma'am," Beth said tiredly. "It appears we're about to be robbed."

"Oh, my!" the elderly woman said.

"Everyone on the floorboard," Beth said, pushing the older woman down to protect her from being shot. She could feel the coach slowing and felt once again as if she were in a dream. Hadn't she done this several months ago?

A lone horseman rode by the window, and suddenly the stage slowed. Shouting between the driver and the bandit caused the driver to pull back on the reins. The stage lurched and bounced, sending the passengers scrambling on the floor to keep from landing on top of one another.

"When we stop, everyone remain calm and step out of the coach. Just do what he says and you should survive," Beth said calmly.

"Have you had this happen to you before?" the older woman asked.

"Yes. As a matter of fact, the last time I traveled," Beth told the frightened passengers.

She shook her head, unable to believe her incredible bad luck. But this time they wouldn't get everything from her. This time her money was in her trunk and her shoe.

The coach finally pulled to a stop, and Beth glanced up to peer through the window. That horse looked familiar. Somewhere she'd seen that animal. From the back, the man talking to the stagecoach driver was about Tanner's height, had the same sandy curls, same Colt Navy revolvers.

For a moment she felt as if the breath had been knocked out of her. Tanner Burnett was here robbing this very coach, now!

He must have heard her gasp because he glanced behind him. Beth ducked down just in time.

"What's wrong?" the banker, crouched down in the seat, asked.

Oh, my God, he was here, right outside the door of the stage, talking to the driver. Her heart was thundering in her chest, and she wished there was some way she could hide.

Suddenly, the door opened, and the passengers all glanced up. Beth's gaze went to the man who had destroyed all her dreams, who even now her excited heart gave a lurch at the sight of.

"Everyone out," he said.

The other passengers scrambled to do his bidding, but Beth only glared at him.

"I'm not moving."

He looked at her. "Oh, yes, you are."

"I am not going to let you rob these poor people." She fairly hissed at him.

"Who said anything about robbing them?" He pulled back the edge of his vest and showed her the tin star pinned to his chest. "I'm here as a deputy of the law."

She gasped at the sight of his badge. "Did you steal that, too?"

"No. Now get out of the stagecoach."

"Why are you wearing that badge?"

"Because I'm here to arrest you if you won't listen to reason."

"That's hardly possible!"

"Beth, don't make me come in there after you. I know you're mad, and you have a right to be. Just come out and hear what I have to say."

"You have nothing to say that I want to hear," she said, hurt swelling until she thought she would drown in pain.

He reached in to grab her, and she took her reticule and knocked him upside the head. "I'm through listening to your lies."

"Ouch!" he said, grabbing for his hat that suddenly went flying to the floor.

She gasped at the sight of the bandage wrapped around his forehead. "Oh, my God, you've been hurt. What happened?"

He reached in and took her by the hand. "Come outside, please."

She quit fighting him, the sight of that bandage frightening her. "I still don't want to hear what you have to say."

He pulled her gently out of the stage. She dug her heels in beside the other passengers. "I'm not going any farther."

Tanner had known she would be upset with him, but he had thought that by now she would have cooled down a little. Yet somehow he couldn't blame her. He'd hurt her badly.

He tugged at her, and she refused to budge. "I thought we could go off in private and talk."

"I've told you multiple times now, I'm not going to listen to what you have to say. I'm not moving from this spot!"

"Fine! Then this is where we're going to talk," he said, determined.

He let go of her hands and stood in front of the three people who had been on the stage, seeing only Beth in front of him.

"I told you that night I was wanted. But I didn't tell you I had made a deal with the governor that if I brought in the Bass gang I would be cleared. I had to leave to fulfill that duty, and I didn't know if I would live to see another day. I had to leave knowing that you would be taken care of, that even if I died, you'd be safe." He paused. "That's how I got this bandage. Sam's bullet grazed me. I thought I was going to die, and I knew at that moment in time that I loved you more than life."

She gasped, and he paused to catch her reaction.

"I realized that you had made me a better man. You had helped me face the death of Carter, to see that I was a good man who had faced some terrible tragedies and made some poor choices."

She stared at him as if she were bored, and he suddenly feared he would never reach her. He took a deep breath, anxious that she hear him.

"Beth, Lord knows I've made a mess of my life. I've done so little that's right, and I realize that I have no right to ask anything of you. But I'm here now to take you back to Fort Worth, to take you back to my family, to keep you safe, watch over you. I have no chance of ever being a man who is worthy of you, who deserves you, but I'm here to throw myself at your mercy and tell you that I love you."

He watched, hoping that he would see a softening of her expression; instead, her eyes flared, and she put her hands on her hips.

"You are the most stubborn, irritating man I have ever met. You tell me that the sacrifices I made during the war were done out of love, and yet the next morning I awaken to find you gone. Gone! What am I supposed to believe?" She took a step closer to him and poked him with her finger in his chest. "Damn you, Tanner Burnett. We shared so much that night, and then in the morning you were gone! Then you ride in here and expect to carry me off like—like some war prize. You're not taking me anywhere unless you do it with a preacher and a ring."

"Huh?" he said, confused. "I don't understand. I said I loved you."

"Ask her to marry you, young man. That's what she's waiting for," cried the old lady.

He glanced at the woman and then back at Beth, who waited. "But how could you want to be married to me? I have nothing to offer you. I'm a deserter, an ex-outlaw. I'm not the marrying kind. How could you love me?"

"You're an idiot for not realizing that I have loved you since I opened my eyes in that hotel room in San Antonio and saw you bending over me. I love you for the gentle man I know is inside of you. I love you for the way you take care of me. I love you for the way you've helped me understand the past. I love you for the things we have in common. I love you, Tanner Burnett, just the way you are. And if we have to spend the rest of our days running from the law, so be it. As long as I'm with you, I don't care."

She was crying. Tears were streaming down her cheeks, and he wanted to gather her up in his arms and hold her, comfort her, but he knew he owed her more.

Feeling like a fool but knowing he would act even more foolish if it would keep Beth in his life, he bent down on one knee in front of everyone that was on the stagecoach.

"Beth, I love you. I love you for the courageous person you are. I want to spend the rest of my life with you. I want us to grow old together, have children. But most of all, I want your love. Will you marry me and spend your life with me?"

All eyes turned and stared at Beth, who was now sobbing. "Yes. Yes, I'll be your wife."

Tanner stood, and Beth flew into his arms. For a moment they merely stood there, enjoying the warmth of their arms around each other, the feeling of being truly together for the first time.

He glanced up and saw the stagecoach driver motioning everyone back into the stage. "Come on, folks, we need to get going, and these folks need a little privacy."

The older woman swiped her hand across her cheek, clearing away her tears. "That was so touching. Best wishes to both of you."

The stagecoach driver saluted them and then stepped up into the box. Within seconds the vehicle was on its way once again.

Still holding each other, they watched the coach roll off into the distance. Beth glanced up at Tanner. "Did you really mean what you said? My past doesn't tarnish me? Doesn't make you think less of me?" she asked.

"Beth, you're the bravest woman I've ever known. You are my inspiration. You sacrificed yourself for your family, and I think you are the most courageous person I know. You gave yourself in an attempt to save the people you love. And I'm so glad that you love me."

"I do love you, Tanner. I really do."

He kissed her deeply, their mouths mating as if they would never part. Finally, they broke apart.

"Take me home," she whispered.

Author's Note

Sam Bass was a legendary outlaw who robbed local stages in the Fort Worth area between 1877 and 1878. During this time, he learned that local cattle traders received large sums of money via the trains; then his focus changed to train robbing, which drew the attention of the Texas Rangers, the Pinkertons, and Wells Fargo. A member of his own gang, Jim Murphy, was working with the Texas Rangers to bring him to justice before he left Fort Worth. The law finally caught up with him in Round Rock, Texas, on July 21, 1878. I have taken the liberty of changing the dates to 1874, to better suit my story.

If you liked THE OUTLAW TAKES A WIFE, be sure to look for Sylvia McDaniel's next release in the Burnett Brides series THE MARSHAL TAKES A WIFE, available wherever books are sold July 2001.

When Tucker Burnett returned to Fort Worth to become the marshal, he thought he'd left his rambling, troubled past behind him. Then Dr. Sarah James rode into town, and the childhood friendship they remembered threatened to become something more, as it had once before. Will Sarah's secrets keep them apart now that they know where desire will lead them?